Lillian's Garden

Lillian's Garden

Carrie Jane Knowles

Winchester, UK
Washington, USA

First published by Roundfire Books, 2013
Roundfire Books is an imprint of John Hunt Publishing Ltd., Laurel House, Station Approach,
Alresford, Hants, SO24 9JH, UK
office1@jhpbooks.net
www.johnhuntpublishing.com
www.roundfire-books.com

For distributor details and how to order please visit the 'Ordering' section on our website.

Text copyright: Carrie Jane Knowles 2012

ISBN: 978 1 78099 830 5

All rights reserved. Except for brief quotations in critical articles or reviews, no part of this book may be reproduced in any manner without prior written permission from the publishers.

The rights of Carrie Jane Knowles as author have been asserted in accordance with the Copyright, Designs and Patents Act 1988.

A CIP catalogue record for this book is available from the British Library.

Design: Stuart Davies

Printed in the USA by Edwards Brothers Malloy

We operate a distinctive and ethical publishing philosophy in all areas of our business, from our global network of authors to production and worldwide distribution.

Also by Carrie Knowles:

The Last Childhood: A Family Story of Alzheimer's

Shoot Me

Searching for Clint Eastwood

Dedication:

This book is dedicated to my husband, Jeff, and my mother, Ruth, two people I love.
Their gardens were wild and wonderful and tangled with dreams.

Acknowledgements

I would like to thank Peggy Payne for her constant and unwavering friendship and support. And, I would like to thank Angella Preston, Sue Shoemaker and Ingrid Wood for their careful reading, comments and help editing this manuscript. A special thanks also to Ingrid for keeping me sane and on track over breakfast every Saturday morning.

I would also like to thank the many caretakers who work tirelessly to help people put their lives back together again when things fall apart. I would especially like to thank the staff of Eloise Hospital, who kept the secrets of so many people and helped them heal, and the staffs of all the other mental hospitals everywhere who continue, in even more enlightened ways, to do so today.

And, most importantly, I would like to thank Neil, Hedy and Cole for believing in me and for having the courage to follow their own wild dreams.

Chapter 1

Linda's mother walked by the library and tapped on the window.

"Your crazy mother wants you," one of the students yelled.

Linda pretended she didn't hear the student and didn't see her mother. Her mother tapped again.

All of the students sitting around her laughed.

Linda picked up her books and moved. Her mother walked away.

"I tapped on the window, didn't you see me?" her mother asked that evening when they were cleaning up after supper.

"Sorry," Linda said. "I didn't recognize you."

Linda's comment nagged at Helen all night long. She couldn't sleep. At 2 a.m. she got up, careful not to wake her husband, Richard, and walked from one room in the house to another, looking for some clue as to why her daughter didn't recognize her. She felt lost. Perhaps there was a door ajar she had never noticed before, or a window she had carelessly left opened where her true spirit might have accidentally tumbled out.

Not finding anything, Helen carefully tiptoed down the hallway to Linda's room and opened the door to see if her daughter was safe in bed and sleeping. Helen also checked to see if Tommy had come home. She was not surprised to discover he hadn't. She went downstairs.

Except for the soft shuffle of her bare feet against the cold wooden floors, the house was quiet. Dead quiet. She had an urge to run outside and smoke a cigarette, as though holding something dangerous like a cigarette in her hand, lighting it, and drawing the sharp smoke into her lungs would magically overpower Linda's niggling comment. Why didn't her daughter recognize her? What had happened to her children? What had happened to her life?

She had found a pack of cigarettes in Tommy's jacket pocket weeks ago, but never said anything to either Tommy or to Richard about finding them. Perhaps if Tommy were home, the two of them could go outside to share a cigarette and look at the stars together and talk. It had been a long time since she and Tommy had really talked to each other.

Lacking a cigarette, she went into the kitchen and lit matches, one after another, striking them against the box. Once lit, she threw the matches into the sink to watch them burn for a brief moment before going out. Each time she struck a new match, she marveled at how quickly the hot flare of sulfur filled the room then just as quickly faded as though the fire and the match had never found each other at all.

Helen fiddled with the spent matches in the sink, straightening them into a neat row like a garden fence. After she'd lit eleven matches she slid the cover off the "Strike Anywhere" box and counted how many were left. There were easily a hundred or more. Enough matches to stand there all night long, watching them burn. Fire and brimstone, sulfur and smoke: this is the smell of everything feeling so wrong and crazy your own daughter doesn't even recognize you when you tap on a window. This is hell.

She pulled a twelfth match from the box and struck it. Just as the fire ignited, she heard Tommy's car creep up the gravel driveway. She tossed the lit match into the sink and turned on the water. Scooping up the spent wet matches she threw them into the trash, pushing them to the bottom of the can. Scurrying up the stairs as quietly and quickly as she could, she disappeared into her room and closed the door. She took a slow deep breath trying to calm the pounding of her heart.

She heard Tommy open the refrigerator looking for something to eat. A minute later she heard him walk up the stairs to the bathroom, go to his room and shut the door. When he was in the bathroom she heard the toilet flush but didn't hear him wash his hands or brush his teeth.

She sat on the edge of their bed for a long time listening, waiting to be sure Tommy had fallen asleep before she allowed herself to slip her cold feet under the covers and close her eyes. Luckily, Tommy's clumsy drunken steps up the stairs hadn't awoken either Linda or Richard.

Helen lay in bed a long time before she finally fell back to sleep. The next morning she waited until Richard got out of bed and dressed before she stirred. After she heard Richard go downstairs for breakfast and Linda finish showering in the bathroom, she slipped out of bed and walked down the hall.

Once safely inside the bathroom, she closed and locked the door. She opened the top drawer of the vanity and rummaged through the hair rollers, bobby pins and lipstick tubes until she found the pearl-handled straight razor that had once been her father-in-law's and now belonged to Tommy.

Pulling the long sharp razor from its leather case, she opened it and held the blade in her right hand between her thumb and first finger the way her father-in-law had taught her to do when he could no longer shave himself and she had to shave him. The weight of the pearl handle of the blade balanced comfortably against her little finger and felt good. She put the razor down, ran water into the sink, and wet her hair. For the first time in a long time she felt sure of herself and what she now wanted to do.

Helen picked up a long lock of her shoulder-length auburn hair and twirled it in her fingers until it was pulled like a tight piece of rope anchored to her head. She picked up the razor. Laying the sharp blade against it, about one inch from her scalp, she pushed firmly until the blade cut through the twisted hair in one clean movement.

Once the first clean cut was made she proceeded with her handiwork, twisting, pulling and cutting as she moved from the front of her hair to the back. She worked quickly across the top of her head and down around her face by her right ear moving blindly over and around the nape of her neck to her left ear.

Her chest tightened. To keep herself from panicking, she started to hum that stupid song about God having the whole world in His hands. Tears streamed down her face. She couldn't remember the last time Richard held her.

She was tired of waiting for God to make her life better.

She wiped her face with the back of her hand and leaned close to the mirror. She turned her head from side to side to look at her profile and her new short hair. She brushed her opened hand along the short curls around her face. When she found a long piece of hair by her left ear she twisted it in her fingers and cut it. Once she was satisfied she had found every stray bit of hair, she wiped the damp blade on a hand towel, flipped the razor closed, slipped it into its case and put it back into the drawer.

Pulling a length of toilet paper from the roll, she wet it in order to wipe up the pieces of hair that had fallen into the sink. She pushed the tissue and all the hair she'd cut into the bottom of the trashcan in an attempt to hide what she had done.

"You look good," she said to her reflection. "It's not your fault Tommy came home drunk again. You are a good mother…you have always been a good mother…you are not like your mother. You never left them."

Taking a fresh towel from the stack under the bathroom sink she rubbed her hair until it was dry. She shook her head and ran her fingers through her short curls.

For the moment, her fresh short hair erased her feelings of anxiety about Tommy and Linda. For the moment, none of that mattered. She felt good about herself, and she thought she looked good.

She reached into the drawer for a tube of lipstick and quickly drew a streak of color on her lips. Calypso Crush: a pinkish coral bordering on bold. Smoothing the color by pressing her lips together, she took another piece of toilet paper, blotted, threw the tissue into the trash and applied a second coat, careful to bring the color all the way to the edges of her mouth. Pressing her lips together to blend the lipstick, she picked up the blood red garnet earrings she had taken off last night before she went to bed and slipped them back into her ears. She forced a smile.

Richard had brought the earrings to her from Italy when he came home from The War. She loved them and wore them everyday as though they were the only part of her soul she was willing to share with the world.

Her wedding ring, a thin gold band set with five tiny diamonds, was in a box in the top drawer of her dresser. It was too big. It had always been too big and would slip off her finger whenever she washed dishes or worked in the garden. It made Richard angry that she didn't wear her wedding ring.

Helen heard Richard's heavy footsteps coming up the stairs. She looked at her watch. It was getting late. She could hear Linda getting dressed in her room. Helen hadn't heard a peep from Tommy.

"Linda," she called out, taking one more look in the mirror at her handiwork before she opened the door. "Would you wake Tommy? We need to get going."

Richard hit the top stair just as Helen opened the bathroom door.

"You cut your hair," Richard said.

"Didn't have time to go into town last week to get it done."

"Guess it wouldn't do any good to say I liked it long."

"Let's not be late for church," Helen said, turning to go into the bedroom to finish getting dressed.

Linda could hear her parents talking in the hallway. She knew by the tone of the conversation it was going to be a quiet ride to church this morning and she had better light a fire under Tommy so the situation wouldn't escalate.

She knocked once, then swung the door of Tommy's room wide open and flipped on the bright ceiling light. Tommy's long lanky body rolled lazily to one side of the bed. He dragged the covers over his head as he did. The room was sour with the smell of sweaty clothes and liquor. Linda pulled the door shut behind her and stepped closer.

"Tommy," she said, shaking his shoulder. "Get up."

"You should 'a come with us last night," he smiled, turning his now uncovered head in her direction. He smelled of cigarette smoke. His pale blue eyes were ever so slightly bloodshot from drinking. His breath was stale and warm with sleep.

"Good idea, glad I didn't, now get up before someone finds out."

"Finds out what?"

"That you've been drinking."

"What time?"

"Time."

"What a time we had last night."

"If I were you, I'd shower twice, just to be sure to get the smell out."

"That bad?"

"That bad."

"Larry and the guys, we were baaaad," he said, laughing. "If coach ever caught us that drunk there'd be no high school baseball team."

"I bet," Linda said, snatching the covers off him. "Now get up before there's a fight about being late for church. The two of them are already at each other."

Tommy took his good old sweet time in the shower. When he at last got into the car, Richard started lecturing. He let it be known in no uncertain terms he hated being late and he wasn't going to tolerate it anymore.

Helen's response to Richard's rant about being late for church was to sit bolt upright, perfectly still and silent, with her head turned to the window, staring off into nothing.

Tommy rested his head against the side window. His legs were sprawled out across the hump on the floor into Linda's space on the other side of the car. Linda, who had the same long legs as Tommy, sat stiffly with her knees pressed together and her hands folded in her lap in order not to take too much space or to push against her brother. Rather than look out the window like her mother, she kept her head down so her long straight brown hair covered her face and eyes. No one spoke.

"The plant is on overtime again," Richard said, breaking the silence. "Been thinking I'd work an extra shift. I want to ask for time off Friday so I can see your game."

"That'd be great," Tommy said, stretching his neck a bit from side to side trying to work out a kink.

"You starting?"

"Yeah, me and Larry for sure."

"Got in late last night?"

"Yeah," he laughed, "you could say that."

Linda rolled the back window down a notch in order to let some fresh air into the car. She didn't want either her mother or her father to smell the alcohol on Tommy's breath and skin. He had showered and put on a good amount of deodorant and after-shave like she'd told him, but Linda was quite sure anyone within ten feet of him could still tell he'd had a heavy dose of drinking the night before.

"You cut your hair," Linda said to her mother.

"Didn't have time to go into town last week," Helen replied, not bothering to turn her head when she spoke to her daughter.

"Looks good short," Tommy chimed in. He was happy to be avoiding a scene.

"Thanks."

Richard drove on in silence.

Rebecca Johnson, who was the head of the Women's Circle, and Edna Wilson, the deacon's wife, were standing in the aisle of the church when Helen and Richard walked in. As Helen passed, the two women stopped whatever it was they were talking about and nodded their heads in greeting.

"Morning," Rebecca Johnson chimed.

Helen nodded in return.

"Blessed day to you," Edna Wilson added.

Helen kept walking. Rebecca raised an eyebrow as if to say, "Well isn't that just like her." Edna snorted a little and the two of them took note of Helen's fresh boyish short hair and the rather garish lipstick pink smeared across Helen's lips. Satisfied they had once again been witness to Helen's general haughtiness and crazy notions, they turned to each other and smiled. Nothing more needed to be said.

Without flinching, Helen walked up to the front of the church and sat down in the second pew on the right, sliding over to the center in order to make room for her husband. Tommy and Linda took seats toward the back with the other teenagers.

Reverend Jacobs signaled for Deacon Wilson to ring the church bell so all the latecomers and gossipers hanging around outside could hurry in to find their places. He seemed anxious to get the morning started. As soon as people settled down, he thumped his right knee with his Bible then began his walk up the center aisle of the church to the red-carpeted altar and the pulpit. Another man, a stranger, walked behind him. Once Reverend Jacobs was firmly situated behind the wooden lectern, the man who had walked down the aisle with him took a seat behind him. Jacobs put down his Bible, lifted his chin, closed his eyes tightly as though the tighter he squeezed them, the closer he could fly to God, and prayed silently to himself. He ended his prayer with a loud and sudden, Amen.

"We are not like our Methodist neighbors," he said, leaning out over the lectern, "who believe salvation is an easy one-way ticket to heaven that's good for a lifetime. Or, like our Episcopal brethren who would like to believe heaven is some kind of birthright given to them with their two car garages."

The same ladies, who had just passed judgment on Helen, now turned to each other and nodded their heads in approval. Their husbands laughed.

"We're not even like those deep-dunking Baptists up the street who believe any good stream of water can wash away the sins of a Saturday night." Pausing for a moment in order to let the laughter grow, Reverend Jacobs smiled while he waited for them to catch on and quiet down. Gripping the two sides of the pulpit, he leaned forward and took a long steady look at his audience as if he had the power to see down through their very souls.

"We're special Baptists. Freewill Baptists, free to ask forgiveness and free to sin with the hope we'll live long enough to ask forgiveness again." Heads nodded and bobbed, women fanned themselves with their Bibles, and everyone seemed satisfied they indeed were righteous to believe so.

"So when my cousin, Joe Nathan from Kentucky, called me up last week to tell me he'd lost his job, I had to laugh." With this, Reverend Jacobs turned to the gangly, black-suited Joe Nathan sitting behind him and gave him a broad wink. "You didn't lose your job, I told him. God took it from you because He wants you here. Here, where you can serve Him better. I believe God does everything for a reason, and the reason he snatched Joe Nathan's job away from him was because we need him. I have heard him preach. He is a powerful man of God. I believe he will be able to show us the wrong of our ways.

"God has given us a gift in Joe Nathan. I believe he has been sent here to stir up a revival of our spirits and a recommitment to God and to each other. Joe Nathan has come so we can once again seek salvation for our sins and our stubborn free wills as well as our Baptist, backsliding ways."

Nodding his head in agreement, a long lock of Joe Nathan's slick black hair broke free of its heavy coat of pomade and dangled in front of his eyes. Joe Nathan swiftly lifted his chin, bearing his turkey-like white neck wobbling loosely in his ill-fitting dress shirt, and tossed his hair back out of his eyes. He nodded again, this time, brushing his hair back into place with his long boney fingers.

"But," Reverend Jacobs shouted, his voice growing stern and parent-like, "Before I introduce you to this holy man who has come to help us find redemption, I need to talk to you about our children."

Bowing his head for a moment as though he needed to pray again in order to have the strength to go on, Reverend Jacobs looked up, leaned out over the pulpit, and leveled his eyes at Tommy.

"The Devil is among us. He is out doing mischief with the children of our fine town." He paused for a moment and raised his right hand as though he was about to swear on his Bible. "How do I know it's the Devil? I know because the Devil does his work when good people aren't looking. The Devil is sneaky. He likes to do his business behind our backs in the middle of the night. He makes his mischief look like fun. He waits for our weaknesses, our taste for alcohol, for lust, for hating, for running wild. That's how he catches people. And the Devil has caught us once again. But, this time his mischief has come not only at night but it came with a baseball bat, and it has popped off a whole lot of mailboxes from their posts up and down the streets of my neighborhood. And when the Devil shows his ugly ways I've got to call him out on this mischief because God is watching. Yes, He's watching and He knows what playing with the Devil can lead to."

People twisted in their seats to get a good look at whom Reverend Jacobs was talking about in the back of the church. Tommy sat up straight as though his name had been called out in honor of some great thing he'd done, and he smiled the same smile that had helped him get through most of the trouble he'd found in his life. Staring straight ahead, Linda bit the inside of her cheek trying not to blink.

Once they had taken a good look at Tommy and Linda, the congregation shifted back in their seats and stared straight ahead to where Helen and Richard were sitting. Standing for a moment in silence, Reverend Jacobs gave everyone the chance to take in the whole of what he'd said.

Richard looked over to Reverend Jacobs and nodded his head as if to say he knew Tommy was involved and things would be dealt with once they were home. Helen did not move, nor did she turn her face to look at Reverend Jacobs to either acknowledge what he had said or give her approval that something would be done to take care of the matter. Holding her head high, she stared out the window. She had other, more important things to think about.

Joe Nathan began to stir. He had done all of the sitting still and quiet he could manage. He rose from his chair to speak. Reverend Jacobs stepped aside.

"I'm a Devil hunter," his raw, raspy voice called out across the congregation as he stood up to approach the pulpit.

"Amen," Reverend Jacobs shouted.

"God made me a Devil hunter," Joe Nathan began to sing out. "I can feel the Devil. I can see the Devil. I can even SMELL the Devil in this church, and I'm gonna find him and bring him to his knees!"

Pulling into the driveway, Richard turned around and told Tommy he should sit tight for a moment. They needed to talk. Helen got out of the car without saying a word and went into the kitchen to put lunch together. Linda got out of the car with her and followed her into the house. While her mother fussed with making a salad and cutting last night's cold meatloaf for sandwiches, Linda set the table.

Richard and Tommy stayed inside the car for a long time.

When they finally got out, they stood in the driveway, close to each other, eye-to-eye. Tommy was as tall as his father, but Richard was heavier built and, at least for the moment, seemed to still have the upper hand.

At one point Linda could hear her father shouting at Tommy. Tommy, she knew without looking, just stood there like he was a warrior covered in armor and could stand his ground and survive whatever came his way. When her father quit shouting, she heard Tommy get into his old Valiant and drive away.

"I hope that's the last of that," Richard said as he slammed through the backdoor into the kitchen. "Drinking and letting off a little steam on a Saturday night is one thing, but deliberately destroying property is another. I'd ground him, but he's too big for that. Too big for everything it seems."

"He's a boy," Helen said, slicing tomatoes and putting them on a platter.

"A boy you let run wild," Richard countered.

"Yes," Helen answered as though he had just asked her if she wanted ice cream for dessert. She felt the room tilt a little and gripped the edge of the counter in order to balance herself.

"Yes," Richard shouted back, then stormed out of the room.

Linda quietly cleared away Tommy's place setting and rearranged the table for just the three of them. While she was putting his plate into the cupboard, she heard another car pull up into the driveway. Looking out of the kitchen window she saw it was the sheriff.

Sheriff Greyjack took his time getting out of the squad car, dusting his hat off across the knees of his uniform as he did. He was only 5′ 10″, a good 3″ shorter than Richard or Tommy, but he looked bigger than either one of them. He was broad and muscular and gave the impression he could wrestle a bear or a drunk to the ground if he needed to, but he never had. In fact, he rarely raised his voice in the line of duty and had only once drawn his gun when some poor unsuspecting drifter thought the gas station next to the sheriff's office looked like an easy mark.

"It's Greyjack," Linda announced.

"I'll go talk to him," Helen said. Wiping her hands on a tea towel, she took off her apron. Before she went outside, she smoothed the front of her dress. Forcing a smile, she wondered what her face with its new haircut looked like. She hoped Greyjack would recognize her.

"Hey, Helen," Greyjack called out waving his hat at her with one hand, while running his other hand through his short cropped silver hair. He and Helen and Richard were all the same age, but Greyjack was the only one who'd gone grey. Rumor had it that his hair had turned completely white the first time he killed someone in the war.

"Hello, Greyjack."

"Sorry to bother you."

"I figured you'd come." She was standing close to Greyjack. Close enough to reach out and touch his rough broad hand, but she didn't.

"You okay?" he asked softly.

"I'm fine." Her voice felt flat in her mouth and buzzed a minute in her ears. She could feel a wave of dizziness creeping over her.

"Good." Greyjack watched her face. "Glad to hear it. Hey, Richard."

Walking down the front sidewalk to the driveway, Richard extended his hand. "Thanks for stopping by."

"When I got the call, I knew it was him," Greyjack answered, looking from Helen to Richard.

"I'm not surprised." Richard said, smiling. "Like Helen says, boys will be boys."

"Could have arrested him, but didn't."

"We appreciate that," Richard said, moving closer to Helen, brushing against her shoulder as he stepped next to her. Helen moved away from him.

"He's a hell of a baseball player. Good arm and he's fast."

"Yep." Richard forced a smile.

"When I picked him up last night I took him back to the station. Didn't book him, just talked to him."

Flinching slightly, Richard touched Helen's arm as though he wanted to get her attention, but he didn't say anything. Tommy hadn't mentioned Greyjack had caught him bashing the mailboxes. The omission stung.

"Told him," Greyjack went on, "if he was going to drink he ought to sit down and do it and stay seated until he felt like he could drive himself home without troubling anyone."

"Seems like good advice to me," Richard said, forcing a laugh. "Don't you think so, Helen?"

"Sure."

"Where's he going after graduation?" Greyjack asked, looking first at Helen then Richard. "Any plans yet?"

Richard glanced at Helen before he answered. "The coach at Eastern Michigan said they might want him to play baseball, but he'd need to take some summer classes to bring up his grades a little before they made their final decision. Tommy doesn't seem too interested in the summer thing."

"The Army recruiter came by the office the other day asking if I might know of any kids in town who might want to join up." Greyjack continued, looking down at his shoes as he let the information sink in a little. "Things seem to be heating up in Vietnam. The recruiter thought the boys who signed up on their own before getting drafted might be treated better and have more choices."

"Might be good for him." Richard looked at Helen.

Helen nodded her head as though they had already talked it through with Tommy and it was all right with her.

"I didn't say anything to him one way or the other, but after last night I thought maybe the Army might not be such a bad situation for him." Greyjack drew in an uneasy breath. "If you want, I can talk with him."

Richard looked at Helen. She nodded her approval.

"The recruiter's a buddy of mine. The Army doesn't want trouble so it won't be necessary to mention everything Tommy's been up to lately. Maybe you can talk with him and tell him to keep a lid on it for a few more weeks before he gets out of school. I told Tommy if he and his friends want to drink they should do it on my watch. Hell, they can even do it on my land. They're not bad kids, just restless and a little stupid right now. A thousand mail boxes in the county and they've got to go and find the one with Reverend Jacob's name on it."

"Thanks, Greyjack," Helen said.

"He's a good kid. Hell of a baseball player."

"He is," Richard said. He shook Greyjack's hand, turned and waited for Helen to come with him.

"Thanks," she said again, extending her hand to Greyjack.

"Happy to help," he said, taking her hand in his and shaking it once hard, the way two fighters might shake right before they went to their respective corners to wait for the bell.

Linda was watching from the kitchen window. She saw her mother hesitate before she moved away from Greyjack and came into the house. She also saw her father turn and touch her mother's arm as if touching her arm was all he needed to do to make Greyjack disappear.

Chapter 2

They waited as long as they could, but when Tommy did not return for lunch, they sat down to eat, and pretended nothing was wrong. After they had eaten what they wanted and the lack of conversation began to weigh heavy in the room, Helen got up to clear the dishes.

Richard offered to help, but in the same breath said if he was going to be able to get time off to see Tommy play football on Friday then he probably should go into the plant and work an extra afternoon shift.

Helen told Richard she was planning on spending her Sunday afternoon in the garden so he should feel free to go on.

Linda had work to do for school. She had originally planned to beg off on her usual Sunday chores, including dishes. But, with Tommy run off to God-knows-where and her father off to work, it didn't feel right to her to just leave her mother with everything.

Linda got up and carried the leftover cold meatloaf and salad to the counter and started wrapping the leftovers. Helen took a fresh plate from the cupboard and put it out on the counter near where Linda was working. Linda uncovered the meatloaf and cut a few pieces in order to make a sandwich for Tommy.

"Thought you had homework?" Helen said.

"Some," Linda mumbled as she spread mustard on two slices of white bread for Tommy's sandwich.

"He shouldn't have been drinking," Helen offered, opening the subject of Tommy's recent escapades and Greyjack's visit.

"He better hope Greyjack doesn't call the coach."

"Greyjack won't. But Reverend Jacobs might."

"He'd be just the type to do something like that."

"Hmmm," Helen let her hands rest in the warm soapy dishwater for a second.

"What does Greyjack think?" Linda asked.

"He thinks Tommy should go into the Army."

"Anyone bother to tell Tommy?"

"I suppose Greyjack's mentioned it to him."

"What do you think?"

Helen wasn't really sure, but it was all she had been thinking about since Greyjack left.

"Do you remember the time when the two of you were little and I took you and Tommy shopping? I think it was for Easter. We went to JL Hudson's department store downtown?"

"Sure. Tommy ran away and hid. We couldn't find him for the longest time. I got so scared I started to cry because I thought he was dead. I couldn't quit crying. Then, just when I thought I'd never see Tommy again, this big lady wearing a dark blue dress came up to us dragging Tommy behind her. She had this real mean look on her face. She seemed to know he was ours without having to ask. Everyone was watching."

"Yes," Helen agreed, "I remember."

Helen had not tried to look for Tommy when he ran away. She didn't even call out for him. She just stood there afraid to move or breathe because the store felt like a long dark tunnel, and the room began to tilt a little underneath her feet.

It was the first time she ever remembered feeling a little crazy, like she'd fallen into someone else's life. Recently, she felt lost and crazy all the time. Whenever Tommy got into trouble, or Linda worried about what Tommy did, or Richard shut down, refusing to talk to her when he woke up from his bad dreams about the war, she got a too-familiar, sick, dark, feeling of being lost in her stomach. When she didn't feel sick with worry she felt invisible. Sometimes she believed she could walk away and no one would notice.

Helen wanted to tell Linda the reason she hadn't recognized her when she was tapping on the library window was because she wasn't really herself anymore. She hadn't been herself ever since the day in the department store. Thinking about it again made the memory rush at her like a tsunami breaking against the shore. She braced her palms against the edge of the sink.

Whenever she thinks of that day, she always hears someone crying but she can't quite get a fix on where the crying is coming from. The crying feels like it is coming from deep inside of her yet at the same time it might as easily be coming from Linda or even Tommy or maybe both of them. She tries to speak, but it is a struggle to find her voice. She has this urge to call out for help because the room has begun to get black and feel cold, but she can't push the words from her mouth. She can't get air into her lungs. She has this horrible feeling, a sense of dread she can taste in her mouth, that she has gone very far away from the world and if she screamed no one would hear her.

In her dreams, she falls head first into a horrible dark tunnel where the racks of Easter dresses and tiny white straw hats spin, and the room turns into a wild swirl of murky blues and greens and a lady in a dark blue dress approaches her. Through it all, she is aware she is holding on to Linda's hand in order not to fall.

The woman approaching her is pulling Tommy behind her. She is wearing a department store badge pinned neatly with a crisp white linen handkerchief at the top of her breast pocket. The badge identifies the woman as the supervisor.

Tommy is screaming and squirming, but the lady is holding tightly to his hand. The two of them are standing in front of Helen, staring at her. Helen tries to reach out to Tommy or to say his name, but she can't do it. She is quite frozen and can do nothing but stare at the name badge the woman is wearing pinned in the middle of that white-white handkerchief.

Helen struggles to come back to the room, to the kitchen where she and Linda are talking. She forces her hands to keep washing the dishes as she lives, once again, through the memory of her failure.

Once again, Helen feels the familiar sensation of being trapped spread up her arms. Her throat tightens and a small warm half-moon of sweat forms under her armpits and down the sides of her clean white shirt. She cannot get enough air into her lungs. A burning sense of shame rushes through her body.

In her mind, she once again sees her daughter, her youngest child, do what she herself was unable to do. Linda lets go of her mother then walks over to Tommy and takes his hand.

Linda saved her that day, and again, each time she relives that moment, Linda is always there to save her, and as she does, Helen is both grateful and ashamed.

"Tommy was a little wild." The memory at last goes blank and Helen takes a slow easy breath in order to steady the beating of her heart. She has always wondered what Linda remembered of that day.

"A little?" Linda laughed. "He was more like a wild animal than a brother, always jumping out of trees and running around yelling like some blood-thirsty Indian on the warpath. He acted so crazy out in the woods with Larry and his friends that I was afraid to play with them. They claimed there were tigers out by the birch trees and bears down by the creek and I believed them."

"Maybe the Army would be good for Tommy, use up some of his wildness. Give him some discipline," Helen said, not really believing it herself.

"Discipline," Linda mocked as she mashed the two pieces of bread around the meatloaf, slicing the sandwich in half and putting it on the plate with some salad for Tommy to eat whenever he finally decided to come home.

"I couldn't do it," Helen whispered in apology. "I tried, but I just couldn't rescue Tommy."

Wiping her hands, Helen took off her apron and went out into her garden.

It wasn't really her garden. It had been her mother-in-law's garden. Helen had never gotten to know her as a mother-in-law, only as Richard's mother when she and Richard were in high school together. Richard's mother's name was Lillian. Helen had always liked the way Richard's father, Thomas, said her name. "Lil-lian," he'd sing out whenever he came into the house or went out to see her in the garden. It was as though each time he called her name he was surprised by the beauty and the music of it.

Lillian was everything Helen's mother had not been. Lillian was short and plump, while Helen's mother was tall and thin. Lillian's face looked soft and freshly scrubbed and she smelled of baby powder and baking soda. Helen's mother's breath and skin smelled slightly sour, and her face was hard and etched with cancer drugs and illness.

Lillian was strong and worked in the garden and cooked and sewed. Helen's mother was sick most of the time and stayed in bed. Lillian laughed a big easy laugh. Helen's mother coughed. She coughed when she tried to talk. She coughed at night and kept Helen awake. In the end, she coughed up blood. She died on Helen's 7th birthday.

In Helen's memory, her mother had always been ill, although Helen wasn't sure this was the truth. It was, at least, what she remembered. She had no memories of her mother playing with her or of her laughing or running, making pickles or even baking cookies with her.

After her mother died, her father gave Helen a picture of her mother on their wedding day. It did not look at all like the mother Helen remembered, but Helen kept it along with the little prayer card from her mother's funeral. The picture and the prayer card were all she had left of her mother. After the funeral, her father took all her mother's clothing and all the things in the house that smelled like her and threw them away.

When Helen was younger, she used to beg her father to tell her about her mother, but he never would. The only thing he ever said was that she was gone. Gone, as if she had run away from both of them.

Helen often had nightmares in which she would be trapped in a long hallway running from one door to the next looking for her mother. Helen could hear her. Sometimes she even thought she could smell her sitting in her room, but she could never find her.

In her heart, Helen knew that part of why she loved Richard was Lillian. It was all going to be just perfect. She would marry Richard, and Lillian would be her mother-in-law. But, Lillian died in 1945, before Richard could come home from the war.

When Richard at last came home, he moved in with his father. By then Thomas, his father, had had a small stroke and his right side was left a little limp and clumsy and he needed help.

Thomas and Richard had both been tall and strong and looked the way some men look as father and son. They were two versions of the same body, distinguished only by years. But the war had changed Richard's body. It made it lean and angular. His waist was newly defined and thin, while his arms and shoulders had grown thick with hard muscles. His face wasn't young and soft anymore, but chiseled and weathered, and his was hair black. Blacker than Helen had remembered. Black like polished boots.

Thomas's stroke had ravaged his strong frame. His body was soft and stooped, his hair, a sullen shade of black streaked with gunmetal grey. It was a little startling to see the two of them together. Their bodies were so different by then, but yet they had the same startling blue eyes.

When Richard asked Helen to marry him, he told her that both he and his father needed her and that the two of them would live with Thomas after the wedding. Helen said she was happy with the arrangement. The war had put her life on hold. There was no money for her to go to art school like she had dreamed of doing, and the little job she had at the drugstore was going nowhere. The prospect of being needed by anyone was exciting. It felt like a new chance at life.

They had a small wedding at the church with a few friends.

After the wedding, Helen went home to live with Richard and his father.

On their wedding night she and Richard slept in his old bedroom, while Thomas stayed in his and Lillian's room. Richard tied the twin beds in his room together with a rope and stuffed his rough wool Army blanket in the crack between the two mattresses. He had tried to make the bed with one of the twin bed top sheets and a blanket but both were about a foot short of each side. All night long Helen found herself cold and uncovered.

The next night, Helen took a double bed sheet and an old comforter from the linen closet and remade the bed. The covers came closer to reaching, but the blanket Richard had stuffed between the mattresses felt like a cautionary double yellow line or a war zone that shouldn't be crossed.

At first, she believed their living arrangements were temporary. Richard had promised her once Thomas was well enough to live alone, they would move out and buy a home of their own. Work was good in the plant and there was plenty of overtime to help put money in the bank. By living with Thomas they were able to save quite a bit of money for a down payment on a house.

Because money was tight and the living arrangements temporary, Helen agreed to continue to live with Thomas and make do with Richard's old twin beds tied together. But, after a few months, when things began to feel more permanent, Helen demanded Richard use some of their savings to buy a double bed so they could sleep more comfortably.

From the very start of their marriage, Richard had trouble sleeping. He tossed and turned and some nights it seemed as though he didn't sleep at all. Helen secretly hoped the new bed would help. It didn't. Richard complained about spending money on the new bed and became angry she had insisted on buying it. Richard told her in no uncertain terms that nothing else in the house was going to be changed.

Helen stayed clear of Richard's anger by working in the garden. She also tried her best to keep everything just as Lillian had left it, hoping that in time, Richard would be happy and everything would work out.

While things were less than perfect with Richard, life with Thomas around was good. Thomas appreciated Helen's company while Richard was off at work. Every morning, when Thomas came down for breakfast, he'd call out for Helen to be sure she was there before he came into the kitchen. He told her once that after Lillian died he didn't eat for a week because he was afraid to go into the kitchen and discover she was really gone.

Helen liked taking care of Thomas. There was something wonderful about having someone to take care of who needed you and appreciated what you did. She learned how to scramble eggs the way Thomas liked them. Which was the way Lillian always cooked them with bits of fried potatoes and green onions from her garden. She also learned how to make shepherd's pie with little puffy mounds of mashed potatoes circling Lillian's cast iron Dutch oven.

All the while she cooked, Thomas would tell her stories about Lillian. He loved to tell her about how they met, and how Lillian would crimp a pie crust by pinching the edges between her thumb and her first finger making it look like a picture in a magazine, how she would sing to the radio and tease him into dancing with her, and how much he missed her.

With Thomas's encouragement Helen carefully worked her way through the large brown envelop of recipes Lillian had written down and left behind. Despite her occasional failures, Thomas never forgot to thank her for each dish and to talk about Lillian.

Helen loved her father-in-law. When she took care of Thomas, Helen often felt like she was playing house, working in her mother-in-law's garden, cooking her mother-in-law's recipes, and making her beds. Almost three years to the day after Helen and Richard were married, Thomas died in his sleep in the big pine bed he and Lillian had once shared.

When Thomas died, Helen had wanted to move. She told Richard the house was full of ghosts and there was no room for them to build a family there.

Richard refused to move. He said he liked the house and felt comfortable there. He also said he thought there was no reason to move. The house was a perfectly good one and except for the taxes, they owned it outright. It made no sense to buy another. Since Helen wasn't working, she found it hard to argue with Richard about money matters. The one consolation to staying put was Lillian's garden.

From the very first, Helen continued to grow gladiolas along the back line of the garden just as Lillian had once done and to keep the large mound at the right corner of the lot for rhubarb. When Helen decided to change the size of the plot to make room for more plants she was careful to plant it the way Lillian had always planted her vegetable garden by surrounding it with a border of flowers. The garden might be bigger, but Helen wasn't willing to part with her mother-in-law's presence.

Shortly after Thomas died, Richard agreed they could move to the larger bedroom. Helen thought about stripping the yellowed wallpaper and painting it a pale blue. Richard said the wallpaper was perfectly good and should be left intact. Helen suggested putting up fresh curtains and buying a new bedspread. Again, Richard refused. They had a terrible fight and in the end, everything in the house stayed just as Lillian had left it.

Helen believed changes would come in time and kept quiet. But, after Tommy was born, she became overwhelmed with the job of being a mother and all thoughts of buying new curtains or moving to a new home vanished.

Tommy wasn't at all like either Richard or his namesake, Thomas. Taking care of Tommy wasn't at all like taking care of

Thomas. Where Thomas was content to sit and be with her, Tommy struggled to get out of her arms and run away. She didn't know how to take care of him. She didn't know how to keep him safe. She didn't know how to be his mother.

Sometimes she was so scared and tired she worried she might get sick and die just like her own mother had done.

Linda stood by the kitchen window watching her mother walk along the string she had staked out to mark a row, working a long shallow ditch with her hoe for onion sets. Linda was supposed to be reading King Lear for English but didn't really feel like mucking through Shakespeare.

"Want some help?" she called through the open window.

"Thought you had homework," Helen called back, working a stubborn clod of clay with the edge of her hoe.

"Just reading."

"Sure."

Slipping on an old pair of tennis shoes Linda grabbed some garden gloves from the back porch before she went out to join her mother.

"Onion sets?" she asked.

"The bucket is over there. The feed store had a new variety of yellow Spanish onions. They're supposed to be bigger and sweeter. Careful when you separate them, only…" Helen started to instruct her daughter.

"Only one per hole. I think I know how to plant onions."

"This garden…"

"Is going to send me to college," Linda completed her mother's next sentence.

"And it will, young lady, if you separate the onions like I tell you to do," Helen said in a mock-stern way.

"And what about Tommy?"

When he was first born and Helen could still wrap him tightly in a square flannel blanket and hold him until he restlessly fell to sleep she dreamt about him growing up and going to college. But, once he took his first step she began to doubt it would happen.

Tommy went after the world in a way that had nothing to do with reading a book or worrying about passing exams. School was too much sitting still to suit Tommy. Helen knew it was a waste of dreams to plan Tommy's life. Tommy did as he pleased from the time he could run.

"Tommy wouldn't be happy in college," Helen said, taking up her hoe and moving chunk by chunk up the string.

"Have you ever asked him if he wanted to go to college? I don't like it when you say the garden money is mine. Shouldn't it be yours too? I think it should be Tommy's as well."

"Has he ever asked you about the money?"

"I told him he could have it."

"Did he say he wanted it?" Helen asked, already knowing the answer.

"Maybe he doesn't know enough to want it."

"Maybe he wants something else."

"Yeah, like a job in the factory with Dad?"

Helen chose to let the comment pass. Linda had always been doggedly fierce in her defense and protection of Tommy.

Working her way a little further up the row away from her daughter, Helen closed her eyes hoping she could magically make all the tension between them disappear.

"Tommy would die in the factory," Helen said, knowing it was true. Tommy would never do well being so confined. "But, for your information, miss smarty pants, your father likes working in the factory."

Richard told Helen once he rather liked the incessant hum of the machinery and the push of the line forcing him to focus on the task at hand. He said it blocked out the memories of the war and the sound of artillery he sometimes still heard in his head. Richard said the hum and the drum of the factory cleared his head and made him feel calm.

Linda kept walking down the row pushing onion sets into the ground with her fingers.

"The Army might be a good place for Tommy," Helen offered.

"Tommy might get killed in the Army," Linda screamed back, the anger and fear in her voice pushing up through her body like an explosion.

"You can't always be there to protect him. None of us can," Helen said, her voice soft and sing-song calm as she dropped the hoe and walked over to soothe her sobbing daughter.

"And if he's lost?" Linda asked, letting her mother's arms swallow up the fear she felt when she thought of Tommy and of how he was always so close to danger, so very far away from where she could go to get him and save him.

"Someone will find him."

Even though she couldn't believe it, Linda wished with all her heart it would be true.

Chapter 3

Pulling into the parking lot the next Sunday, Helen was surprised to see the visiting preacher, Joe Nathan, standing on the sidewalk greeting people.

"Praise Jesus," he called out, his gangly right arm waving wildly like the clapper in the bell of his ill-fitting suit as the Sunday worshipers got out of their cars. "The Lord is good to me!"

With each new arrival, he called out the same greeting, hitting the "me" in the sentence extra hard as though everyone who had come to church that morning had come just to hear him.

Helen had not liked the looks of the man the first time he stepped up to the pulpit last Sunday. He had the kind of sharp angry face that no big smile or friendly waving hand could wipe away or hide. She knew for certain that he was someone she wouldn't unlock the door for if he came knocking late at night.

She had no desire to get to know him better. In fact, she had no desire to know him at all. Turning her head away from his fast approaching presence, she silently prayed she'd disappear or lightning would strike and take away the madman before her. Richard touched her leg as if to say she should behave herself and accept his Christian greeting. She didn't move.

"We're here." Richard said happily as he let the car roll to a stop in the parking space.

"We are here," she replied.

Tommy rolled his eyes and punched Linda in the arm. "Welcome to the God show," he said under his breath.

"Tommy," Richard snapped.

"What'd I say?" he laughed.

Helen did not want to get out of the car and receive a blessing from Joe Nathan. On the other hand, there wasn't much point in staying in the car listening to Tommy and Richard fight. She opened the door and got out before Richard could come around and let her out. Seeing Helen get out of the car, Joe Nathan moved in her direction, waving his hand like a flag. It would have been impossible and also rude for Helen to ignore him, so she stepped forward in order to meet him. Getting out of the car, Richard came around to stand behind Helen. Tommy and Linda took the opportunity to get into the church without being accosted.

Joe Nathan nodded a greeting towards Richard without shaking Richard's outstretched hand. Instead, Joe Nathan grabbed Helen's hand in both of his and began to pump it up and down as though he was trying to prime a well. Helen pumped in return, and as she did she noticed there were two women standing with him.

"Nice to meet you, ma'am," he sang out loudly, "this here is my wife, Mrs. Nathan, and this is my daughter, Melinda, but we call her Mindy."

Mrs. Nathan pulled her shoulders up and looked down at her shoes as she extended her hand to Helen as though she was reaching into a box of snakes and was afraid to see what she might touch. Mindy, on the other hand, kept tossing her hair from side to side, smiling like someone in a shampoo commercial.

"I'm Helen Nichols," Helen said, shaking off Joe Nathan's vigorous grip and taking Mrs. Nathan's offered hand. "This is my husband, Richard."

"Pleased to meet you Mr. and Mrs. Nichols," Joe Nathan's wife said.

"Feel free to call me Helen," Helen said.

"Yes, ma'am," Mrs. Nathan responded, without offering her first name as if she didn't have one.

Mindy didn't seem to notice either Helen, Richard or her mother and just kept tossing her hair and smiling at people as they passed by. Every couple of seconds or so, Joe Nathan would touch his daughter's arm. Mindy would turn to her father and the two of them would smile like they were just happy in the Lord to be standing there together welcoming the world to worship. Mrs. Nathan, on the other hand, stood off to the side, trying to stay out of the way, while her husband and daughter continued with their cheery greetings.

An awkward silence clung to the air.

"Shall we go in," Helen said to Richard, taking his arm in the hopes of steering clear of this odd welcoming party.

"Nice to see you, Mrs. Nathan, and you, Mr. Nathan," Richard said.

"Just call me Preacher, yes, that will do, just call me Preacher. And, for sure you'll be seeing us, all right," Joe Nathan sang out so that everyone around them could hear. "Me and my wife and my little girl are here to stay."

Before Richard could respond, Joe Nathan and his daughter were already heading towards the next family. Mrs. Nathan trailed a few steps behind.

"We should go inside," Richard said, putting his hand in his pocket to protect it from the fact that it had gone unshaken.

Once inside, Linda and Tommy took seats in the back. As Helen and Richard walked past them, Helen squeezed Tommy's shoulder as if to say she hoped there wouldn't be any more surprise announcements like there had been last Sunday. Tommy looked up and flashed a smile. Helen walked on.

Tommy let the smile shine out for a minute or two just in case any of the good ladies of the church were craning their necks in order to see what was going on. When he was satisfied no one in particular was looking, he put his arm around Linda and whispered in her ear.

"Bet'cha two big ones he's not a real preacher."

"Tommy," Linda hissed. "Gambling's a sin. In case you hadn't noticed, we're sitting in a church."

"Aren't sure, are you?"

"He's here to preach, isn't he?"

"Preaching don't make you a preacher. Now, are you going to bet me or do I have to tell Mom about that time you went drinking with Larry and me?"

"I had one sip of one beer," Linda said under her breath.

"Drinking is drinking whether you've had one sip or ten, so you might as well of finished the bottle."

"Oh, all right. I say he's a preacher or he wouldn't be here."

"Got some money you're willing to part with?"

Unsnapping her purse Linda pulled out two one dollar bills then folded them in the palm of her right hand like she was thinking about slipping them into an offering envelope. "Here's mine," she said, "now let me see yours."

"Hot dog," Tommy said, reaching into his wallet. Like Linda, he folded his two dollars and held them in his hand. "I love it when you lose."

"Let's see who wins before you start planning on how you're going to spend this fortune."

"You're a tough one," Tommy teased, "a real gambler."

"Shhh," she warned.

When everyone was seated and Joe Nathan was somehow divinely assured all of the good people God was bringing to him this morning had arrived, he pranced down the aisle with his wife on one side and his daughter on the other. As the three of them worked their way up the aisle, Joe Nathan continued to wave his hands in blessing, and the two women dutifully handed out mimeographed sheets to the congregation.

Once they had reached the front, Mrs. Nathan and Mindy took their seats on the very first pew next to Reverend Jacob's wife, and Joe Nathan stepped up to the podium. Reverend Jacobs sat down on a folding chair to the right of Joe Nathan.

"Now my wife and my daughter have handed you all the Bible verse for this morning's worship. But, before you get too comfortable this fine Sunday morning," Joe Nathan said, rattling his piece of paper with the Bible verse and smiling at Reverend Jacobs. Jacobs rattled his paper back at Joe Nathan as if to say he had his, too. "You might want to get on your knees for a moment so you can hear what the good Lord has to say to you today. I always think you can hear better on your knees than you can resting on the seat of your pants."

"Amen," Reverend Jacobs offered, as he promptly stood up and turned to face the seat of his folding chair and knelt. As he stood, everyone else stood, fumbling with the kneelers and their papers. Since Mrs. Nathan, Mrs. Jacobs, and Mindy, were sitting on the very front row and there was no pew in front of them with a kneeler attached, they stood, turned toward their seats, and knelt on the hard linoleum floor.

"I'd advise you," Joe Nathan said, standing at the pulpit, "to close your eyes and find an easy resting place on your knees this morning because you're going to be here for a while. Before we commence praying, I will read these words that came to me by the inspired hand of Jesus."

Joe Nathan paused. Once the congregation was settled, he started to read.

"The in-spir-ed hand of the Lord," he sang out, hitting hard on the word inspired. "I have learned in years of sinning and repenting to let Him guide me," he said. Then he paused again.

Helen decided to quit pretending like she was praying, and read the verse on the paper she was holding in her hand. At first glance, it did not seem to make sense, so she peered up over the top of the pew in front of her in order to get a look at Joe Nathan as if looking at him would clarify the meaning of the words in front of her. He glared back, like the great wizard-trickster Oz, indicating she should not be looking, but should have her eyes closed and start praying instead. She held his gaze.

Joe Nathan stirred a sense of rebellion in Helen. He angered her but she didn't know why. The anger felt good. It felt like a warm fire inside of her that had been smoldering for years.

"I have learned to be still," he said, looking straight at Helen as though she were wiggling restlessly in the pew or otherwise causing a stir. "To stay on my knees until He talks to me." Helen didn't flinch. Joe Nathan turned his head from Helen and closed his eyes. She turned her head away and looked out the stained glass window.

"He talks to me," Joe Nathan sang out, "oh, He does, yes He does. He talks to me." Then Joe Nathan started to hum a kind of drone-like hum. Helen looked at Joe Nathan. His eyes were squeezed shut and his head was thrown back so his Adam's apple quivered like a small bird trapped in his throat.

"I hold my Bible tight in my hands until I can't hold it any longer and I pray to Jesus to give me guidance. I ask Him to show me the way." Joe Nathan's humming got a little louder. Reverend Jacobs let out a loud, "Amen."

"Je-sus, I called out the other day to my friend. Give me some words to guide these good people."

"A-men," Reverend Jacobs gave a shout.

"No sooner than I had asked for guidance, my Bible flew open," Joe Nathan said, opening his eyes wide and leaning out over the pulpit, "and these are the words the good Savior gave me."

Helen wanted to stand up and tell the congregation that this man was a charlatan. She wanted to shout, to scream, to wake up the people around her. She had never had such an urge before. She felt both unhinged and powerful. She started to move to stand. Richard grabbed her hand. She tried to pull away. Richard tightened his grip on her. She rested her knees back onto the kneeler again. She looked down at the paper in her hand. Others in the congregation were reading their papers as well. There was a fluttering of paper and hands and a swell of whispers all up and down the aisles of the small congregation as people began to read the verse under their breath.

"What'd I tell you," Tommy said as he finished reading his paper.

"One verse doesn't prove anything."

"Read it and weep," Tommy teased, "read it and weep."

"These are the thoughts of Jesus," Joe Nathan called out in warning as though he feared the whole congregation might misconstrue their meaning. "The Lord has brought these to you to put in your hearts. He wants you to memorize these words so they will be with you in your time of need. And you will need them as well as you will need Him. Because we all need Him." Then his humming started coming in short bursts as he started rocking back and forth on the heels of his shoes.

Tommy tugged teasingly at Linda's two dollars. Linda held tight and shook her head. She needed more proof.

Closing his eyes, Richard let Joe Nathan's humming transport him into a place of prayer. Helen read over the verse a second time then looked up from her paper and watched Joe Nathan's amazing Adam's apple as it bobbled and jiggled up and down his neck to the rhythm of his humming. She wanted to laugh.

"And it came to pass," Joe Nathan sang out, his eyes closed and his head thrown back so he could show that he'd already committed 1st Samuel 4:18 to memory, "when he made mention of the ark of God, that he fell from off the seat backward by the side of the gate, and his neck brake, and he died: for he was an old man, and heavy. And he had judged Israel for forty years."

Pausing for a moment as if he was awaiting some response from God, Joe Nathan rocked a little more and hummed and called out the verse again. His oversized black suit jacket flapped open then closed as he rocked. He could have been a bird, perhaps a big crow, rocking back and forth in the wind, wings resting by his sides.

Helen looked up in amazement. The verse made no more sense to her upon hearing it a second time than it did the first time she read it. She was aware, however, that the air around her had become filled with Joe Nathan's humming and felt heavy and still the way she thought it must feel right before an earthquake. She held her breath.

Rocking harder, Joe Nathan's palms slapped against the podium as his body swung violently back and forth. His humming got louder then all of a sudden he gave out a great shout, "Thank you, Je-sus," he cried. Reverend Jacobs answered with a loud, "Amen," and threw up his right hand like he was spreading pixie dust into the air.

When Joe Nathan finished humming, he stopped rocking and leaned out over the pulpit to speak.

"These are the words of Jesus. This is His message to you today. Listen with your hearts. You know what Jesus has to say to you today. You and only you know what sin you have to confess, what evil you have to offer up before you can find salvation. Let us feast on what Jesus has put before us. Let us use the call of these words to get our hearts right with God."

Reverend Jacobs gave out another "Amen." A couple of other people threw in an "Amen" or two, or a "Praise Jesus", and then the whole congregation began to shift a little on their kneelers.

"You can get up now," Joe Nathan said, his hands rising as if to help the congregation to their feet. "Forget about bringing your Bibles to church with you for now. Listen to Him as you listen to me. Let your hearts be opened. Let us sing."

The organist played the introduction to "The Old Rugged Cross." One by one, the congregation joined in with Joe Nathan. He moved his hands to the music as if he were directing a heavenly choir. When the hymn was over, he held up both of his hands, indicating everyone should take their seats again. Once the sitting and shuffling of feet was done, Joe Nathan began to preach.

His preaching was as odd as his choice of Bible verses. He rocked, hummed, and called out what he referred to as the words of Jesus in his heart. He never explained who fell off what seat beside what gate and broke his neck. He just rocked and hummed and called on Jesus to fill their hearts. Each time he took up some new phrase, his voice started low and soft then got louder and louder until it shook the room.

Linda squirmed. Joe Nathan's sermon had now gone on for about twenty minutes, and nothing he had said made sense. It was, however, hypnotic, and every once in awhile someone from the congregation shouted a loud "Amen." These little outbursts of "Amens" jolted Joe Nathan. Whenever one of them rang out, he'd stop rocking for a second, pull up his chin to let his Adam's apple dance a bit in preparation for him to shout back a hearty "Praise Jesus, I feel the spirit moving." He'd nod to the person who had called out then wave his hand back and forth as though he was giving them a blessing. Then he'd start in once more with a low kind of moan and begin his plain song again.

Tommy turned and smiled at Linda. Linda, in turn, handed over her money then folded her hands in her lap.

"Thank you," Tommy whispered sweetly as he folded her money with his and tucked it into his pants pocket.

"If he's not a real preacher, then maybe he's the Devil," Linda hissed quietly.

"Maybe. But we didn't bet on that," Tommy smiled.

By this time, Linda was pretty sure Joe Nathan was not a real preacher. The length of his sermon, however, made her groggy. She noticed the little ones sitting next to their mothers had quit squirming in their seats. The warm hypnotic drone of Joe Nathan's voice had quieted the whole congregation. Even Tommy, once his bet was secured, was lulled by Joe Nathan's words and leaned into Linda's shoulder for a rest. Linda didn't bother to push him away.

Helen had let her mind drift. Her body and her mind had temporarily detached themselves. She felt oddly at peace. She was somewhere else and it felt easier to be there than any place she had ever been before. She didn't understand what Joe Nathan had stirred in her, and for the moment she didn't care. She felt comfortable.

Just as the whole congregation was nodding off and heading in some direction other than where Joe Nathan had intended for them, his talking and rocking reached a new pitch and his voice became high and far away like those women in Africa who are said to cry out in the night when someone dies. Just as Joe Nathan's humming reached a fevered pitch, Reverend Jacobs stepped up beside him at the pulpit and raised his hand with a loud and definitive, "Amen."

Joe Nathan hushed.

"Is there anyone here," Reverend Jacobs called out, his hand sweeping the room, "who has anything to confess? Is there anyone here who needs to speak to Je-sus?"

Joe Nathan's humming started anew like a low rumble. His body rocked violently back and forth, his eyes squeezed shut and his head thrown back as if he was in a trance.

"Is there anything," Reverend Jacobs shouted out above the hum of Joe Nathan, "you need to get off your heart so you can get right with Jesus? Does anyone feel the need to testify?"

"I have something to confess," Richard said, coming slowly to his feet, his hands resting on the back of the pew in front of him as though he needed help to stand. At the sound of his father's voice, Tommy jolted awake. Linda felt her cheeks flush, while Helen kept her head turned away from Richard as though she was not willing to give up looking out of the window no matter what might happen next.

"Tell us," Joe Nathan sang out.

"I have not always been a good husband."

"Hmmm," Joe Nathan hummed, his eyes closed, his head thrown back and his Adam's apple jumping. "Lead us NOT into temptation," his voice whipped through the congregation like a cold wind. People's heads began to nod in agreement.

"I have not always been a good father."

"SPARE THE ROD," Joe Nathan shouted, "and you will SURELY spoil the child."

All eyes turned from Richard to Tommy then back to Helen, who had not even flinched as though she was deaf and couldn't hear what was being said. Heads quit bobbing and the whole church got quiet.

Helen could feel their eyes like mosquito bites itching her flesh. She did not turn, however, but blinked for a moment to look down at her hands in her lap. She then straightened her shoulders and resumed looking out the window again.

Richard began to cry quietly to himself, tears making a slow trail down the front of his face. Joe Nathan's hard boney hand slicked his hair back across the top of his head. He leaned out across the podium in an attempt to show he wanted to be close to Richard, to reach out and touch him.

"Je-sus has heard you. He knows your troubles and feels your sadness. He will forgive you."

Richard nodded his head then slowly lowered himself back into the pew. Helen moved slightly in her seat making room for Richard to sit down.

"Is there anyone else?" Reverend Jacobs called out. "Anyone else who needs to talk to Jesus?"

Heads turned slowly from side to side. No one spoke. Helen reached over and touched Richard's arm. Her eyes never left the window.

Chapter 4

Sitting down, Richard inched his hand over to Helen, hoping she would take it. He felt her fingers brush against it. He opened his hand so she could let hers rest in his palm. He felt her hand withdraw. He turned and saw she was not looking at him, in fact, was not looking at anything in particular. She was just sitting there, looking out the window at nothing.

He wished he had told her he liked her short hair.

Linda looked to the front of the congregation where her parents were sitting. Her mother was looking out the window. Linda looked at her father and wondered what had just happened.

A wave of anger washed over her. She was angry with her mother for not doing something to stop her father from standing up. Her father's words were ringing in her ears like a bell. I have not been a good husband. I have not always been a good father. She could not let them go. They kept playing over and over in her head like the pulsing singsong preaching of Joe Nathan. What if she hadn't been a good daughter?

"Forget it," Tommy whispered in her ear.

"Why'd he say that?" Linda hissed.

"Just forget it. Joe Nathan's not a preacher. He's crazy, and crazy people can make you do crazy things. I mean, look at that weird Bible verse. What was that supposed to mean?"

"Dad's not crazy," Linda said, her teeth clinched, trying hard not to scream.

"Look, I'll give you your money back." Tommy reached into his pocket.

Linda didn't respond.

"Come on," Tommy pleaded, touching her arm. "Don't go floating off like Mom."

"I'm not like Mom," Linda protested, snatching her arm away.

"Okay, you're not like Mom. Take the money." Tommy pushed the money into her hand.

"Why did he say that? And why did she just sit there. What's wrong with her?"

"Just forget about it."

After church, Linda and Tommy went to the car and climbed into the backseat. Tommy wanted to roll down the windows to let some air in while they waited for their parents. Linda said she thought it was a bad idea.

"Pretty scary stuff, huh?" Tommy said, pulling at the edge of Linda's dress to get her attention. "Look, I told you he's no preacher. Plus, there's something creepy about him and the way he kept saying things over and over like he was hypnotizing us. Like he was a snake charmer or something. Maybe he hypnotized Dad. You ever think of that?"

"What are we supposed to do now?"

"Who knows," Tommy said, "I sure hope Mom and Dad won't want us to sit in a circle holding hands praying or something weird like that."

"Maybe Joe Nathan will come over after lunch to bless our house."

"Over my dead body," Tommy said.

"Don't say that."

Linda and Tommy could tell by the way their parents got into the car the topic of what had happened during church was not up for discussion. At first there was an icy silence, then once they had pulled away safely from the church parking lot their mother spoke.

"Beautiful day for gardening," she said as though they had all been talking about the weather. "Listen, Dad's got to go to the dedication of the war memorial at Civitan Park this afternoon so I thought we could stop at the market and pick up some cold cuts and Kaiser rolls for lunch. Have something simple like chips and sandwiches then Dad can be off on time for the dedication and I can do a little work in the garden."

"Sounds great," Tommy said, relieved they weren't going to be asked to form a prayer circle. "Larry and I were thinking about getting a game together this afternoon."

"What's up with you, Linda?" her dad asked.

"Nothing," and then, because she worried she had not been a good daughter, she added, "can I come along with you to the park?"

"I'd like that," he said, looking in to the rearview mirror, smiling.

"Brown nose," Tommy whispered in her ear.

After lunch, Richard went upstairs and changed into his old Army dress uniform. All the veterans of the town had been asked to come to the ceremony in uniform. Those who couldn't fit into them anymore were asked to wear their hats and medals. Richard's uniform was tight, but it still fit. It made him feel uncomfortable to have it on again. The smell of moth balls and the aging wool made him queasy.

He wished there had never been a war. He wished he'd never had to hold a gun or kill anyone. He wished he could sleep at night without hearing the sound of gunfire or seeing how the bullets he shot would knock a body back off its feet. So many bodies. So much blood. He used to worry all the bodies he saw fall were the ones he hit, that somehow he was responsible for all the pain and death scattered on the ground. Twice he killed at such close range he could see the person's face and watch the shock of the bullet as it burned through them. Those were the deaths he dreamed about over and over again.

He wondered what his life would be like now if he had never fought in the war. He wondered why he had kept the uniform, why he hadn't thrown it away or burned it with the trash he raked up from the lawn.

He envied the Catholics in his battalion who, after each battle would stumble in exhaustion with blood still on their hands and uniforms to the priest's tent and count the dead, letting them go one at a time, like rosary beads, into an eternity of forgiveness.

When they arrived at the ceremony, Richard took his seat with the other veterans sitting on folding chairs in front of the memorial. On either side of the veterans were seats for the boy scouts, girl scouts, safety patrol boys and town officials. Everyone else was expected to stand. Linda took a place toward the back of the crowd under the shade of a tree.

The high school marching band was there in their fancy new uniforms. They started the ceremony with a medley of military songs ending with the national anthem. Once the people in front were again seated, the mayor stood up in order to open the ceremonies and to introduce the president of the Civitan Club.

"This day," Mayor Arnold called out across the small crowd, "has been a long time coming. Much too much time has passed for us to honor the men before us who fought so bravely for our country and for those men who were killed in action during World Wars I and II as well as the Korean War. So it is with great pleasure that I present to you this humble memorial." The mayor let his hand rise slowly as he pulled the canvas away from the small stone and bronze obelisk. "I hope it will bring honor not only to those men who have fought to keep our country free, but to our town for raising such brave and honorable men."

People applauded.

"So, without further ado, let me now introduce George Taylor, president of the Civitan Club."

Mr. Taylor, the owner of Taylor's Hardware, stepped forward. He had fought in World War II with Richard, but unlike Richard he could no longer fit into his uniform so he wore a dark blue suit with his serviceman's hat. When he came forward, he removed his cap and tucked it under his left arm like a riding crop.

"I'm not good at speeches," he said, looking down at his shoes, "and I know there are many people to thank for making this memorial possible. So, thank you."

A soft ripple of laughter worked across the crowd.

"I thought it would be a fitting thing for us to hear the names of the men who are engraved here on this monument, so I've asked one of the members of the high school Drama Club to read us the list." With this, he stepped aside and Cynthia Martin, the president of the high school drama club, stepped forward.

"The names I will read today," Cynthia said, pausing to give the various scout and safety patrol participants a chance to quit squirming in their folding chairs and bring themselves into the right frame of mind for the occasion, "are the names of those who were our friends, our family and our neighbors. They were honorable and loving people who lived among us and died protecting us.

"Let us remember them for their brave deeds."

The afternoon air was warm and Linda was beginning to feel a little drowsy. She closed her eyes for a second and let her mind drift. Cynthia's reading of the names washed in and out of Linda's consciousness.

"And, let us remember Warren Emerson Greyjack, older brother of Sheriff Greyjack."

Linda's head snapped to attention. She had always known Greyjack had a brother and his name was Warren. Her father talked about Warren being in the boat ahead of him when they landed in Normandy. She knew Warren had been killed before he made it to the beach with the others. Often after her father talked about the war and Warren getting killed, he would get in the car and drive around until long after dark. Sometimes he would go out into the shed and work by himself for a few hours, or go up to his room and shut the door. Eventually, he would call Greyjack and the two of them would go out and get drunk.

Cynthia's sharp precise enunciation of Warren Emerson Greyjack's name stunned Linda. Suddenly, Greyjack's brother was a real live person, and he had a name, and Linda could see him getting off the boat and knew he moved like Greyjack. She could hear her father calling out to him, and she could hear him calling back right before he got shot and she knew he sounded just like Greyjack. Her mother told her once that when Warren Emerson Greyjack died a part of her father and a part of Greyjack died as well.

Linda looked over at her father sitting in the front row in his uniform. He was sitting straight upright as though he were at attention. His chin was up and his face forward, staring off into the distance, tears streaming down his face.

Greyjack wasn't sitting in front with the other men. Instead, he was standing to the side near the back. Linda looked for him. She saw he had moved away from the crowd. He was dressed in his sheriff's uniform, and was leaning against a tree. Linda looked at him. He saw her and tipped his head in recognition. Then he walked to his squad car and drove away.

After the last name was read, one of the trumpets from the band stepped forward and played taps and the ceremony was over. Richard came over to Linda and said they should be going. Her father rarely hung around anywhere in order to talk to anyone.

Shortly after they got home, Greyjack came by, and her father drove off with him in his squad car. Later, when it was time for supper and her father hadn't returned. She started to get worried.

"There's nothing to worry about," her mother said, making a plate of food for Richard when he came home.

"He's been gone a long time."

"Greyjack and your dad are probably out talking about the war and having a drink."

Linda didn't like it when her father drank. Her friend Connie's father drank and often came home drunk. There'd be a terrible fight and sometimes Connie's mother would get hit. When things got really bad, Connie would call and ask to come over and spend the night.

"He's not like Connie's father," Helen said as she put the plate she made for Richard into the refrigerator. "He's just having a couple of drinks. It helps him remember, and it helps him forget. And he's never hurt me. I don't think he's ever hit anyone. You know that. He's not like Connie's father."

"I wish he didn't have to get drunk," Linda said.

"They were very close. He really misses Warren."

When Linda was getting ready for bed she heard Greyjack's car pull into the driveway. She looked out her window. She saw Greyjack help her father out of the car. Her mother went out to help Greyjack. It took both of them to bring Richard into the house and up the stairs to the bedroom. Tommy had been downstairs watching television when he heard them come in, and he offered to help. Greyjack thanked him, but told him they were fine.

After her mother and Greyjack got her father upstairs and into bed, they went back outside and stood in the driveway for a long time talking. Linda watched them from her window. Greyjack had taken his hat off and thrown it on the hood of his car. Standing there hatless in the moonlight with one foot resting behind him on the base of the car wheel and his arms crossed in front of him he looked young and handsome. His head was bowed slightly like he was talking quietly, seriously about something. Linda's mother stood in front off to the side a bit as though to make room for Richard if he woke up and came down to join them.

Every once in awhile one of them would laugh about something, their heads thrown back and bodies relaxing for a moment. The moment of laughter would pass and they'd get tense and quiet again, whispering secrets. Eventually, Greyjack picked up his hat and got into his car and drove away. When her mother came into the house she came up to Linda's bedroom and stood in the doorway.

"It's a good thing Dad went out with Greyjack tonight," she said, pushing her short hair back behind her ears and fiddling with her garnet earrings a little. "A good thing."

"Good," said Linda. She shook her head to indicate she understood even though she was not quite sure what her mother was talking about.

"Men sometimes don't have a very good notion of how to be friends, so, when they need to be friends, they sometimes need a drink."

"Sure," said Linda.

"Warren was Greyjack's older brother. He and Greyjack were more like best friends than brothers. Your dad and Greyjack and Warren did everything together. Warren was really special. He was funny and smart, and he had this way of making everything seem bigger than it really was, or better. You could be down by the lake with friends not doing anything in particular. Then Warren would come along and it wouldn't feel like nothing anymore, it would feel like a big party.

"A bunch of people would just walk by. Before you knew it Warren would be choosing teams, and they'd all start playing football and laughing and you'd just think that you were having the best time in your life. But, all you'd be doing was hanging out with friends out at the lake like you always did.

"Everybody loved Warren. Sometimes your father and Greyjack don't quite know what to do without him. Do you understand?"

"Sure," Linda said.

"I know what you're thinking. You're thinking your father is going to be like Connie's father, drunk all the time. But he won't. I promise you. I know he won't."

"Does Greyjack have a first name?" Linda asked.

"Yes," said Helen, looking away for a minute as though she was trying to find a good name for him, "his name is Francis."

Chapter 5

Helen fiddled with her hair. It had grown out a bit since she had cut it. It was floppy and messy. It irritated her. She was thinking about locking the bathroom door again and getting out the razor, but she knew she didn't have time before church. She wet her hands and ran them through her curls, trying to tease them into something that pleased her. She wanted to cry.

She usually didn't care about pleasing anyone else, especially not anyone from the church. It was Richard's church, not hers. Before marrying Richard she didn't even go to church. Her father had quit taking her when her mother died. He said they had no reason to go because God didn't listen to the prayers of the likes of them.

Church was something she did for Richard although she really didn't know why because she didn't like it. She could not stand the way the women at the church acted so holy and proper, yet talked behind each other's backs. Helen sometimes wondered if the women talked about her. More than anything, she hated this morning that she cared.

The last two Sundays had brought more attention to her and her family than she liked, and she knew people would be looking at her. Helen had the feeling they were always looking at her, watching her as though she was somehow different from them.

Given all that had happened, especially Richard's confession of last Sunday, it didn't come as any surprise to Helen that Tommy and Linda were dragging their feet getting up and out the door for church. She didn't blame them, but also didn't feel like she could tell Richard none of them wanted to go because he had made such a public display of their lives.

"Get up," she called out again for the third time. "It's almost time to go."

"Gettin' up," Linda snapped back.

"What about your brother?"

"Tommy," Linda screeched.

"Go away," he shouted.

"Come on, let's go," Helen said brushing her hair back over her ears again then getting out of the bathroom so Tommy and Linda could get washed. When she went downstairs she smeared peanut butter on two pieces of toast for the kids to eat in the car.

When they finally made it to church, Helen was relieved to discover Joe Nathan was not outside greeting everyone in the parking lot. She was equally happy, as the morning unfolded, that the service seemed to go on without any further mention of Tommy's mischief or Richard's failings as a husband and father.

She was not at all pleased when she saw Mindy, Joe Nathan's daughter, stride up the aisle when the service was over tossing her hair from side to side, her hand outstretched to meet Tommy.

When Linda saw Mindy come down the aisle to meet Tommy, she tugged on the sleeve of his shirt and stepped in front of him as if to shield him from her. Linda could see by the easy way Mindy walked with her hand outstretched, as if anyone who saw it would be glad to take it, that she was just like Tommy.

Linda found herself caught between Mindy and Tommy and stepped aside. She realized she would not ever be able to stop what might happen between Mindy and Tommy, so she didn't even try.

"Hello," Mindy said, smiling at Tommy. Tommy smiled back but didn't speak.

Linda tugged again at his sleeve.

"This is my sister, the quiet, cautious one, Linda. When she gets wild we call her Priscilla." Tommy slid his arm around Linda and pulled her close to him, all the while never taking his eyes off Mindy.

Linda felt the sting of his words flush across her face. She did not like it when Tommy called her Priscilla. It made her feel like she was somehow half alive compared to Tommy, even though the way Tommy lived sometimes scared her to death.

"Mindy," she said, not looking at Linda, but holding her hand out to Tommy, "short for Melinda. But, only my parents call me Melinda."

"Hello, Melinda." Tommy said taking her hand.

"Hey, Tommy."

"Jailbait," Helen said, turning her head around from the front seat of the car on their way home from church. She was looking straight at Tommy when she spoke. "Let me remind you, young man, you are 18 and legally responsible for your actions. She, however, is maybe 16, at most 17. Just what you need to carry you straight into trouble."

Tommy laughed.

"Totally innocent," he said with the brush of the back of his hand and a smile. "Nothing to worry about. We're going to have an ice cream at United Dairy this afternoon. I told her I'd invite Larry. She's new, doesn't know anyone. Seemed like the right good Christian thing to do."

"You'll take your sister with you," Helen responded, snapping her head back to the front of the car indicating there would be no further discussion of the matter.

"I don't want…" Linda started.

"Love to," Tommy said, throwing his arm around Linda and punching her in the arm.

When Tommy and Linda drove up to United Dairy, Mindy was standing outside and Larry was nowhere in sight.

"Such a cute place," Mindy gushed as they got out of the car.

"Good ice cream," Tommy said.

"I mean the whole town," Mindy offered. "Daddy likes it here. That's why Mama and I came to join him. We found this adorable little house right down the street from our cousins, Reverend Jacobs and his wife. Daddy took a job with the post office. We plan to settle for awhile."

"Settling sounds like a good thing to me."

"You all's high school is such a big place. Maybe you can introduce me to some of your friends, Linda," Mindy said, turning to Linda with a big smile. "It's so hard coming to a new place, especially so late in the year. You all were so kind to invite me out this afternoon."

"I'm sure Linda will show you around." Tommy gave Linda a gentle nudge. "Right, Linda?"

"Love to," Linda said.

"Larry ought to be here soon," Tommy said taking Mindy by the arm. "Why don't we go in and get some ice cream while we're waiting?"

"Sounds good to me," Linda chimed in, feeling like a fifth wheel with a flat tire.

When they sat down Tommy slid into the booth next to Mindy and Linda took a seat alone on the other side. Mindy kept up a light patter of chitchat all through the ordering. Tommy asked for a root beer float, and she ordered one, too, saying it was her favorite. Linda ordered a dish of butter pecan.

"My daddy's a wild one," Mindy said, pushing her straw with the tip of her finger into the blob of vanilla ice cream in her glass, watching it bob and melt into the root beer. "Done just about everything from preaching to pipe fitting. This time he's got himself a job at the post office as a mail carrier. He says it's God's will. That it's His way of calling him to get out and walk among the people. And, like my mother says, it really doesn't matter whether he welds pipes or delivers mail. He always manages to stir up the Devil around us."

"I can imagine." Tommy broke out his best and warmest smile.

"Daddy says his real job is stirring up the Devil, and everything else is just stuff to make money and fill up the days. Says he likes nothing better than to get the Devil on the run."

The whole time Mindy talked, she poked her straw into her ice cream. Tommy was watching her hands like they were some great mystery or maybe the first hands he'd ever seen. Linda didn't like the way Tommy was paying attention to Mindy, but didn't know what to do about it so she just ate her ice cream.

Linda didn't care much for her brother's friend Larry. He was too quick with his hands and had a creepy kind of way of making her feel uncomfortable about whatever it was she was wearing. Right now, however, she wished he'd get here as fast as possible to snatch Tommy back to his senses.

Just when Linda thought she was going to have to say something to Tommy about the way he was watching Mindy's hands, Larry showed up.

"Sorry I'm late," he said, sliding into the booth next to Linda, giving her a playful peck on the cheek while running his hand down her back, pausing for a moment at the clasp of her bra.

"Stop it," Linda said, pushing him away.

"You know you love it," said Larry, blowing into her ear just to annoy her.

"Hi," Mindy said, dropping her straw for a moment and pushing her hand across the table towards Larry, "I'm Mindy."

"Yeah," Larry answered, "I'm Larry."

Linda's stomach felt queasy with the easy way Mindy had charmed Tommy. However, she could tell by the way Larry answered he had sized up the situation pretty quickly and knew Tommy was moving a little too fast for trouble with Mindy. Linda hoped Larry would know what to do.

"Hey, listen," said Larry. Tommy barely looked up from Mindy's hands and her soda to notice his friend. "Some of the guys are playing a little ball this afternoon."

"Mindy's going to be settling here for awhile," Tommy offered.

"Daddy's got a job at the post office," Mindy told Larry as she continued to poke at her ice cream with the straw. "Daddy says the post office suits him fine, says the pay is good, and he gets his Wednesday nights and Sundays free for preaching."

"Suit you, too?" Tommy asked.

"Suits me fine." Mindy said pulling the straw up to her mouth until it touched the edge of her lips.

"Got to go," Larry said, sliding out of the booth.

"Bye," Linda called out after him, wishing she had someplace else to be also.

After Larry left, they stayed around the Dairy for an hour or more. Eventually Mindy said she had to get home. Walking towards the door, Mindy grabbed Linda's hand.

"Where shall I look for you tomorrow?" she gushed at Linda as though they had just become best friends.

"I'll be in the library before school," Linda answered.

"Then I'll see you there," Mindy said, leaning forward a little as though she might hug or kiss Linda.

"See you tomorrow," Linda said, stepping back and away.

"See you, Tommy," Mindy cooed, as she turned to leave.

"See you," Tommy called out.

Mindy waved goodbye, walking down the street tossing her head just enough to make her hair swish from side to side.

"She's got the prettiest hands."

"Sounds like Joe Nathan is here to stay," Linda said.

"Sounds good to me," Tommy said, unlocking the car.

Sliding into the passenger side of the car Linda folded her hands in her lap like she was waiting for someone to ask her to dance. She knew her mother would ask about what happened. She didn't know what to say.

Chapter 6

The sharp edge of the wooden kneeler cut into the thin blade of her shinbone, so Helen rocked back a little and shifted her weight onto her toes in order to take the pressure off her legs.

"Shut your eyes!" Joe Nathan roared from the pulpit. "Shut them tight so you can't see anything at all except those floaty black spots behind your eyeballs." Then he chuckled as though he had just said something funny.

Helen shut her eyes. She had no desire to look at his ugly face or the ridiculous way his Adam's apple bobbled as he pranced and chanted his crazy sermons. She thought she felt his shadow move across her face.

"Je-sus wants you to listen, and He knows you can't listen with your eyes jumping all over," he said, bending over Helen as though he was trying to warn her to stay still.

Helen didn't move. Just before she thought she couldn't be still a moment longer, she felt Joe Nathan turn away from her. She breathed a deep slow breath, pushing back whatever strange fear the edge of the kneeler and his haunting voice had bubbled up inside of her. Her heart pounded in her ears. She could hear Joe Nathan, his arms swinging by his sides, the soles of his rough leather shoes brushing against the worn linoleum floor like a blind man kicking out before him as he walked down the aisle.

"Today is the first Sunday of Lent. We're on our way to Easter. To the cross! To salvation! What have you given up for Je-sus? What of your pitiful life have you offered to Him?"

Joe Nathan's scuffling footsteps came to the end of the aisle at the back of the church. His hands swirled out like a whirligig, twisting him around. "Are you listening? What do you hear? What do you see?"

What Helen could see when she thought about Lent were the Catholics walking around town with ashes on their foreheads and the people lined up outside the fellowship hall of the Methodist Church to eat pancakes on Shrove Tuesday. She also saw the Episcopalians who felt they had a toehold on eternity. Secretly she envied them and wished she had been born Episcopalian. They seemed to have everything in this life and the next. They were proud and wealthy, ate pancakes on Shrove Tuesday, got ashes on their foreheads on Ash Wednesday, danced, drank, prayed on thickly padded kneelers, never seemed to have the need to testify or be saved and had the nerve to wear their best clothes to church-hats, gloves and fancy jewelry every single Sunday of the year, not just on Easter Sunday morning.

Helen covered her mouth with her hand to muffle a giggle when she suddenly realized she'd worn her best dress, her best shoes and was carrying her best purse to go to a church where she didn't feel like she belonged to listen to a man she was beginning to think was a freak. It all seemed so wrong.

"Look in your hearts," Joe Nathan called out as he worked his way back up the aisle to the pulpit again. "What do you see?"

Helen tried to imagine her heart, but what she saw instead was this little white clapboard church with the poorly lettered hand-painted sign. She also saw the cheap yellow stained-glass windows and the gossiping people hiding behind their paper fans who kept going to church Sunday after Sunday as if they had no where else to go and who believed that showing up and sitting in a pew was all you had to do to get to heaven.

"I see a garden," Joe Nathan sang out.

Helen rolled her head a little from side to side. Her eyes were still shut. She could see a garden. Lillian's garden. She could also see the notebook of plans she and Linda kept for the garden, where they would work out the various plots for peas, corn, potatoes, radishes, broccoli, zucchini and tomatoes. Every garden she ever planted was in the notebook, and along the margins of each garden plot she had carefully written down the name and variety of every plant she and Linda had ever grown and how well it had done.

Every year, she turned to a fresh page and carefully drew out where things had been planted the year before so she could rotate the crops so the plants wouldn't deplete the soil. She diligently moved everything every year except the melons. Lillian always had melons at the back of her garden.

Helen wouldn't change that. Besides, the melons were rather indiscriminate about where they wandered, so she always put them exactly where Lillian had put them and hoped she could keep them confined. But, despite her efforts there were times when a warm soaking rain and a couple days of sunshine would send them twisting down through the careful rows of the tomatoes and up the first cornstalk or bean pole they could find.

Joe Nathan swung his bony body around and began walking up the aisle to the front as if he were going to attack. Helen quickly pushed her garden aside.

"It is no accident," Joe Nathan announced, the flat of his palms slapping down against the podium as he took his place back at the altar. "The very first story Jesus tells us in the Bible is about Eden. THE garden. The first garden. A garden full of beauty. A garden full of hope. A garden full of pride."

"Amen," a voice from the back of the church shouted.

"Now, there are times for shouting," Joe Nathan snapped back. "And there are times to be listening. This here is a time to listen."

An uncomfortable silence blanketed the sanctuary.

"I believe Jesus was trying to tell us our lives are like gardens. Listen to what Jesus has to say to you this morning and look deep in your heart. What are you growing in your garden?"

Helen tried to ignore Joe Nathan. She closed her eyes and shut him out and began to figure her list of things she'd need to order from the Burpee catalogue. She already had her onion sets from the hardware store in town, along with her potatoes sets and her snap bean seeds. She had already pressed the seeds for spring lettuce and spinach into small peat pots and put them in the cold frame out by the garage along with the tomato seedlings and the hot chili peppers she used between the rows of cabbage and broccoli in an attempt to control bugs. She made a mental note to check the Farmer's Almanac to determine when to put everything in the ground.

"Take a walk with Jeeee-sus," Joe Nathan cajoled, "into the garden of your heart."

Helen gladly let Joe Nathan push her back into her garden. She could see Lillian's tall gladiolas along the back of the plot. This year, Helen planned to add snapdragons, cockscomb, zinnias, daisies, and baby's breath. She'd plant corn and beans and around the perimeter and plant bright smelly yellow marigolds throughout the rows of tomatoes in the hopes of discouraging tomato worms.

If she had to be honest with herself, she'd say the flowers were the pride of her garden. Every morning, before anyone else was up or the sun was hot she'd go out to cut every full blossom she could find. She'd bundle them into tight bouquets with rubber bands, put them in buckets and old coffee cans she'd filled with water, and set them in the shade to sell on her stand. She loved the way the rough stems felt in her hands and how the bright petals of the flowers were so soft that when she brushed her hand against them she had to close her eyes to feel them.

Her flowers were the prettiest in town. People came by her stand early every day to be sure to get them, and while they were there they'd buy pole beans and cabbage or a sack full of tomatoes or fresh picked corn. The flowers were like a lure to bring people in to buy vegetables. She almost never had flowers left over for her own home.

"How does your garden grooooow?" Joe Nathan crowed.

It grew because she planted it, and she planted it because she wanted Linda to go to college. The garden was like a dream she didn't get to have, and the plants were like little pieces of the world she never got to see. She pored over the catalogues every winter looking for seeds and plants from far away places. She loved her big French rosemary even though none of her customers ever bought sprigs she'd cut from it because they didn't know what to do with it. They did, however, buy the pungent sweet Italian basil, the broad-leafed fresh-hay-smelling Mexican cilantro, her delicate French sage, and the beautiful firecracker starbursts of dill heads you needed to make German Kosher Dills. Her garden was filled with far away places and delicious dreams.

Richard's dreams were dangerous. He rarely talked about them, but she knew they were filled with bloodshed and death. She also knew his dreams were filled with images of people dying. Richard tossed fitfully though the night and whenever he accidentally fell into a deep sleep he could hear gunfire and screams. Night for him was a living terror.

Helen, on the other hand, welcomed night. She had wonderful dreams. She had dreams for her garden and dreams for her daughter. The first thing Helen had ever taught Linda in the garden was how to lay out a straight row with sticks and twine. She taught her how to put in onion sets, how to tell when snap beans were ready to pick and how to pinch suckers from tomato plants. And, while they worked together Helen told her daughter about books to read and places she could go once she left home and went to college.

"How does it grow, how does it grow, how does it grow…" Joe Nathan chanted clapping his hands to the rhythm of his chant until his voice and the clapping of his hands were like thunder and lighting, or gunfire. Helen inched closer to Richard and covered her ears with her hands as though covering her own ears would protect Richard from hearing the sharp gunfire of Joe Nathan's clapping.

"Be careful how it grows," Joe Nathan pranced and shouted. "Because someday Je-sus will call you and He will tell you it is time to reap what you have sown."

Helen felt the vision of her beautiful garden slip away.

"You will surely be called by Je-sus," Joe Nathan called out then clapped his hands twice, hard, as if to wake the congregation from their dreaming. "To reap what you have sown."

Helen opened her eyes. Her face was covered with tears.

"Get off your knees," Joe Nathan sang out, "and go work in the garden with Jesus."

Joe Nathan's ranting sermon had stirred an unwanted storm into Helen's life. She neither liked nor trusted the man, but for whatever reason, she could not stop thinking about what he said about the garden. Her hands itched with the need to be out in her own garden digging and doing. Her mind was buzzing with Richard's horrible dreams, her own dreams, and the dumb blue dress she'd worn to church. She'd seen the dress last year in a store window and bought it on a whim thinking she and Richard might go out to dinner or take a trip together to celebrate their 20th anniversary. Since that never happened, she decided she'd wear it to church.

The dress was fitted at the waist and came down tight around her knees. It was better suited for dinner and dancing than it was for prayer. As she struggled to rise gracefully from the kneeler back into her seat, she knew she wasn't where she wanted to be. She wanted to run from the church and go to her garden. She couldn't make her mind be quiet. She felt restless, out of place and angry.

When they got home from church, she went straight to her room and changed her clothes. After lunch, she went out to the garden alone. She put on her gloves, got her tools, and marked a new row with two sticks and a line of string. All afternoon, she worked from one end of the string to the other digging holes. It was early to be planting tomatoes, but fine for lettuce, spinach and marigold seeds.

When the last plant was in and the last pinch of flower seeds covered up, she sat down at the end of the row. Something didn't feel right. Her line was neat and straight. The plants were evenly spaced. It was a perfect row of seedlings, a row full of promise. Instead of being happy with what she saw, the newly planted garden made her feel edgy and agitated.

Looking down the taut string of her work, she knew, before the first tender leaves of lettuce were plucked until the last bolted stem of spinach was pulled to make room for tomato plants and cucumbers, she would walk this row a hundred times. She would pick and pinch. She would also chop back the weeds with the sharp edge of Lillian's old smooth-handled hoe.

But, no matter how hard she worked or how well her garden grew, no amount of digging and weeding would ever be enough to quell the uneasiness Joe Nathan had stirred in her. Helen wondered, for the first time in a very long time, if she was happy.

On Monday, when Linda came home from school, she was surprised to find her mother wasn't in the garden. At dinner the night before all her mother could talk about was the garden, and how she wanted to build up the melon beds and plan for another row of tomatoes. She had big plans for tomatoes.

Her mother was always anxious to get her garden in before Easter but this year she seemed especially anxious, almost edgy. The garden was piled thick with leaves and compost, ready for tilling. Linda called out thinking her mother might be in the garage putting things away. There was no answer.

When Linda walked back to the garden she saw there was nothing new except for one fresh pile of compost dumped at the back edge of the garden. It looked as if her mother had thought about building the melon beds, but left in the middle of it to do something else.

When Linda went into the house, she was surprised to find

her mother standing on a ladder painting. Everything on top of the cabinets or counters had been cleared away, put onto the floor in the corner and covered with an old sheet. The stepladder from the garage was pushed next to the back wall and her mother was standing on it, her short-cropped hair covered with an old scarf. She was painting the kitchen bright orange. Not peach or melon, but bright pumpkin orange.

"I hauled a load of the winter compost over to the back of the garden where we talked about putting in the melon patch," her mother said to her as Linda stood frozen, watching her paint. "Looks a little rich to me. You'll want to mix in some leaves extra and stuff before you build your beds. Be sure to make the beds good and thick with mulch. Keeps the melons from rotting."

"Nice color," Linda said.

"Pumpkin," Helen said.

"Orange," replied Linda, not sure what else she could or should say.

"Pumpkin. That's what the color swatch said, Harvest Pumpkin."

Linda was making her second haul of leaves from the compost pile and was walking by the back of the house when her father came home from work. She saw him pull into the driveway, heard him walk through the house to the kitchen. She stopped what she was doing then moved her wheelbarrow a little further to the right so she could get a better look through the big kitchen window and see his reaction. He'd be angry. She doubted her mother had consulted with him about painting the kitchen. She'd never known her father to agree to change anything about the house. It was as if there was something sacred about the way the house was, and they were never allowed to change it.

"Nobody," she heard her father say, the words clenched so tightly in his teeth he had to shout in order to push them out of his mouth, "in their right mind would paint a kitchen this color."

Gripping the handles of the wheelbarrow, Linda inched it forward a little in order to hear them better. She knew she shouldn't be standing there watching.

"Then I guess," she heard her mother say, as she dipped the brush into the paint and cut a swath of orange like a blaze of fire down the kitchen wall, "I'm not in my right mind, and you ought to think about getting out of my way."

Linda held tightly to the handles of the wheelbarrow and quickly made her way back to the garden. She could hear her father walking through the house, slamming the front door behind him. She heard him get into his car and drive off. Looking back over her shoulder she saw her mother through the kitchen window. She was still on the ladder painting. The streaks of orange coming together like a great orange sea washing down the walls.

About an hour later, Tommy came home. Linda tried to catch him before he went into the house to warn him, but she didn't move quickly enough to stop him. She wanted to know, however, what his reaction would be, so she moved back over to the edge of the compost pile and pretended to be mixing leaves and mulch so she could see through the kitchen window and watch him. Tommy didn't seem to be surprised, in fact, she could see Tommy laughing, handing their mother a glass of water. Then he moved away from the window, and a minute later he came out into the garden.

"Hey, Priscilla," he called out. "How about we go into town to get some dinner?"

Linda didn't say anything, but waited until he got closer and she could speak without being heard by their mother in the kitchen.

"What do you think?"

"I think she's crackers." Tommy answered, twirling his fingers around his ears.

"Don't say that," she hissed.

"Okay, she's nuts."

"I've got a couple more loads of leaves to move," Linda said, grabbing the wheelbarrow in the hopes of changing the subject.

"Okay," Tommy said, taking the handles from her, "let's get it done."

"You in the garden!" Linda said with surprise.

"Better than standing around waiting for you to get your butt into gear while Mom goes screaming off the deep end."

It took them twenty minutes to finish the mulching and after they were done they washed up using the garden hose instead of going back into the house. Then they got into Tommy's car without saying goodbye and drove into town for shakes and burgers at Daly's Drive In. They sat for a long time in the car at Daly's talking about school and the upcoming baseball game. Linda tried to ask Tommy about the mess with the baseball bat and the mailboxes and Greyjack's idea about Tommy joining the Army, but he said he didn't want to talk about it. He said he'd rather talk about Mindy. Linda said she thought Mindy was trouble. Tommy called her Priscilla and told her she shouldn't believe everything Mom told her.

After they finished, they ordered a burger and a drink to take back to their mom. They figured she probably approached painting the same way she did gardening and wouldn't stop until it was done. They also figured their dad was probably out with Greyjack having a drink and wouldn't come home to eat, so he was on his own.

When they gave Helen the sandwich and drink, she thanked them and asked them if they had any homework. They were happy to have some excuse not to help her, and went to their rooms.

When Linda went to bed at 11 p.m., her mother was still on the ladder moving down the walls in the same methodical way she planted onions. Linda didn't hear her father come in. When she woke up Tommy for school the next morning she asked him if he'd heard their father come in and he said he hadn't heard anything.

When Linda came downstairs for breakfast, the first thing she saw as she hit the bottom stair was the explosion of color in the kitchen. It felt like a wild eruption of hot lava that had blown up through the house and covered the walls. The house felt both changed and charged like something had happened but nothing had happened.

Everything in the kitchen was back in place. Her mom was standing by the counter packing lunches and frying eggs. Tommy and Richard came down the stairs behind her for breakfast. No one said anything about the orange walls. Over in the trash, Linda could see the drink cup from Daly's was empty. She also saw that half of the hamburger she and Tommy had bought for their mother was wadded up in the wrapping and thrown away.

Chapter 7

"Wear stockings," Helen said, calling up to Linda. It was the Saturday afternoon before Palm Sunday. They had just finished working in the garden and had come into the house to get ready to go shopping.

"I'll just use the store footies," Linda called back.

"And a slip."

Linda took off the dirty jeans she had been wearing to work in the garden and got out a pair of stockings and a slip from the top drawer of her dresser. She also took out her best skirt and blouse from the closet. She knew if her mother had wanted her to wear stockings and a dress she was also expected to wear dress shoes. She also knew her mother was down in the kitchen switching her wallet and keys from her old purse to her good one that matched her Sunday shoes.

Earlier, she had heard her mother fiddling with her hair in the bathroom and she was certain her mother had brushed her curls into some tamed arrangement and put on some lipstick. She knew her mother would expect her to do the same.

"Ready?" Helen called up the stairs again.

"Almost."

"Brush your teeth. Did you turn off the sprinkler on the melons?"

"Right before I came in."

"And…"

"Moved it to the tomatoes," Linda said, finishing her mother's sentence.

"Then let's go."

When they got into town, Helen parked the car near Kresge's then turned off the ignition.

"First stop," she announced, "will be underwear."

Linda was delighted by her mother's new upbeat spirit.

"What's the plan?"

"You need new underwear. Plain or fancy? What's your pleasure?"

Linda had needed new underwear for quite a while, but was embarrassed her mother had noticed. She hesitated before answering.

"Fancy," she said at last.

"That means a trip to Winkleman's."

"Then lunch?" Linda begged. She'd been working in the garden since 7 a.m. and was starved.

"The lunch counter at Kresge's?"

"Of course," Linda answered, knowing they might dress up to go downtown, but they preferred to eat at the dime store. Whenever they were out together, they always sat in a booth and had lunch at Kresge's.

While walking to Winkleman's, Linda slipped her hand into the crook of her mother's arm. Helen set the pace, walking slowly, taking her time. She had an urge to tell Linda things, things about herself. It was time, she felt, for her daughter to know more about her.

"When I was 16," she told Linda, "my father sent me to visit my Great Aunt Willa in Akron, Ohio. She was my mother's oldest aunt and she was rich. At least, richer than we were, and she was old, and I was her only 'girl-child.' After my mother died Aunt Willa paid extra attention to me. She always called me on my birthday, sent presents at Christmas and invited me to come for a visit. She had two sons, and her sons had only managed to produce grandsons for her. She always told me I was the girl she always wanted and treated me like I was her own. I really loved her.

"My father sent me on the train by myself. It was the first time I had ever traveled alone, and he made long lists of instructions and double-checked my luggage to make sure I had packed only my best clothes. He was a little sensitive about being both a mother and a father and was quick to hear criticisms about the way I dressed or if my hair wasn't combed so he went out of his way to make sure my clothes were always good and always clean. At the last minute I started getting worried about not having enough underwear for the trip so I snuck in all of my underwear, both the good and the not so good. I had decided I'd wear the rattiest underwear the first few days then my best underwear as the week wore on. For the life of me I can't remember now why I thought this was a good plan, but it felt like a good plan at the moment, and it was something I'm quite certain I didn't discuss with my father. He would have been mortified."

Linda listened intently as she walked with her mother. Her mother never talked much about herself, and Linda was aware she knew little about her mother's childhood.

"Great Aunt Willa was wealthy and haughty enough to have a full-time maid, a black woman named Sadie, who wore a uniform. My father thought it was scandalous and a ridiculous way for her to throw her money around. A couple of days after I arrived for my visit, Sadie went into my room and gathered up all of my dirty clothes, including my ratty underwear. Aunt Willa and I had gone to the market that morning, and when we came back my ratty underwear, along with the rest of my clothes, had been washed and hung up on the clothesline in the backyard. When Aunt Willa saw my old cotton underwear hanging in her yard, she was furious. 'A woman's wash,' she scolded me, 'shows the whole world what kind of lady she is and everyone knows what kind of woman wears ratty underwear!'"

"What did you do?" Linda gasped.

"Nothing. She told me to put the groceries on the back porch and instructed Sadie to take my underwear off the line and throw it away. She said the only thing cotton underwear was good for was dusting a piano. She then told me to get back into the car. She drove straight into town and took me to this fancy ladies store and bought me the most beautiful silk and satin lingerie I had ever seen or imagined."

"She threw away your underpants?" Linda gasped, as they stepped into Winkleman's and walked to the back section where there were slips, panties and bras.

"It was the best thing anyone had ever done for me. Nice underwear," Helen said, sifting through a stack of silky flowered briefs, "can get you through the worst of times. I'll never wear ratty underwear again, and neither should you. Cotton or silky?"

Linda really wanted silky underwear like her mother wore but had never had the courage to ask for it before. Despite her mother's preference for jeans and cast-off dress shirts, her underwear was another story. It was far from old or hand-me-down and not the kind of underwear Linda could imagine the ladies of their church wearing. Her mother's underwear was silky and filmy and either soft tan, pink, or pale-pale coral, never stark white. Her underwear was pretty, very pretty, and soft. It was as if her mother had some private life, some other side of her hidden in her underwear that no one ever saw.

The way the flimsy wild-flowered nylon bikinis were stacked next to the more substantial white cotton ones on the counter made Linda feel crazy. She wanted to touch the fancy underwear, but was afraid to pick them up and say she wanted them because they felt so private and sexy. It made her blush.

"Look at these," Helen said, picking up a little pair of yellow and lime green flowered bikinis and waving them in the air. "Aren't they great? Let's buy some."

"They're beautiful," Linda said, reaching over gingerly to touch them.

Helen picked out a few pairs for herself and insisted Linda get a dozen for her and a half dozen matching bras. She had Linda try on the bras. The sales lady helped with the fitting and suggested she needed to move up a size. She also suggested a lightly padded bra to give her breasts more definition. Linda found the fitting process embarrassing. She'd never had anyone examine her breasts before.

"You'll get used to it," her mother laughed. "Besides, you have beautiful breasts, you should be proud of them."

"Could I get a new slip too? My old one feels tight."

They picked out a beautiful beige slip that was fitted at the bodice and lightly flared around the hips. It was trimmed in peach-colored lace at the top and on the hem.

"There," her mother said, as the cashier wrapped their purchases in tissue and carefully placed them in the bag. "As soon as we get home, you need to throw your old underwear away."

"Or turn them into dust cloths."

"If we had a piano." Helen countered.

"I forgot about the piano."

"Lunch?" Helen offered.

"I'm starved."

With their purchases in hand, they headed back to Kresge's. They took seats in a booth and placed their order. Linda ordered a grilled ham and cheese with tomato and mustard and a Coke. Helen ordered a BLT with black coffee. Linda couldn't remember a time when she felt happier being with her mother.

"How about we share an apple dumpling?" Helen asked.

"Sounds good," Linda replied, stuffing the menu into the rack behind the napkin holder.

"One apple dumpling and two spoons," Helen told the waitress.

"One more year," Helen said to her daughter, once the waitress had left their table and they were alone again, "then off to college."

"What about Tommy?" Linda asked. "He graduates in June, you know."

"Probably go into the Army, unless Mindy gets him first."

"She's not so bad," Linda said, coming to Tommy's defense.

"I'd prefer Tommy doesn't know I don't approve of Mindy," Helen said, bringing her coffee cup to her lips. "Disapproving of her is the quickest way to drive him to her. She's not bad, just young. She's your age, but you'd think with the way she flips her sassy hair around, she was a grown woman. Tommy ought to know better than to get mixed up with someone like her."

Linda didn't know for sure what her mother meant, but she chose not to challenge her. Linda was relieved when the waitress came with their sandwiches. She was happy to have something to eat so she wouldn't have to talk about Tommy and Mindy. She still hadn't told her mother about the day in the Dairy when Tommy nearly killed himself watching Mindy's hands while she poked her soda straw into her blob of ice cream.

They ate in silence for a moment.

"Whatever happened that afternoon at United Dairy?" Helen asked.

"We had ice cream. Larry came, but didn't stay for very long. Mindy said her father had gotten a job with the Post Office and that they liked it here."

"What happened between Tommy and Mindy?" Helen pushed.

"They just talked."

"Tommy wasn't interested in Mindy?"

"I guess he seemed a little interested."

"A little interested?"

Linda felt backed into a corner. She hadn't promised Tommy she wouldn't say anything to their mother about the day at the ice cream shop. Telling her would not be breaking a promise, but the whole thing made her feel queasy. She wanted to protect Tommy but had never been able to lie to her mother about anything.

"It was like he was trying to memorize what her fingers looked like," Linda confessed. "Like Tommy believed he could make Mindy part of himself just by looking at her hard."

Helen picked up her cup and leveled her eyes over the rim

before she took another sip of her coffee. "Sometimes men think just because they love you, they own you."

"Does Dad ever look at you like that?" Linda asked.

"He has," Helen said, reaching over the table to touch her daughter's face, "and it's very flattering when it first happens. But, if a man ever looks at you like that I want you to run the other way. He's not a man you want. He's trouble."

"I can't believe Dad has ever been trouble," Linda said defensively.

"All men can be trouble. You just need to know when to run."

Linda jumped. Her mother had hit the word run hard and fast like a racehorse breaking free of the starting gate.

Helen could see a shadow of worry in her daughter's face. Helen was sorry she'd said what she'd said. Pushing her half-eaten sandwich away, she took her daughter's hand.

"Mindy probably isn't really that bad," Helen said, smiling, "but Tommy isn't that good either. In some ways they're a lot alike and, with or without each other, they're capable of making their own kind of trouble. By next spring you and all the money from your garden are going to be packed off to college. You're not going to need a man. You'll be fine all by yourself. You don't need to go looking for trouble like Tommy and Mindy. They are who they are, and you are who you are, and you don't need to worry about them. They're not your trouble. I shouldn't have asked you to tell what I already knew."

Linda finished eating her sandwich in silence. Her mother got another cup of coffee when the apple dumpling came. While they shared the apple dumpling, they talked about the garden. Helen took her paper napkin and sketched out a possible new arrangement putting the tomato plants along the edges of the garden and the cabbages and cucumbers inside, using the tomatoes and their tall wooden spikes as a kind of fence to ward off the rabbits and deer.

"You should think about putting in an extra row of corn this year and another big mound of cantaloupes," Helen said finishing the drawing then pushing it across the table for Linda to see where she was talking about putting in an extra row of corn. "Almanac says it's going to be a good year for sun and rain. Perfect for corn and cantaloupes. You always sell out of corn before noon. Even if people have room in a garden for a few tomatoes and some onions, most don't have room for corn or cantaloupes. Besides, yours is better than anyone else's and everyone knows it."

Watching her mother draw on the napkin, Linda couldn't stop thinking about what she'd said about how you had to know when to run. It was like she had thought about saying it for a long time and was just looking for the right time to tell her. The kitchen had something to do with it. Linda knew it to be true even though she couldn't say why.

"Ready?" Helen said at last, putting a stack of quarters on top of the check for a tip and snapping her purse closed. "I say let's go to Stuart's to find a pretty dress."

"Stuart's?" Linda said in surprise. Stuart's was the best women's store in town. She'd never had a dress from Stuart's before.

"You get one good dress a year, so why not get the best?"

"Why not?" Linda responded, cheerily.

"Don't forget the underwear," Helen warned, pointing to the bag sitting on the bench in the booth.

Linda picked it up and followed her mother out of the store, linking her hand, once more, through the warm crook of her arm.

"What about this dress?" Helen asked Linda, pulling a pale peach dress from the rack at Stuart's.

"Too springy," Linda offered.

"Or this?" she asked.

"Too old-looking."

"How about this?"

"Too prissy."

"Well," Helen said, sitting down in the big cushy chair by the changing room. "What are you looking for? What do you want?"

"Something different."

"Different," Helen said, with more patience then Linda had ever seen in her mother before.

"Grown-up but not old. Pretty but not prissy. Maybe sophisticated," Linda said, hoping not to seem foolish or too fancy.

"Sophisticated," Helen smiled, getting up from the chair and returning to the racks along the wall. "Then we better look again."

Helen got up from her comfortable seat, and they continued to sift through the rack together. Linda tried on a few of the dresses her mother found just because it was easier than saying no to everything she showed her. Linda made countless trips into the changing room then back again to stand barefoot in front of the big three-way mirror trying to imagine how she would look on Easter morning.

Hanging around Mindy had made Linda want to be more attractive. She wanted to be noticed the way people noticed Mindy. She wanted boys to smile at her the way Tommy smiled at Mindy.

Helen looked on patiently. When Linda didn't like what she'd tried on, Helen would suggest maybe they could look for something with a longer hem or a shorter hem, wider collar or no collar, short sleeves or long sleeves, anything to help Linda find what she wanted.

"What about a black dress?" Linda offered as she rejected yet another pale flowered dress her mother handed her.

"Black is for older women and funerals," Helen quickly responded.

"I think black is classic," Linda said, determined to stick to her guns.

"Black is classic," Helen conceded.

"I could wear it for my college interviews."

"You could also wear something like this," Helen said, holding out a sweet pale blue linen dress with a delicate lace collar.

"That," Linda said laughing, "looks like something an old woman would wear."

"I thought you wanted to look grown."

"Sophisticated."

"Black is," Helen laughed her agreement, "sophisticated. Okay, let's look."

Helen let Linda try on one black dress after another. Alone in the dressing room Linda let the dresses slip over her head with her eyes closed so when she opened them she'd see herself in the mirror as though it was someone else, not herself. Linda hoped a black dress would make her more interesting, more self-assured than she was when she worked in the garden in her old jeans and tennis shoes.

Lately she had been noticing the changes in her body, her softer hips and small hard breasts. She wondered if her mother had noticed, or maybe if Tommy had noticed. Her new hard breasts embarrassed her. She thought bras were uncomfortable. She didn't like the way she smelled when she got her period. She wished she had her mother's soft curly hair. She ran her hands down her long legs. If she got a dress, a grown-up black dress, she'd shave her legs for Easter Sunday.

What she wanted from a black dress was a glimpse of the woman in her, but when she came out of the dressing room and stepped up to the mirror to examine her new self, she felt uncomfortable with the complicated half girl-child, half woman in the mirror.

Helen could see her daughter struggling.

"Maybe it's time for you to own a suit. A suit would be nice for your college interviews."

A suit was about 180 degrees away from what Linda had in

mind when she was dreaming of a tight little black dress to transform her life. However, she recognized, a suit was a face-saving way out of a black dress she wasn't comfortable wearing yet, and it was a far better offer than the usual flowered Easter dress trimmed with lace.

She turned from side to side examining the latest black dress in the mirror. It was too black. Too severe for her pale freckled skin. She could see that.

"A suit?"

"A good light-weight wool would carry you from Easter into fall," her mother offered, as though a suit was some means of transportation.

Linda tried on several Chanel-type suits with tight straight skirts and short nipped jackets. There was a black and tan hounds-tooth check suit that made her look like one of the Episcopal ladies Linda quickly rejected. She also rejected a prim navy blue trimmed with a white linen collar that looked like it was ready for a honeymoon voyage as well as a soft grey tweed befitting a judge.

None of the suits seemed sophisticated enough for the Easter Sunday Linda was imagining. What she wanted was a suit that would turn heads when she slid into a pew at the back of the church. Then, as if her mother had been waiting for the exact moment when at last Linda's will was broken and she was too exhausted to look one more outfit further, she brought her another suit. It was a deep honey-tan linen suit printed with flowers. The jacket was fitted at the waist and draped softly over the hips. It had 3/4 length sleeves and would probably look best with the jacket buttoned up and worn without a blouse.

As Linda stood in front of the mirror on tiptoes, her calves high and tight beneath the hem of the straight skirt, examining the top button of the jacket where the V-neck flirted with the edge of her collarbone, she thought she looked good. In fact, for the first and maybe only time in her life she liked the curve of her hips and the way the jacket fit tight around her waist then flared softly at her hips.

"Do you like?" Helen asked, seeing the woman in her daughter.

"What do you think?"

"I think it makes you look pretty. Very pretty. I think we should buy it."

They bought the suit and a pair of beige high heels with a matching purse and a pair of nude stockings. Linda had rejected the idea of buying an Easter hat. Hats were for little girls and old women. Besides, she wanted to wear her hair down and have it dance softly around her shoulders when she walked.

It was 5 p.m. by the time they finished. On the way home, Linda suddenly realized her mother had not bought a dress for herself, only underwear. They had been so busy talking about the garden and looking for a suit, they hadn't stopped to buy a dress for her mother.

"What are you going to wear?" Linda asked her mother as they pulled into the driveway.

"Don't worry about me," she said, "I don't really need anything new for church this year. I have my dress from last year. It still looks good. Put on your suit," she said, grabbing the bag with the underwear and shoes, "and go stand by the garden so I can take a picture of you."

"We can do that on Easter." Linda insisted, not wanting to take off her clothes again.

"Come on, let's do it now, over by the garden. The light is good. It'll be perfect."

When Linda came down dressed in her suit, Tommy was just pulling into the driveway and getting out of the car.

"Whoa, Priscilla, don't you look pretty!" Tommy teased, coming up beside Linda and putting his arm around her newly defined waist.

Linda punched him hard in the arm.

"I could still knock you down if I wanted to," Linda responded. "So watch it, buddy."

Helen asked Tommy if he'd come over and take a picture of them standing together. Tommy took several poses of his mother and Linda, then Helen took the camera saying she wanted a picture of Tommy and Linda together.

Tommy put his arm around Linda's shoulder, and she leaned her head against his arm. When she did so, Helen couldn't see Linda's face in the viewfinder.

"Put your chin up, Linda, and pretend you're looking off into the future," Helen called out before snapping the last picture.

It was a funny thing for her to say, and it made them all laugh.

Chapter 8

Helen pulled into the drugstore parking lot, took the camera out of her purse, and rewound the film. When she hit the part where the film clicked free of the sprockets, she kept winding. The small black camera clicked and whirred rhythmically in her hands. The sound and the feel of the clicking and winding had a calming effect and kept her mind from wandering into sadness and her hands from shaking.

Her hands had been shaking ever since she had gotten into the car to drive into town. The only way she could keep them still was to hold on tightly to the steering wheel while she drove. They had first started shaking when she looked through the tiny square viewfinder in order to take Linda and Tommy's picture. Helen had not been particularly sad or even melancholy when she suggested she take their pictures. In fact, she had felt rather buoyant as though things were good, and for a moment she felt a sense of hope and ease in her life she hadn't felt for a long time.

She kept winding the camera. Click, whirr, click, whirr, click whirr. It was like one of those Tibetan prayer wheels she had once read about. She closed her eyes and prayed.

"Please, God, don't let me be sad. Don't let me cry. Don't let me cry. Don't let me be sad. Don't let me be sad." The words tumbled through her mind like water over rocks.

Once she felt sure of herself, she stopped praying, tugging at the lever to open the camera in order to get out the film. Failing, she tried again. Her hands began once again to shake. She closed her eyes again. This time her prayer was a desperate wish.

"I'm fine, I'm fine. I won't cry. I don't want to cry. I'm fine. I'm fine."

The push of tears at the back of her throat had started when she wasn't successful getting both Linda and Tommy into the picture. She moved back a few steps, then to the side, but still something was wrong. Linda's face was in the shadow of Tommy's shoulder. When she managed to get a good view of Linda's face, Tommy's head was chopped off. They'd stood stiffly waiting for her to snap the picture. They laughed and struck a yearbook-like picture when she told them to look like they were staring off into the future.

And when she snapped that picture, the one of them looking off into the future, a strangling, choking feeling at the back of her throat made her feel like she was going to scream.

Looking through the lens, her children didn't look like her children anymore and her garden looked barren rather than newly plowed and planted. It gave her an odd and unsettling feeling like she was seeing something other than just her children standing at the edge of her freshly turned garden.

When she finally managed to get both of them into the frame together, she felt as though she hadn't managed to capture her children at all but rather two people she hardly knew standing somewhere without her.

After the last picture was taken, she felt like she had to get away from home in order to keep the flood of tears that had been building up inside of her from bursting out of her throat.

"I want to get this developed," she called out to them. "I'll be back in a little while."

"Do you want me to come with you?" Linda asked, shading her eyes from the sun.

"No," Helen answered.

"What about dinner?"

"Order pizza if you want," Helen said, her stomach feeling queasy, "I'm not really hungry. Dad is working tonight. Maybe you can grab a bite in town."

"Pizza sounds good to me," Tommy offered, tugging on Linda's sleeve. He was ready to get out of the garden and on with their lives.

"I'll leave a twenty by the phone," Helen called then waved, the camera still in her hand.

"Damn it," Helen swore under her breath. The car felt warm and stuffy. She had thought about rolling the window down but didn't. She felt a little paralyzed. There was a raw thin edge of tears growing in her throat. She had an unsettling feeling she was going to cry even though she couldn't think of any real reason to cry.

She stopped fiddling with the camera for a moment and closed her eyes. She needed to gain a little balance within herself. She was desperate to stop the crazy flood of tears that had recently taken up residence in her life.

The house made her feel crazy. There was no place to sit down. No place in the house where she felt comfortable except the kitchen. The kitchen with its bright orange walls was hers. Last night she woke up because she was having trouble breathing and came downstairs and just stood in the kitchen in the moonlight struggling to catch her breath.

The rest of the house felt suffocating. It was like she was stuck in a long dark tunnel and no one could hear her. Sometimes the garden felt like the only safe place in the world. The garden listened. When Tommy and Linda were at school and Richard was at work, Helen would go into the garden. While she weeded, watered, planted and mulched, she would talk to the tiny onion seedlings. She would ask if they thought Richard loved her. She whispered to the empty rows about how worried she was about Tommy and what he might do or become. She complained to the long furrows she dug in the hopes of planting tomatoes about how Tommy was too young to be so very serious about a girl as foolish as Mindy. She also gossiped to the onions about the fat women in the church and how they were so arrogant. She bragged to the melon bed about Linda's good grades. And, whenever she gently pushed a new seedling into the ground, she thanked it for what it would do by summer to help Linda go to college.

Sometimes in the afternoon, Greyjack would come by and she would talk to him. He didn't come often, but whenever he came around she'd stop whatever she was doing and just talk.

She had always been able to talk to Greyjack. When her mother died, her father spent many evenings at the Greyjack's house, drinking and talking with Greyjack's parents while she and Warren and Greyjack played tag in the woods, told ghost stories or pretended like they were hunting bears.

Whenever Greyjack held his head intently to one side, the way he always did when he was listening, it was as though they were ten years old again and wild friends waiting for twilight to come so they could go catch lightning bugs. Lately when she talked and Greyjack listened she felt as though Warren was there inside of Greyjack listening too. Once, when she thought she saw Warren flit across Greyjack's intent face, she reached over and touched his cheek. Greyjack didn't pull back and he never said anything about it.

Sometimes she dreamed about Warren. When she was ten years old she thought she was in love with Warren. But, then again, everyone loved Warren. He was shorter than Greyjack but very handsome and funny. Every girl in town loved Warren and believed they would grow up to marry him.

She never told Richard or Greyjack about Warren. She never even told the garden.

The windows of the car were beginning to cloud up with the warmth of her breath. She fumbled with the camera. Her hands were slippery with sweat. The latch of the camera was stuck, and the ragged thin edge of her thumbnail was not strong enough to budge it clear of the catch. There was a fresh cascade of tears rolling down her hot face.

She knew she was crying too much lately. It made her feel crazy out of control, like she had either fallen out of her life or woken up to discover her life was somehow over. Everything about her felt empty. Even the house felt empty.

It was raining too hard to work in the garden. Tommy and Linda were at school, and Richard was off running some errands before he left for work. The emptiness of the house and the relentless pounding of the rain against the window made Helen feel restless and out of sorts. She didn't know what to do. She considered putting on an old slicker and working in the garden in the rain, but she was afraid her muddy feet would do more damage than good to the newly turned earth.

She went into the kitchen to make a fresh cup of tea for herself, but she felt so jittery she didn't want to sit down so she stood by the stove to drink it. She had painted the kitchen just a few days before, and she was pleased by the way the warm orange color of the walls filled the storm-darkened house with light. She put her teacup down and tore a corner off a grocery sack sitting on the counter and started to make a list of other things she wanted to fix in the house.

Richard had gotten quite angry when she painted the kitchen. They had a terrible fight. It was one of the first terrible fights she could ever remember having with him. It ripped a vulnerable place in her life letting other scary things push through. They were things she didn't necessarily want to think about and had kept hidden in the back of her heart for a long time.

When they were first married, and she moved into the house with Richard and his invalid father, Thomas, the house felt fragile. It was the kind of house where people neither screamed or laughed or made loud noises at all.

When the alarm clock went off in the morning on her side of the bed, she was expected to get up to make breakfast for Thomas and Richard without turning on the lights or making any noise. When she cleaned the kitchen after dinner, she was expected to do so quietly. If she played the radio, she was to play it softly so only she could hear it.

She did not whistle or hum while she worked. She moved through the house like a ghost, while Richard and Thomas made their way from room to room as though they walked on some minefield strewn footpath only they could see. Whenever they talked, their conversations were confined to careful comments around the dinner table about the weather and the news.

After Thomas died and Tommy was born, Helen had at first welcomed his wild baby screams and busy explorations throughout the house. She was, however, careful to keep him quiet when Richard was sleeping or home from work. Whenever Tommy woke up in the middle of the night hungry, scared, or wet, she was the one to comfort him as though she alone was the guardian of the stillness of the house.

The stillness of the house, its refusal to change to be something new or fresh or just different year after year, wore on her. She felt hungry for something different to happen in the same way she sometimes felt hungry for a crisp apple or a slice of warm buttered toast.

The first time she thought about painting the kitchen, she imagined a bright white or even a deeper shade of yellow than it had been before. But, when Richard refused to even entertain the idea of changing something so little as the color of the walls in the kitchen she had been cooking dinner for him in for nearly twenty years, she felt crazy. Crazy like her hair was on fire. Crazy like she wanted to grab her purse and get into the car and just start driving as fast as she could to some place that wasn't painted a dirty yellow. She wanted to run away to someplace where she could breathe.

When Richard turned away from her while she was trying to talk to him about painting the kitchen, she went out into the garden and started working on building the melon patches. By the time she got to the back corner of the garden where she always planted melons, she was nearly gasping for breath and fighting back tears. But, as she worked on, digging deeply into the earth, her breathing got easier. As the breath in her lungs came in deeper and deeper gusts of wind and her head quit spinning and her heart quit racing, she got the idea to paint the kitchen a bright pumpkin orange.

Beautiful, outrageous orange. Orange so bright it would wake up the whole house. Orange bold enough to drive out whatever spirits filled the corners of the house. Orange outrageous enough to be able to force a breath of fresh air into her lungs. Room to breathe. She felt delirious with excitement. At the same time, she was afraid of what Richard would say.

She had been right to be afraid. When he saw what she was doing in the kitchen, he screamed at her in a way he had never screamed at her before. And then, because she felt so restless and crazy, she screamed back and kept painting.

She dumped her cup of cold tea into the sink and went to the cupboard to pour a teacup full of brandy. She sat down at the kitchen table and wrote out a list on her scrap of paper of everything she'd ever wanted to do in the house; strip the wallpaper in the dining room, living room and the bedroom, paint the hallway, get rid of the ratty over-stuffed furniture and rearrange the living room, buy a new couch, buy a bookcase and fill it with beautiful brand new hardback books.

Everything on her list seemed too big. Her throat was feeling hot from the brandy, and her head jumpy and fuzzy. Nothing in the house or her life felt safe or right. She considered screaming just to hear something other than the sound of her heart pounding in the quiet, quiet, dead house.

She went into the living room and picked up the morning paper Richard had left in the chair. There, in the women's section, was an article about spring-cleaning. She felt inspired and decided she'd clean the linen closet.

She had never, in all the years she had lived in the house with Richard, cleaned the linen closet. She didn't do it when Thomas was alive because it would have felt like she was intruding in his home. The linen closet also felt like Lillian's place. Helen didn't want to disturb whatever spirit of Lillian's had lingered in the house after her death. She was pretty sure she didn't do it after Thomas died. And, of course, after Tommy came along she was so busy chasing him and trying to keep him quiet she didn't have time to think about cleaning the linen closet. It was crazy, but she had been living in Lillian's house for almost twenty years and had never had the time or the courage to clean the linen closet.

Helen went into the kitchen and pulled out a handful of garbage bags from underneath the sink. The article had been very clear about throwing out or giving away everything you didn't need. It suggested, when you did your spring-cleaning, you should not only be preparing your house for the coming year but also preparing it for new things to happen. Therefore, you should throw away some things, give some away, and keep only what you really need or really love.

Helen took the bags and went upstairs to the closet. Opening the door wide, she started sorting, tackling the bottom shelf first. Bathmats, towels, old bedspreads and musty pillows came tumbling out. Most of the linens were worn and ratty.

She flipped on the hallway light in order to get a better look. She was amazed at how thin the linens had become. None of them looked good enough to keep, but if she threw them all out then they wouldn't have any left, so she tried to sort them into piles. She quickly tore the worst ones into rags so she wouldn't be tempted to save them or keep them for some terrible emergency.

She pushed these newly torn rags into a bag. That left three piles of towels. Those that were slightly worn, those that were a bit more worn or maybe stained, and the ones that were thin but still usable. She was hesitant to throw the thinnest ones away because they were just the right thickness to wrap around her head when she first got out of the shower.

She looked at the piles. She hadn't really gotten rid of very much. She started to sort through the stacks of towels again, but after a few minutes of being unable to make any new decisions, she pushed them aside and began pulling out things from the other shelves. She decided she should sort through everything before making final decisions as to what to keep and what to throw or give away.

She pulled out the sheets and pillowcases and the little rag rugs stuffed in the very back of the closet on the floor. She got on her hands and knees in order to pull out everything from the bottom of the closet, then got a chair from her bedroom and stood on it in order to reach the very back of the top shelf. That's when she found all of Lillian's embroidery.

There, in the back of the top shelf, were pillowcases, luncheon napkins and tablecloths, all neatly stacked and bundled in a yellowed plastic dry cleaning bag. When Helen unfolded the bag she discovered the pillowcases and napkins were brand new. At some time, Lillian had embroidered them, washed them, and starched them then tied them into sets with yellow satin ribbons. Helen cleared a space and laid out the sets on the hallway floor.

There were six sets of pillowcases and two sets of luncheon napkins. Each luncheon set had four napkins, and a large square tablecloth embroidered to match. Standing on a chair, she reached back into the closet to be sure she'd found everything. That's when she discovered a bridge set with a small square card table cloth and four tiny cocktail napkins embroidered in red and black with diamonds, clubs, hearts and spades, wrapped in a second bundle.

Even after all the years of being wrapped in plastic and stuck in the back of the closet, they still smelled like Lillian. When Helen put her face against the cool smooth linen cocktail napkins she could smell Lillian's hands full of baking powder and cinnamon as though she'd been baking cookies and had forgotten to wash her hands before she folded the linens and wrapped them and put them away.

Helen untied the pillowcases from the first bundle and sat down on the floor so she could unfold them in her lap. They were meticulously embroidered and the crocheted edging had been dipped in starch and pressed flat so she was able to see each tiny looped stitch in the lacy patterns.

Finding them was like finding a part of Lillian she hadn't known existed.

"Oh, Lillian," Helen said to the empty hall, "when did you do these?"

She brought the pillowcases up to her face and breathed in Lillian's smell. Helen could imagine Lillian sitting at the end of the couch, the little reading lamp turned on so she could see as she embroidered. Helen also imagined the dinner dishes washed and stacked on the drain board in the kitchen, the evening meal done and put away, the counters wiped clean, the dish cloth hung over the bar on the door of the stove.

Lillian would have cleaned the kitchen before she ever sat down in the evening. Everything would have been in order and ready for the morning. Maybe Thomas would already be in bed, and she'd be watching the news by herself or listening quietly to the radio. Lillian always had the radio on as though she too needed something or someone else in the house with her in order to be comfortable.

The delicate napkins, the playful card table set, and the lovely pillowcases adorned with blue birds and twisting vines all looked like they were made for a special occasion.

"Why didn't you use them?" Helen asked, spreading the pillowcases out onto the floor so she could look at them better. "Why didn't you use these pretty things?"

She started to cry, maybe for Lillian at first, but later for herself. For the first time she realized she had been waiting all her life for a special day to come. She had been waiting for a day where she would put on her best blue dress and go out to dinner, a day where she would have to make cream cheese sandwiches with the crusts cut off and tiny chocolate frosted cupcakes to serve with sweet iced tea over a game of cards with friends, or a night fit for fancy pillowcases upon which she and Richard could sink deep into each others arms.

Helen picked the beautiful pair of pillowcases with the blue birds and pushed them aside. Then she carefully folded the rest of the beautiful linens and retied all the ribbons and put them back into the closet. She sorted through the other piles of towels and sheets she'd taken from the closet, throwing the worst of them away then folding the others and restacking the shelves.

Once she was done, she went into their bedroom and stripped the bed and made it fresh with some nicer sheets that had long ago been crammed into the back of the shelf and forgotten. Then she put the sweet blue bird pillowcases on their pillows. They looked so pretty she didn't pull the spread up over them to hide them.

"Where did you get these?" Richard asked, later that evening, as he got ready for bed.

"Found them when I cleaned the linen closet," Helen said, admiring the way they looked, wondering if using the pillowcases could turn this into a special day.

"They're stiff," Richard said, running his hand over the starched pillowcase. He then pulled the blue bird pillowcase with its delicate rose colored hand-worked lace off his pillow and threw it on the floor.

"Mom is dead," he said, looking away. "Using her fancy stuff won't bring her back." He went out into the hall to get a different pillowcase.

Helen picked up the pillowcase from the floor and carefully folded it and put it on her dresser. She then took off the one on her pillow and folded it also.

Chapter 9

Helen didn't know if she had been dreaming about running away or if the idea had just come to her in the brief moment before she woke, but it was stuck in her mind, and she couldn't shake it. She pushed it aside while she brushed her teeth and showered. It came back to her again when she was making the bed. What if she ran away? What would happen? Who would care? Where would she go and what would her new life be like?

Thinking about running away made her feel good. It made her feel different. Bigger somehow. Alive. Anxious but happy. Her heart raced. She had to keep this a secret.

She waited until Linda and Tommy had gone to school and Richard had left for work before she let herself sit down in a chair and really consider the options. When the house was at last empty, she turned on the radio as loud as she could and let the music fill the rooms. She looked around the house. Nothing had changed in all the years she lived in it except for the fresh coat of orange paint in the kitchen. The curtains were the same. The furniture was the same and stood in the same place Lillian had placed it before she died. Helen could hardly tell she had ever lived in the house at all.

Linda's room had once been her grandmother's sewing room, but somehow Linda had made it hers. She had picked the pale pink paint color and the dark plum bedspread. She'd hung old travel posters on the walls she'd gotten from the library for helping with shelving books after school.

Tommy's room was his too even though it was Richard's old room and none of the furniture was new except for the double bed she and Richard had bought before Thomas died. Tommy, however, had left his mark with his clothes strewn across the floor, his room crammed with years of baseball trophies, and broken baseball bats: trophies of hard hit homeruns. There was no mistaking the room as his. The room not only looked like him, it smelled of him.

Helen squinted her eyes and looked around the house again, trying to find her place. She wasn't in the big brown overstuffed couch or the rickety magazine rack by the side of the reading chair under the crook-necked floor lamp. She wasn't in the worn flowered carpet or the fancy china hutch filled with Lillian's pink English stoneware dishes with pictures of bridges and castles and running hunting dogs. She wasn't anywhere to be found.

There were no books or bookshelves in the house. Richard thought buying books was a waste of money. There was a perfectly good library in town and the bookmobile came to their front door every two weeks. Besides, he always argued, once you read a book, it was useless and troublesome.

Richard also believed books on shelves got dusty and cluttered up the house. He hated clutter. He didn't like things sitting on the coffee table or crowding up the mantel over the fireplace. He wouldn't even let her put Tommy's baseball trophies in the living room.

Helen had trouble arguing with Richard, so did the children. Richard was not one with whom to have a discussion about anything. Just rules. Tommy kept his trophies in his room. Linda kept to herself in her room. And, Helen didn't buy books.

Helen agreed with Richard that the library was a good one. She also liked the bookmobile, but sometimes her heart ached to hold a book that was hers and only hers. She wanted a book she could write her name in, or underline some passage that meant something to her, or just read and reread a favorite book until the pages wore out.

The first thing she'd do when she left, she decided, was to buy a book. But which book? One she'd read before and loved? One she'd never heard of? Maybe she'd buy a book about finding happiness?

She went into the kitchen and took out a piece of scrap paper from the drawer by the phone. She needed a list. She'd start with a list of books she wanted. She knew she didn't want paperbacks. She wanted real books with real covers and beautiful dust jackets. She'd need a bookshelf too. Something sturdy made of wood. Not high and towering, but maybe low, with a nice wide top where she could put a vase of fresh flowers every week.

Her house would be full of books and beautiful colors and comfortable chairs. She hated the squat, square kitchen table with its four sturdy chairs and their hard wooden seats. She never sat in the living room because the only comfortable chair in the room was Richard's chair. She never sat on the couch because it smelled of years of dust and boiled corned beef and cabbage and was just too low and lumpy to be comfortable to sit on and too short to lie down on for a nap. She hated it.

She went upstairs to shower and get dressed. She fiddled with her hair. She pulled one blouse from the closet, put it on, took it off then chose another. She folded her nightgown and tucked it into her top drawer. She put on her jeans and found fresh socks to wear. She tied her shoes, then untied them, and tied them again, this time pulling the laces tight so they felt firm on her feet. Firm and secure so they could carry her away.

She found a set of fresh sheets in the linen closet and made the bed, smoothing the covers with her hands until there were no wrinkles, no tugs or pulls, just a smooth, fresh surface waiting for the day to unfold. Making the bed momentarily made her feel relaxed and happy.

It was thrilling to close her eyes and imagine how good it would feel to just walk away. So thrilling she couldn't think about anything else. She also couldn't think of any reason not to go. Tommy certainly didn't need her anymore. He hadn't for years and Linda was nearly grown. Linda seemed to be gone from her as well. That's what Helen had seen in the viewfinder when she was taking Tommy and Linda's pictures. Her children were grown and ready to be gone from her.

Linda would be fine without her. Maybe she'd even be better. Helen could see now how her unhappiness was flooding their lives and drowning everyone in their house. Linda would be better off without her. They would all be better off without her. Once she found a place that made her happy she would write to Linda asking her to forgive her for leaving. Helen thought she might even ask Linda to come live with her. Maybe they could both learn to be less cautious and happier in the world.

Helen gave a shudder. She'd been having thoughts of really leaving the world. These thoughts were not like the thoughts she was having about running away. The thoughts of killing herself were so terrible she tried every trick she knew to not have them. Whenever she sensed these bad thoughts, she ran out into the garden and sang to the flowers, dug holes, picked up rocks, hauled mulch and worked so hard her muscles twitched and stung. Sometimes working in the garden drove the thoughts of suicide away, and sometimes it didn't.

The growling, sneering, thoughts of suicide had reared their ugly head the day Richard refused to talk about changing the color of the kitchen. In response, she chose to paint the kitchen the brightest boldest color she could find. It had been a crazy thing. She knew it now, but at the time, driving to town, picking out the color, clearing the countertops, washing the walls, and stirring the paint drove the thoughts of suicide away. The prospect of painting the kitchen orange made her feel alive and full of hope.

When she began to paint, her arm moving from paint bucket to walls became like a pendulum, the bright orange paint lighting up the room with each new stroke. As she worked, she couldn't help but realize she had waited twenty years too many to paint the kitchen. Twenty years to claim the house as her own. Twenty years for something to happen in her life. And as she painted, she tried her best to push the anger and tears she had held for all these years in the dam of her body from bursting up through her arm through her hand, to the walls.

At one point, she felt as though the paint was going to swallow her or that maybe she might just choose to fall into the refuge of the inviting bright orange of the walls. Fall like Alice down the rabbit hole. Down, down, down until she disappeared. But she didn't fall. She kept her balance. When Richard came home and yelled at her, she stood firmly on the ladder and drove her brush deep into the paint can and let the paint splash out against the walls in defiance. But even in anger, she couldn't let those horrible thoughts of suicide take over her mind. She couldn't let herself fall. She didn't have the courage to do it.

The black moment was past now. The kitchen was painted. Things were washed and put away. The fresh new kitchen would be her present to Linda. It would be a sign to her daughter that she was well and happy. She didn't want Linda to worry about her. She wasn't going to kill herself. She was going to run away but she would return. She could return anytime she wanted, but right now she wanted to leave so she could breathe. She ached to feel alive.

Her stomach tied itself into a knot. She pulled Lillian's pale blue satin spread up over the head of the bed and tucked it deep under the pillows forming a hump across the top of the bed like a neatly dug mound in her garden, the kind that would have been a perfect bed for tomatoes or beans or even marigolds.

When Richard made the bed he didn't care about pulling the spread tight around the pillows. He also didn't take care to smooth the blankets so they fell cleanly and evenly over the sides as if he didn't need to take care of the lives they shared together in bed. He just gave the covers a yank and pulled them any old which way up over the pillows.

She didn't sleep well when Richard made the bed. She never told Richard. He would not understand. She used to try to talk to him about painting a room or buying a new couch, but whenever she did, Richard either got angry or said he wasn't interested.

Eventually, she quit trying to talk to him about the things she wanted and believed she needed to be happy.

Everything that had ever happened in her life had happened without her consent. Like her mother dying when she was seven. She hadn't wanted her mother to die, and she couldn't stop it from happening. She had cried and prayed and done everything she knew to do to make her mother live. But Helen couldn't keep her mother safe, and from the moment her mother died, Helen was aware she didn't have any control over what happened in her life. Before Tommy was born she thought she would be responsible for him growing up, but even that wasn't true. Tommy wasn't hers to keep any more than her life had been hers to keep. Instead of being happy, she often felt like she was trapped on some horrible conveyor belt slowly but surely moving her from one place in her life to another without pause or consideration. She felt trapped in Richard's life.

She had been thinking a lot lately about why she married Richard. She could no longer remember when she decided to marry Richard. In fact, she wasn't sure she ever had decided to marry Richard or to do anything in her life for that matter. Perhaps if Warren hadn't died she would have married him and she would be happy. But, then, she probably wouldn't or couldn't have married Warren because she also loved Greyjack the same way she loved Warren. Sometimes she thought she had married Richard was because she couldn't have ever chosen between Warren and Greyjack.

She loved the quiet way Greyjack moved through the world as though the world needed him to listen. Greyjack had a place in the world. Greyjack felt comfortable both in his place and in himself, and sometimes she wanted him to just hold her for a moment so she could let the calm beat of his heart penetrate her body.

Whenever she talked to Greyjack she wanted to stand close to him. She didn't want to be with him as much as inside of him as though he were a big safe cave where she could hide. She would have married Greyjack, but Greyjack hadn't asked her. He had stood by watching her marry Richard. She often felt him watching her as though he was some great guardian angel. His watching calmed her. She often wondered why Greyjack had never married.

Of the three men she thought she loved, Richard was the one who asked her to marry. She could remember, even now, the way he smelled when he asked her. They were sitting in his car in her driveway. They had been out to dinner. He had just come back from basic training and was going to be shipped out to the war the next week. He had called in this funny formal way and asked her to go out to dinner downtown. He told her he'd be wearing his dress uniform.

They had never gone out to dinner together before. In fact, she had never been out to dinner at a fancy restaurant with a man before. She thought it was funny the way he called and offered his stiff invitation to have dinner with him at a restaurant downtown, telling her what he was going to wear. She remembered thinking the war had made him a grownup.

She didn't know what grownups wore to have dinner downtown, and she didn't have anyone to ask. She looked in her closet, and everything she owned looked like something you'd wear to a high school basketball game.

She didn't have anything fancy or formal to wear. She thought maybe she should have something more elegant than a plaid wool skirt and a sweater.

She found her mother's old sewing machine in the back of the closet. She also found a length of dark rose grosgrain material. It was just enough material to make a skirt. When she gathered the rose colored grosgrain around her waist, it fell neatly to her ankles. She liked the way it made a swishing sound when she walked. She added a pale pink satin sash around the waist. She tied the sash to one side in a neat knot and let the ends fall to her knees. She wore her best white blouse. Even her father said she looked beautiful.

Walking to the front door to greet Richard, her hips swayed from side to side so the long skirt swished and brushed against her legs as she walked. When she opened the door he laughed at her and made a joke about her looking like she was going to a high school prom. The way he said it wasn't nice. It felt mocking and demeaning. She would have run up to her room to change, but she didn't have anything else to wear. Instead, she smiled and thanked him and said she wanted to look as nice as he did for their special dinner.

She had wanted the dinner to be special. She really had, even though she didn't know why it mattered to her so much. His comment made her fidget with her skirt and sash all the way to Detroit and back home again. She smiled a lot during dinner and crossed her legs at her ankles and tried to look seductive and grownup. When they were seated, the waiter lit the candle at their table. Helen felt like she was in a movie. It was the first time she'd ever had dinner by candlelight.

The waiter brought them a basket of hot garlic bread. She picked up a piece of bread from the basket and ate it slowly, tearing off one little bite at a time with her fingers. Richard ordered a scotch on the rocks even though he wasn't yet twenty-one. The waiter nodded toward Richard's uniform and asked if he had already been in the war. Richard said he was going next week. The waiter didn't ask for his I.D. and gave him the drink and said it was on the house.

He offered Helen a drink on the house as well, but she didn't accept. She had never had a drink before, and she worried she wouldn't like it or she might choke and sputter the way people did in the movies when they had their first strong drink.

Richard ordered lasagna and a salad for dinner. She had wanted to order spaghetti and meatballs. She loved spaghetti and meatballs, but it sounded childish. She was also afraid she might get sauce on her new skirt. She didn't want Richard to laugh at her again so she ordered the linguine with clam sauce because it sounded more adult than spaghetti with meatballs. She didn't order a salad because she thought it cost too much and she wasn't sure how much money Richard had or what they would do if he didn't have enough to pay the bill.

She hadn't cared much for the linguine or the little white rubbery bits of clam in the watery sauce, but she ate it all and smiled so much while she chewed her face hurt.

Richard didn't talk very much. In order to fill up the long silences between bites, Helen told him about everything that had happened at school while he was off to basic training. She was nervous. The whole evening had made her feel anxious and childish.

When he pulled into the driveway beside her house she became uncomfortable sitting in his car waiting for him to kiss her. Before he had left for the Army, they had held hands and had kissed. They had even played around in the back seat of the car, necking, and stroking each other until the windows had fogged up and she was aware of the way their breath smelled. But that was before he wore a uniform. That was before he was grownup and going to war. He no longer seemed like the same skinny boy she used to kiss.

She was playing with the sash of her skirt, weaving it in and out of her fingers when he reached over and touched her shoulder. When she turned her head to look at him she realized his hands smelled of garlic and fresh bread. It had surprised her so much she unwound her fingers from her sash and smelled her own hands. They too smelled like garlic and fresh bread. She liked the way his hands smelled. They smelled like spaghetti and meatballs as much as they smelled of bread and garlic.

"Our hands," she said, putting her hands up to his face so he could smell it too, "smell like garlic bread and spaghetti and meatballs."

He took her hands in his, bringing them to his lips. He kissed the soft rounded tips of her fingers.

"Will you marry me," he said, his eyes focused not on her eyes but on her hands.

The question startled her. She hadn't expected it. She wondered if that's why he wore his uniform and she had sewn a new skirt. Perhaps they had both known this would be the night they would decide to marry and they had to dress the grownup part.

She ducked her head down so she could look up into his eyes to see if he was just playing.

"Will you marry me?"

"Yes."

She had said yes because she thought she shouldn't say no. After all, they had just eaten dinner in a fancy restaurant. He said he wanted to give her a ring, but he didn't know what size to buy. She said she didn't want a ring. She hated the way all the silly girls in her class were always busy showing their tiny diamond engagement rings. All of the girls in school had to take home economics, and the ones who were engaged couldn't wait for their future husbands to come back from the war so they could start cooking dinner.

The tiny chips of diamonds in their plain little rings made Helen feel sad. There was nothing beautiful about them. Instead, there was something terrible and strangling in the tiny diamonds they twisted and admired while they were supposed to be doing homework. A diamond said someone owned you. Helen didn't want to be owned. She didn't want a diamond ring, no matter how big or small the diamond.

Richard and she argued about the ring. She tried to make him laugh. He said he wanted everyone to know she was going to marry him. She told him she didn't want everyone knowing her business. She said she didn't want a diamond. She didn't tell him wearing an engagement ring felt like making a promise she couldn't break. Instead, she said diamonds were for old ladies.

"Do you want to marry me?"

"Yes, I said yes, didn't I?"

"Why won't you let me buy you an engagement ring?"

"I don't want to be EN-gaged."

"Then what do you want," he asked, his voice urgent and strained as though he had to catch a train and couldn't wait around for her to come to her senses.

"Garnet earrings," she said, triumphantly. "I want a pair of garnet earrings." She hadn't known she wanted garnet earrings before she asked for them but once she did, she was certain she wanted them. Garnets were rich and solid and they felt serious and fancy without being old. He didn't like the idea that they would seal their engagement with a pair of earrings, but he agreed he'd buy them for her. He said he was being shipped out to Europe and he would buy them there. He wanted the earrings to be special.

She had only half believed Richard was serious about marrying her. But, when he came back from Italy carrying a tiny black box lined with satin with a pair of gold and garnet earrings, she took them, put them in her ears and kept her promise of marriage.

She ran her hands over the top of the spread. She wanted to remember what their bed together felt like. She walked to the dresser mirror and looked at her face. It was a soft face but a sad face. She was wearing the earrings. She would take the earrings. They were hers. She adored their deep sassy color and the way other women looked at them as though they knew she had a secret.

She would leave her wedding ring. It was in a box in her top dresser drawer. She never wore it. Linda could have it. It slipped off Helen's finger and got in the way when she gardened.

Other than the earrings, she wouldn't take much, just a few

clothes and the pictures she'd taken of Tommy and Linda the other day. She'd also take one of the sets of napkins and another of the pillowcases Lillian had embroidered. Richard would never miss them.

She would put the pillowcases on the pillows in her new life. She would use the napkins when she ate, folding them carefully and putting them by the side of her plate when she set the table. She would paint her new house any color she liked. The walls would be like a garden of flowers. They would be blue and bold, bright and yellow, glistening deep honey colored. She'd open the windows every morning, even on the coldest winter morning. She'd let the fresh air dance through the rooms. She'd drink tea from thin china teacups with prissy little handles. She'd eat whatever she wanted when she wanted. She'd stay up all night reading, and sometimes she'd sleep late and no one would bother her.

She thought of packing but decided she couldn't do it because Richard might sense what she was planning to do and try to stop her. There were other things she needed to do. She needed to prepare the rest of the garden for planting. She needed to get some money from the bank. She needed to write a note for Linda to make sure she understood all the money from the vegetable stand was hers for college. She'd also write a note to Tommy.

She didn't know what she'd say. She wished she knew her son better. Her head was spinning. She was worried he was headed for danger, but she didn't know how to stop him.

She had to make a plan. She'd leave Saturday night, before Easter. She'd write notes and put them in their Easter baskets. She'd leave in the middle of the night when they were all sleeping. She didn't want anyone to wake up and hear her leave.

Chapter 10

Helen decided she'd cook a fancy dinner. She planned to leave in the middle of the night after everyone was asleep, and she wanted Linda and Tommy and Richard to remember her as a good mother. She was making Richard's favorite meal: a big pot roast with oven-browned potatoes, green beans and Waldorf salad. There was also an ambrosia fruit salad for dessert with coconut, green grapes, canned pineapple and whipped cream she'd seen a recipe for in a Woman's Day magazine. She wanted it to look just like the ambrosia in the magazine, so she carefully washed four of Lillian's best crystal compotes and filled them with the creamy salad and put them into the refrigerator to chill. She topped each of the ambrosia servings with a bit of toasted coconut.

While the roast was in the oven she ironed a tablecloth and took Lillian's good china dishes with their pretty pink scenes from the dining room hutch. She was going to set the table in the dining room but decided the dining room felt too formal. Instead, she draped a freshly ironed tablecloth over the kitchen table and set it with the good dishes.

They rarely used Lillian's china so it had to be washed before she could set the table.

"What's the occasion?" Richard asked coming into the kitchen.

"No occasion," Helen lied, her stomach jumping with excitement.

"Then why all the fuss?"

"Tomorrow's Easter Sunday," she challenged, surprised and a little afraid of the edge she could hear in her voice.

"That's tomorrow. This is today and all this fancy stuff looks like another one of your crazy ideas," Richard said tossing his head towards the bright orange paint on the walls.

"I wanted to make a special meal."

"It looks nice." With that, Richard walked out of the kitchen and into the living room to listen to the evening news.

Helen's hands were shaking. Richard's words, "It looks nice," worked their way through her hands and her flesh, stinging the lids of her eyes with tears. Her heart was pounding in her chest. She was frightened. What if she was making a mistake? What if Richard's admission the table looked nice was his way of trying to tell her he understood and he wanted to be different with her? What if she left and he regretted her going? What if she was wrong? What if Tommy and Linda really did need her? What if she could be happy with Richard?

She held her hands under the faucet and let the hot rinse water coming from the tap burn them. The water stung her fingers, but she continued to hold them there as though by burning them with the water she could forget how she felt. She closed her eyes and swallowed the rush of tears in her throat. She would not cry. She could not cry. Not now.

She finished washing the dishes and stacked them into the drain rack. She pulled the plug in the sink and watched as the soapy water went down the drain. She basted the roast with the pan drippings, careful to baste the potatoes as well so they'd develop a dark golden brown crust. She put ice in the water glasses and sliced bread from the long French loaf she'd gotten at the grocery store that morning. Then she went to the pantry and took Tommy and Linda's Easter baskets from the shelf.

She'd bought chocolate rabbits, jelly eggs, little chocolate coconut nests and boxes of yellow Peeps for them just like she did every year. She also bought one large dark chocolate fruit and nut egg for Richard. It was his favorite and she bought him one every year.

She dug little holes into the green shredded Easter grass and planted the large chocolate rabbits in the center of the baskets then poured jelly eggs around the base of the rabbits and put the

Peeps off to the side. She rolled a twenty-dollar bill and snapped it into a large plastic egg and put it into Tommy's basket. For Linda's basket, she carefully rolled three pair of pretty pastel-colored underwear into three of the larger plastic eggs and tucked them into the grass around the edge of the basket. She took two more plastic eggs and put them aside. She'd written notes to each of the children telling them she was leaving. She had these notes folded and pressed deep into the pocket of her slacks. She would wait until they were all asleep to put them in the eggs for their baskets. She didn't want them finding them before she left.

She'd written a letter for Richard too and planned to put the note along with his chocolate egg on his dresser by his keys. She wanted him to find the note before he went downstairs so he'd be prepared just in case Tommy and Linda would have gotten up before him and found theirs. She had it all worked out.

Tommy and Linda had gone into town together earlier in the day to see an afternoon movie. She told them she wanted them home for dinner. Linda didn't want to go at first, but Helen had insisted she get out of the house. She told her it was her Easter vacation and she should do something fun for a change. She hoped having Linda along would keep Tommy out of trouble. Also, by having Linda and Tommy out of the house it was possible for her to get things ready so she could leave. Richard was already at work by then, and as soon as she was alone, she packed a few things into a suitcase and then hid the suitcase in the back of the closet.

Hearing Tommy and Linda pull up in the driveway, she quickly put the filled Easter baskets into the pantry and closed the door. She still had the notes she had written to them in her pocket.

"Hey," she called out as they came into the house.

"Smell's good," Tommy called back, coming through the backdoor to the kitchen, "hope you don't mind company for dinner."

Mindy came in behind him, then Linda, her shoulders hunched together as if to say it wasn't her idea.

"No, of course not," Helen said, a little surprised, "there's plenty. Linda, would you get another plate from the hutch?"

"Whoa," Tommy gasped when he saw the table, "what's up?"

"Nothing," Helen said, reaching into the refrigerator to take out the four ambrosia salads she'd put in earlier to chill. She'd have to steal a bit from each dish to make another serving, but she probably had enough coconut to go around again to top it all to make it look like five full servings. "Could you bring me another compote dish?" she called out to Linda, careful not to look at either Tommy or Mindy.

"It looks like a party," Mindy drawled sheepishly, tugging on Tommy's sleeve.

"No, no party. Just dinner. Glad you could come." Helen said, forcing herself to smile. "Maybe you should call your parents and ask if it's okay for you to stay. Let them know you're here."

"We found Mindy at the movies," Tommy offered, squeezing Mindy's hand.

"Hmm," smiled Helen, scraping the bits of ambrosia from the four chilled dishes so she could remix them and portion them out as five servings. She opened the cupboard and took down the bag of coconut then went into the refrigerator and got a few more grapes.

"They won't mind," Mindy said, smiling her best smile for Helen. "Momma's at her sister's, and Daddy's generally pretty edgy on Saturday night. He'll be in his room working on his preaching for tomorrow. Best to not bother him."

Linda came into the kitchen carrying the dishes her mother had asked for and went to the sink to rinse them. She kept her head down.

"How was the movie?" Helen asked, turning toward Linda.

"Fine," she said.

"What'd you see?" Helen pressed.

"Well, we saw Mindy and we decided not to go to the movies."

"What'd you do?"

"We just walked around," Linda said, turning her head away from her mother in order to look over her shoulder at Tommy.

"Showed Mindy downtown," Tommy offered. "Took her to the library and then to the dime store to get a soda.

"Sounds nice." Helen smiled.

"You have a real pretty town." Mindy said. "We don't have a real library in Shelby, Kentucky where we come from. Just a bookmobile that comes out from Paducah to the school once every two weeks."

"We have a bookmobile," Linda blurted out. "Ours comes every two weeks too." She said, happy to have something to talk about rather than the movie they didn't see.

"You like reading?" Helen asked.

"Yes, ma'am."

"What kind of books?"

"Adventure stories."

"About?"

"About far away places. I plan to see the world when I grow up."

"That's a good plan," Helen said, mixing the fresh grapes in with the ambrosia in order to make it stretch.

"Hey, Linda, want to show Mindy your garden?" Tommy asked.

"Sure," Linda said, putting the extra plate and place setting on the table and handing the compote dish to her mother.

Tommy waited to speak to his mother until he could see Mindy and Linda out the kitchen window, standing at the edge of the garden.

"You don't like her," he said.

"I never said I didn't like her," Helen responded as she

carefully dipped ambrosia into the thin glass bowls.

"She's better than you think."

"She's pretty."

"Mindy's smarter than she looks, and I like her, and I want you to be nice to her."

Helen put the spoon in her hand down on the counter, "I'm glad you brought her home for dinner. I was just a bit surprised when she walked in."

"She's working hard to graduate from high school. Wants to do something, maybe own a little shop someday, maybe a children's bookstore, or work in a nursery school. She likes children. Says they're so innocent and so sweet. I've never known anyone like her before."

Helen looked at Tommy. His face seemed softer and smoother than the one she had remembered seeing the other day in the camera. He looked like a little boy, not the boy she knew who sometimes took money from her purse to buy beer or the troubled kid who skipped school or who got drunk and decided to take batting practice on a line of mailboxes. He was just a kid in love with the wrong girl.

"I'll be nice," she said, "but that doesn't mean I'll quit worrying about you."

"There's nothing to worry about."

The roast was a bit dry, but the potatoes were perfect. Richard and Tommy took seconds while Mindy daintily ate through her helping, and Linda hardly touched hers at all.

Richard made a funny snorting sound when Helen got out the glass compote dishes with the ambrosia salad.

"What are we supposed to do?" Richard smirked. "Pick it up and drink it or eat it with a spoon?"

"A spoon," Helen said, picking up hers and smiling across the table to Mindy.

"My momma makes ambrosia," Mindy said, lifting a tiny

spoonful to her mouth. "But yours is sweeter. I like the coconut on the top. Daddy doesn't like coconut so Momma never puts coconut on hers."

"I like coconut," Tommy piped in.

That's when Helen knew for certain Tommy was in love: he hated coconut.

Mindy had offered to help with dishes. Helen let Linda and Mindy do the washing and drying, and she took on carrying the plates from the kitchen back to the dining room. Tommy put them in the hutch. Richard didn't offer to help. He went into the living room and turned on the television.

When they finished, Linda begged off and went to her room. Tommy said he should be getting Mindy back to her house. Helen knew he would probably take Mindy out to the lake or somewhere and have a couple of beers and neck.

"Here," she said, opening her purse and taking out ten dollars, "you might need some money for gas or something."

Tommy took the money.

"Thanks," he said.

"Thanks for dinner," Mindy added.

She had thought about telling Tommy not to be out too late but she knew it wouldn't make any difference. She'd just have to wait up until he came home before she finished with putting the notes in the baskets and leaving.

"Glad you could come by," Helen said, "say hello to your mother and father."

"Yes, ma'am," Mindy said. She squeezed Tommy's hand and smiled at him, and the two of them left.

Helen heard Tommy come in around one o'clock in the morning. She lay there in bed waiting for him to go to sleep. Linda had been in her room since dinner. Her light had been on when Helen came upstairs. When she knocked on Linda's door, to say goodnight, Linda said she was going to read for a while longer. Helen told her to be sure to turn her light off when she finished. Richard came up to bed around ten. Helen had thought they might talk a little. She wanted to tell him he'd been a good husband. She asked if he wanted to make love, but he wasn't interested. He said he was tired and wanted to go to sleep.

She waited until around 2:30 before she got up. She had left her clothes on the chair by the dresser so she wouldn't have to turn on the light to find them. She slipped her shirt and pants on in the dark. Her shoes were down in the kitchen by the back door where she'd left them when she came in from the garden that afternoon.

Opening the closet as quietly as she could she reached in and pulled out her suitcase. She took the letter she'd written for Richard out of her pants pocket and put it on his dresser underneath his wallet. She could hear her heart beating in her head. She felt dizzy and had a little trouble catching her breath. Her lungs burned.

She had gone to the doctor last week. She had told him about having trouble breathing. She said it felt like there was something wrong, something tight in her chest, like an elephant was standing on it all the time. He listened to her heart and lungs. He tapped her on the back and told her to take a deep breath then he sat back into his chair and told her he couldn't hear anything. He said it didn't mean there was nothing wrong with her. He asked if there was anything going on at home, if the kids were giving her trouble or if Richard was acting funny. She said things were fine at home. But, as she spoke she felt her face flush and her heart begin to race. Her chest tightened and she thought she might faint.

The doctor listened to her chest again. She wondered if he could hear her heart trying to tear itself loose. He shook his head then took out his prescription pad and said maybe what was happening was not in her body but in her head.

"A lot of women feel the way you do sometimes," he said. "There's nothing to worry about. It passes. Take one of these when you're beginning to feel like you just described. It will help you relax."

She went to the pharmacy and had the prescription filled. She didn't tell Richard about seeing the doctor. In fact, she didn't tell anyone. The pills were little round red ones. The pharmacist had smiled when she gave him the prescription. "Mommies' little helpers," he said, when he gave her the bottle. "They work like a charm but don't take them too often. Only when you need them like the doctor said."

Having them in her purse made her feel dirty. When she came home she put the pills in the bottom of her underwear drawer. She had taken one right before she started to cook dinner just to keep her hands from shaking. She had never taken more than one in any one day before but now she was finding she needed another because she couldn't breathe again. She tried to straighten her shoulders to force the air into her burning lungs. She could taste the tears in the back of her throat. She tried to put her hands together out in front of her in the dark of the closet and as she did she could feel her fingers shaking. She put her hands down to her sides and quietly backed out of the closet with her suitcase in her hands.

"That was yesterday," she said under her breath to herself as she quietly put the suitcase on the floor. "Yesterday I took one. This is today. I can take one for today." Then she slid the dresser drawer open and lifted the bottle of pills out from under her clothes and unscrewed the lid. She took one of the pills and put it into her mouth and threw back her head and swallowed it. Capping the bottle again she put the rest of the pills in her pants pocket.

She walked over to the bed and pulled the covers up over Richard's shoulders. She had thought about kissing him but didn't want to risk waking him. He was a restless sleeper.

She carried her suitcase to the end of the hallway and put it down at the top of the stairs. She opened Linda's bedroom door and peeked in. Linda had pulled the covers up over her head. Helen stepped into the room and gently pulled back the covers so she could see her daughter's face.

Linda was sleeping on her side and her dark straight hair had fallen across her face like a curtain. Helen pulled her hair back. It was cool and silky in her hand. She kissed her daughter's forehead. Linda stirred a little but didn't wake. Helen adjusted the covers up over her shoulders and gently tucked her in.

She closed Linda's door. Tommy's door was slightly ajar. She pushed it open. His clothes were thrown in a pile on the floor. She stepped near his bed. He smelled of cigarettes and beer. She pulled the covers up over his shoulders and touched his hair. He didn't move. She stood there by his bed for a long time watching him sleep. She wondered what would happen to him. She wished she would have known how to be a better mother for him, but she hadn't. She bent down and kissed his hair and whispered that she hoped he understood she had done her best.

When she left Tommy's room she opened Linda's door one more time and looked in. Linda was sleeping peacefully. Helen worried Linda hadn't recognized her that day at the library because she was ashamed of her. Helen kissed Linda and brushed the hair from her face. Linda was so beautiful. Helen hoped she wouldn't hate her for leaving.

Helen picked up her suitcase and crept down the stairs. She put the notes she still carried in her pocket for Linda and Tommy into the baskets and placed the baskets on the dining room table. After putting on her shoes she unlocked the back door and left.

She didn't want to take a chance of making too much noise, so rather than opening the trunk and putting the suitcase there, she put it on the front seat, sliding it into the passenger side. She took one last look at the garden.

Her garden was beautiful in the moonlight. She could see the barest new lime-green shoots coming from the ground where she'd planted the snap beans and the corn. The long rows of onions Linda had planted were already upright and strong looking. Along the back edge of the plot she could see the first signs of her gladiolas pushing their way through the thick black mulch of leaves surrounding them. It would be a good garden this year. She could feel it. The soil was black and rich from years of mulching and turning, and the weather just damp and warm enough to give it a good early start.

She put the car into neutral and let it slide down the driveway, waiting until she was in the middle of the road before starting the engine. When she was halfway down the road and could no longer see the house in her rearview mirror she started to cry.

It wasn't a hard shaking sobbing crying, but rather a rush of tears burning her throat and falling down her face to the front of her shirt. Part of her felt cut clean from her life. She was scared.

She let the car take her down the road. She pushed on the gas pedal hard with her foot and felt the car fly forward out into the night. Then she'd ease her foot off and let the car coast as though she had just crested a hard steep hill and was silently drifting down.

The tears came in streams down her face. She could taste the salt water in her throat. She felt a little like she might drown. She didn't have a plan.

She gunned the engine then drifted. Gunned then drifted, for what seemed like an hour or more. She went downtown and drove the empty streets. The stores were dark and there was no one on the sidewalks. All the little restaurants were closed. She ran red lights twice just to see what would happen. No one was there to see her. Nothing happened.

Her body convulsed with sobs. Her face felt raw from the tears. Her nose ran and she didn't even bother to wipe it with either a tissue or the back of her hand. She could hear something that sounded like an animal caught in a trap. The sound was coming from her throat, from her lips, but she didn't recognize them as her sounds. It was as if she had at last let the crying grab control over her, and once she had let go, she became someone or something else.

Suddenly the car stopped. The headlights pointed off into the woods. She wondered if she had driven off the road or was in trouble. She opened her door but didn't get out. The night air was cold against her wet face. She looked around and realized she had driven to Greyjack's house.

Greyjack recognized Helen's car. He turned on the front porch light and grabbed a flashlight. He walked toward her, shining the light out in front as he came in order not to frighten her with his approach. He could sense she was in trouble.

She saw a beam of light coming towards her car. Greyjack called out her name. She couldn't move. She let the car stall until it sputtered and turned off. She could hear Greyjack calling out to her. She tried to answer him, but she couldn't. Her voice was lost somewhere in her head.

"Hold on," Greyjack called out.

Hold on to what? Helen thought. She could hear Greyjack calling but it sounded like he was yelling through a long tunnel filled with running water and the rushing sound of the wind. She tried to move her hands but couldn't find them. It was as if her body and her mind had left each other and she was forced to decide which she would inhabit: her head or her heart.

Greyjack opened the car door, put his arms around her and pulled her from the driver's seat. Helen let her head fall onto his shoulder. His body felt like a warm blanket. She tried to tell him she was tired, and she wanted to go to sleep, but the words came out all funny.

He saw her suitcase sitting on the passenger side of the front seat.

"Going somewhere?"

Helen tried, but couldn't answer. She was sobbing again.

He kissed the top of her head and tightened his arms around her.

"Do you want me to take you home? Does Richard know you're here?"

Helen shook her head no. Then she shook her head and shook her head and shook her head.

"It's okay, Helen, it's okay." Greyjack hugged her tighter and then slipped his arm under her legs so he could carry her to his house. He was surprised how light she felt when he picked her up. She didn't feel like a grown woman in his arms, but more like a skinny teenager, the same skinny teenager he and Warren used to play hide and seek with for hours on end in the moonlight when they were kids.

Helen draped her arms around Greyjack's strong neck and let the gentle back and forth motion of his walking rock her body into a deep sleep where she couldn't hear and couldn't feel and didn't want to speak.

Chapter 11

Richard woke up at 4:30 a.m. and discovered Helen was gone. He went down to the kitchen looking for her. When he didn't find her in the house he went out to the garden knowing she wouldn't be there, but also knowing he had to go out there because he had to be able to say he searched for her. He knew she'd left him.

The house felt strangely hollow. He went back to his room and looked at the bed. He could see the place where Helen had been sleeping. He ran his hands over the sheets hoping to feel some small trace of her warmth. He wondered how long she'd been gone and why he didn't wake when she got up to leave.

He opened her dresser drawers and looked in the closet. He could see she'd taken some clothes, but not all of them. He found her ring box in her underwear drawer. When he opened the box, the ring was there, still shiny, hardly warn. He hadn't really expected her to take it, but it hurt him none-the-less to know she'd left it.

He searched the room, looking at everything, making a mental note of what was taken, what was left, looking for clues as to where she might have gone. That's when he found her note stuck under the chocolate fruit and nut egg on his dresser. It was such an odd thing, the chocolate egg. She bought him one every Easter and always left it in the same place. It was a funny little ritual that made him feel a bit uncomfortable since he never remembered to get her anything.

The note said she wasn't feeling like herself and needed to go away because she was having trouble breathing. She signed the note: Love, Helen.

It didn't make sense to Richard. She had seemed plenty strange lately, but not sick. She hadn't said anything about not feeling well or having trouble breathing. He wondered why she hadn't seen a doctor. He wondered if that's what she wanted to talk about last night before he went to sleep. He felt a little sorry they hadn't had sex last night. The phone rang. He went downstairs to get it.

"She's here," said Greyjack, "but I don't think she's in good shape. She's sleeping right now."

"She left a note," Richard said angrily. "Why'd she come there, to you?"

Greyjack chose to ignore the question.

"Looks like she's been driving around for awhile," he said. "Her car is nearly out of gas. Her suitcase was in the front seat."

"She left me."

"I figured as much."

"You sleeping with her?"

"You can really be an jackass, Richard, you know that? Do you really think I'd sleep with your wife?"

"You and Helen are old friends."

"I thought we were all friends."

Richard took a deep breath.

"Greyjack, I..." he wanted to apologize.

"She's sleeping. She had some pills in her pocket. Looks like a prescription for some kind of tranquilizer."

"How many did she take?"

"I can't tell."

"What'd she say?"

"The little of what she's said hasn't made much sense. I think she maybe had one or two of the pills. The bottle was still pretty full. My guess is she didn't have enough to hurt her. The pills seem to be the least of what's going on. She seems pretty depressed, pretty sad and confused. Keeps saying she had to leave because she couldn't breathe. I don't think it would be wise for me to bring her back. At least not right now. What do you want me to do?"

"What do you suggest?" Richard said as coolly as he could manage.

"I think she needs to see a doctor."

"What's wrong with her?" Richard almost screamed into the phone.

"It looks to me like she's having some kind of nervous breakdown. I think the best place for her right now is the County Hospital."

"The mental hospital?"

"They've got good doctors who can look after her there. I don't think she knew what she was doing when she left you. Throw the note away. Don't read it. She wasn't herself when she wrote it. I'm sure of it. The woman who came to my house isn't Helen. She needs help."

"You take her then," Richard said, not wanting to talk anymore.

Greyjack had known Richard would be angry. He wasn't surprised Helen had come to his house. As far as he knew she didn't have many women friends. Greyjack always figured it was hard for Helen to be friends with other women because her mother had died when she was only seven, and after that there were only men in her life. He figured you learned girl things from your mother the same way you learned boy things from your father.

"Look," Greyjack said, trying to get his friend to make the right decision. "Helen came here asking a friend for help."

"Right, and we're such good friends she left me, remember?"

"She needs help. Help neither you or I can give her right now and if you'd like I'll take her to the County Hospital for you."

"What do you suggest I tell Linda and Tommy?"

"That's up to you."

"I don't want them to know you took her to a mental hospital."

"No one has to know. I'll tell them at the hospital that you want this kept quiet. There will be some papers to sign."

"Will she come back?"

"She might. It's hard to know."

Linda was the first one to come downstairs. She found her father sitting in the living room like he had been sitting there all night waiting for her to walk down the stairs. He was dressed for church.

"Your mother's gone," Richard said, not looking up.

Linda knew without asking that her father meant her mother was gone forever, not just gone out to the garden or to the store or maybe to visit a friend.

The house felt still the way an open field feels still before a big storm tears through it. The clock in the living room ticked louder than she could ever remember it ticking before.

"You should get dressed. I don't want to be late for church."

Linda stood counting the ticks of the big grandfather clock waiting for him to say something else. She had always waited and counted the ticks after her mother or father had spoken to her before she answered or left the room. Ten ticks were enough, she always thought, to be sure the conversation was over. Ten ticks were enough, she reasoned to give her time to think about how to respond. And, when she had a bad dream or her parents were fighting, ten ticks were enough to make her feel safe again.

Her father turned away.

Tommy was still sleeping, so Linda went upstairs and woke him and told him their Mom had left. The news didn't seem to shake Tommy much. He asked where Dad was and she told him he was sitting in the living room dressed for church. Tommy didn't say anything. Linda could hear the clock in the living room and wondered if Tommy was counting the ticks as well.

While she stood there waiting for Tommy to respond, she had the strangest feeling they weren't doing it right or at least the way she'd read about in books or seen people in the movies do when someone left or died. They should be screaming or crying, but instead they were being quiet and contained like they were all listening to the clock tick and wondering if ten ticks were enough to bring them back to where they had been before. No one seemed surprised she had left. It was as though she'd been talking about it every morning at breakfast for as long as any of them could remember.

Linda was standing in the doorway of Tommy's room waiting for him to tell her what they should do. She really hoped he would say something. It seemed to her Tommy had spent his whole lifetime not doing much else but working some great outfield play in his head, and as soon as everyone shifted into the right places he'd know where to throw the ball. He didn't move.

"What should we do?" Linda asked, still waiting, hoping he had a plan.

"I guess we ought to get ready for church," he said, pulling back the covers and dropping his feet to the floor.

"You want breakfast?" she asked.

"Do you?"

"Not really."

"Let's get this church thing over with," he said.

Linda left his room. She didn't go downstairs again to ask her father if he wanted her to cook breakfast. She figured none of them could either be hungry or want to go into the pumpkin-colored kitchen to eat.

She and Tommy took their time getting ready for church, staying in their rooms with their doors shut until they heard the clock chime and their father get up from his chair to call them to come down.

They left the house without looking in their Easter baskets.

The drive to the church was deadly. Richard drove with both hands on the wheel like he was afraid to let go. Linda watched him from the backseat and thought he drove as though he was afraid if he loosened his grip at all, the car would careen off the road and crash into a ditch and kill them all. She kept from screaming by smoothing the front of her new skirt, tracing the tangle of roses and vines in the intricate pattern on her suit with her fingertips. Tommy sat in the front seat and kept his head turned away, looking out the window the way their mother had done so often before, so he didn't have to talk to anyone. No one spoke.

When they pulled into the parking lot, Joe Nathan was standing there waving his long bird-like arms like he was about to take flight.

"Hallelujah," he called out as each new car eased into the parking lot.

"Praise Je-sus," he sang out, prancing up and down the sidewalk greeting people as they came up the walkway.

Linda jumped out of the car as soon as it came to a stop. She wanted to avoid being greeted by Joe Nathan. She went into the sanctuary without waiting for either her dad or Tommy. She wanted to sit by herself.

She slid into the empty back pew. When she thought no one was looking, she took a sidelong glance to the other side of the church where Tommy took a seat with Mindy. Linda looked to the front and saw her father sitting alone.

Heads were turned and people in the congregation were whispering and staring at her father. He was crying. Linda could see these onlookers staring at him then twisting around in their seats to first find Tommy then her as though they expected them to get up from their seats and do something about their father crying. She kept her head down and avoided their eyes. When Joe Nathan pranced up to the podium, all the whispering and staring stopped.

Halfway through the service, a new ripple of whispers swept over the congregation like a rustle of wind. All heads turned and looked at Linda. She looked up in defiance, realizing as she did that Greyjack had just slid into the pew beside her.

Greyjack was not a member of their church. In fact, he was, as far as Linda knew, not a member of any church. Her mother had once said that when they were growing up neither her family nor Greyjack's went to church. She had said her father refused to go to church after her mother died and Greyjack's family didn't go because Mr. Greyjack didn't believe God lived in churches. Mr. Greyjack was a Menominee Indian from the Upper Peninsula and Mrs. Greyjack was of Irish descent and had left the Catholic Church when she got married.

Greyjack looked more Irish than Indian. He had a strong, short, stocky body and soft blue eyes. He was quiet, however, and had a disquieting way of coming up on you without you seeing him. Linda had heard a number of devout church-goers in town call him the "Indian" behind his back in the same way you might use an ugly word for a black man.

Greyjack sat very still next to her, looking straight ahead so if anyone turned to look at her they'd see him instead and quickly turn around to mind their own business. There was something about having him next to her that gave Linda a kind of raw courage. She didn't drop her eyes, but stared out at the people who were staring at her. People began to whisper Greyjack's name. As the wave of whispers hit against the back wall, her father turned around and saw Greyjack.

Greyjack just sat there waiting.

"Je-sus works in mysterious ways," Joe Nathan shouted across the congregation as if he was declaring he had somehow invoked the power of Jesus to bring Greyjack to church this morning.

"Your mother asked me to come here," Greyjack said, putting his hand on top of Linda's. "She wanted me to talk to you."

Greyjack's touch was like a fire shooting through Linda's arm to her brain.

She didn't respond. She sat still, her head held high, her eyes looking out into some distant place.

"Where did she go?"

"Away for a while."

"Where?"

"I can't tell you right now."

"When can you tell me?"

"You can call me."

Tears welled up in her eyes. Greyjack took a clean folded handkerchief out of his pocket and put it in Linda's hand. He slipped out of the pew and left the church.

Joe Nathan stopped shouting his declaration that Je-sus works in mysterious ways. The whole congregation quit their squirming and nodding and turned their heads and held their breath as Greyjack made his way out the door.

Reverend Jacobs had called Joe Nathan early in the morning telling him Helen Nichols had been admitted to the psych ward. Reverend Jacobs also told him Helen was having a nervous breakdown and had left her husband.

When Joe Nathan got off the phone, he dropped down to his knees right there by the telephone in the kitchen, and he started to pray and to listen for what God wanted him to do.

Jacobs had told Joe Nathan the family wanted it kept quiet, but when Joe Nathan started to pray, he felt a nagging pull by Jesus. Wanted what quiet? That she had run away and was in a mental ward? That she'd abandoned her husband and her children?

Joe Nathan couldn't abide a man who didn't have the guts to make a woman obey, and he didn't have any respect for a woman who would just up and leave her husband and children. It was not what God intended. Joe Nathan felt Jesus nudging him to ignore what Reverend Jacobs had told him and to tell the truth instead. And, if he told the truth and the congregation understood why this had happened in their church, then they could help this family heal. Yes, Jesus wanted him to use Helen as an example for the whole congregation. Joe Nathan was sure of it.

When Greyjack stepped out of the sanctuary and the big front door to the church clicked shut, Joe Nathan took a deep breath and a hard left turn off Jesus' mysterious ways. He leapt into a storm of hell fire and damnation. The spirit blew through him like a mighty wind.

His eyes were wide and wild and he was leaning out over the pulpit looking straight at Richard when he spat the words:

"This is the day I should be talking about a stone and a tomb and a heap of salvation. Instead, Je-sus spoke to me and told me to tell you that hell is full of Jezebels whose husbands couldn't control them. God made man, THEN God made woman FOR the man."

A flutter rippled across the congregation as people shut their hymnals and fanned themselves, but kept their heads down low in order to whisper to one another.

Joe Nathan was on fire. He paced. Wiping his sweating face with his big white handkerchief, he stomped and praised.

"Hell is full of Je-zee-bels," he sang, his head thrown back, "and who's responsible? Who? What does Je-sus ask of us? What does He want for all the salvation He's offering us with his wounded hands?" Joe Nathan shouted.

"To love AND O-bey. That's what."

When he said obey he slung the word out like a lead weight: an anchor put there to keep good Christians everywhere from drifting.

"When we were thrown from the garden," Joe Nathan paced and spat, "Je-sus intended for the man to be the head of the house. The MAN. His first creation. Not the woman who plucked the apple and created temptation. Not the woman who couldn't or wouldn't obey. It was MAN who God made in HIS image. MAN was the FIRST creation. Woman was the second. Man first, then woman second, because the man was to be the head of the house and the wife his support. His servant."

The church was electrified.

"But Je-sus was a wise man, a smart man and He told us that if," and with this pronouncement, Joe Nathan spun on his heels,

"IF the man wasn't strong enough, wasn't man enough to take control, the woman would do what she had done in the garden. That's what that story is trying to tell us: left to her own devices, a woman would cast aside her God-intended role. SHE would leave the path. SHE would pluck the apple. SHE would spit in the face of God and leave."

His fiery words blazed through the congregation. They were a warning to all the men.

Linda didn't know how Joe Nathan knew her mother had left but it was clear he did and he planned to use her leaving to teach everyone a lesson. Linda hated her mother for it.

Joe Nathan rocked back on his heels, spread his hands out over the top of the pulpit and sucked on his big front teeth before he looked at her father again and said, "Hell is full of Je-zee-bels whose husbands couldn't make them obey."

Linda looked out over the congregation and saw her father sitting alone at the front, his head bowed and his shoulders as still as a hot afternoon. No one had come to sit down beside him. He was alone and looked like he had been beaten, or lost an arm or a leg or maybe had seen his best friend die.

Linda looked at Tommy and knew her mother had been right: Tommy and Mindy were the same and whatever was going to happen between them was already in play and there was nothing anyone could do about it. Tommy didn't need Mindy to take him into trouble and Mindy didn't need anyone to help her play out her life.

Her mother had also been wrong. Mindy and Tommy needed each other and right now, Linda was glad they had each other and wished she had someone herself.

Without thinking about the fact that it was Easter Sunday and Joe Nathan was still preaching, Linda stood up, smoothed the wrinkled front of her new suit jacket and skirt and made her way up to the front pew where her father was sitting. She knew everyone was watching her, so she walked like she had someplace to go and something to do when she got there. Linda put her hands on her father's shoulders and helped him stand.

Joe Nathan stopped preaching when Linda walked with her father down the center aisle.

"You okay?" Tommy asked as she passed where he and Mindy were sitting.

Linda nodded her head. She turned around to face Joe Nathan and spoke as loudly and as clearly as she could manage.

"You go on and say whatever it is you want to say about my mother. I'm taking my father home."

Linda drove while her father sat in the passenger seat, staring out the window much the same way her mother had stared out the window just a couple of weeks before.

When they got home, she helped her father out of the car and walked with him up to his room. She took off his shoes and his socks for him.

"You need to sleep," she kept saying, her voice cooing and soothing. "You'll feel better when you wake up. I'll be downstairs. If you need me, call."

She didn't expect him to answer, and she didn't bother to give him a chance to do so. She just kept talking because she was afraid of the silence between them.

When he put his head on the pillow and closed his eyes she pulled the blanket at the foot of the bed up over his shoulders. He needed to get some rest, because nothing was ever going to be the same again.

Linda stood in the hallway by her father's door for a long time just listening. Once she was certain he wasn't crying and was probably asleep, she went into her room to change her clothes. There was a large square mirror hanging over her dresser, and she stood in front of the mirror watching as she unbuttoned her jacket and took off her skirt. The house was quiet, completely quiet, except for the ticking of the grandfather clock in the living room.

She put her Easter suit, the one her mother had bought for her just the other day, on the wooden hanger it came on from the store then took it to the closet and hung it up. Turning towards the mirror she looked at herself again. The person she saw looked more like a woman than she had ever remembered seeing before. She had rounded breasts and round hips and soft brown hair hanging smooth from the crown of her head, nearly touching her soft shoulders. She was thinking she should feel sad her mother had left them. Instead, Linda felt a kind of satisfaction and fascination that she now looked grown. She could take care of herself. She could take care of Tommy and her father too. If her mother wanted to leave them, then fine. Linda didn't need her.

She pulled off her slip then sat on the edge of her bed and took off her nylons and pulled on her jeans and a fresh shirt. She found a clean pair of socks in her drawer and slipped on her old tennis shoes, pulling the laces tight before she tied them. She then went into the kitchen and called Greyjack.

She told him she wanted to talk to him and that her father was sleeping so it would be better if he came over and they didn't talk in the house.

"Have you eaten?"

"I'm not hungry," she said.

"You need to eat. Have you looked in your Easter basket?"

Linda thought it was a strange question. She hadn't even thought about her basket since the moment she came down to get it and found her father sitting there dressed for church.

"No."

"Want a hamburger?"

"Ketchup and mustard, no pickles or onions."

"Straight up," Greyjack said, "no nonsense."

"No nonsense."

When she hung up the phone she went into the dining room

and found her Easter basket. Tucked in between a large chocolate rabbit and the big plastic eggs were two savings passbooks and a note.

One of the passbooks was in her mother's name and the other was in hers. The one in her mother's name, which had $2,000 in it, had been closed out on Thursday. The other, in her name, had a little over nine thousand dollars in it, including a deposit for $1,500 made on the same day the other account had been closed.

The note was written on a page her mother had torn from her garden notebook. It said:

Dear Linda:
I never went to college so I don't really know how much these things cost. I would think the money left in the bank should cover four years of tuition, room and board, and books. You have two more gardens to grow just in case.

I took $500 with me. I always figured the money from the garden I put away in my account to pay for the plowing and seeds really belonged to you. As soon as I can, I will pay you back.

I'm sorry I had to leave you. I couldn't breathe anymore. I had to go. I hope you'll understand. I know you will be okay. Take care of yourself and be yourself at whatever cost.

Love,

Mom

p.s. It is not your job to take care of Tommy and Dad. They are both grown men and should be able to take care of themselves.

Linda folded the note and put it in her pants pocket. She put the bankbooks in the back of the silverware drawer in the buffet. She took the chocolate rabbit out of the box, broke its head off and ate it. Linda had never in her life eaten any part of her chocolate rabbit on Easter morning. She used to save it as though there were sacred rules governing the consumption of something so fine as a large chocolate rabbit.

She heard Greyjack's car pull into the driveway. She went out to meet him.

"Let's eat by the garden," she said with a nod of her head, indicating they shouldn't go inside.

Greyjack had stopped by a burger joint in town on his way over. He got out of his car carrying two large white bags. Without saying anything, he followed Linda. There was a stand of trees by the side of the garage. They sat down to eat.

Before she knew what she was doing, Linda had eaten her hamburger and all the fries in the bag as though she had been looking all morning for something to fill her up and make the emptiness go away.

"I found the bank books," she said.

"She wanted you to know the money belonged to you."

"I bit the head off my chocolate rabbit."

Greyjack laughed.

"My mother said Tommy and Mindy together are just two people looking for trouble."

"She might be right."

"Tommy has someone at least. Mindy's here."

"And your mother's not."

"She was wrong. Tommy's plenty capable of getting into trouble on his own. He doesn't need a girl to help him."

"Your dad and I will take care of Tommy. His trouble isn't yours to worry about."

"Mom always used to say this row of onions is going to buy you books and this row of corn another class. She talked crazy like that all the time. It was like she lived in this fantasy world where potatoes were ideas, tomatoes were classes, and radishes were places I'd go. Where I'd go, never where she'd go. She never talked about going anywhere."

"She wants you to go to college."

"I'm never going back to that stupid church again."

"Don't let your anger close doors."

"Why did she leave?"

Greyjack waited a long time to answer. Linda sat still, waiting for him to say something.

Greyjack looked away from Linda towards the garden.

"People are going to talk, but you don't have to listen," he said slowly. "I guess you could say she left because she couldn't stay."

"Is she with you?"

"No."

"Where is she?"

"She needs a little time."

"Will she come back?"

"It's too early to know," he said. Then he picked up the wrappers lying about on the ground and he put them in the bag. He helped Linda to her feet.

He told Linda her mother loved her.

Linda said she found that hard to believe and walked away from him and into the house.

Chapter 12

The aide knocked lightly on Helen's door, and walked in.

"See you're in here for a bit of a rest," she said. "Wouldn't mind a little rest myself, but you better believe I wouldn't do it here. Can't get much rest here, everyone always banging around and them crazy ones screaming all the time. Can't rest with them around."

Helen closed her eyes. She didn't want to listen to the woman. She didn't want to listen to anyone. Her brain felt a bit thick. Her tongue was swollen and no longer fit comfortably in her mouth. Her mouth was dry. She remembered getting a shot. She wasn't sure if it was in the middle of the night or noon. The shades were pulled and the room was always dark. Helen cleared her throat and tried to swallow but discovered she couldn't.

"Water," she whispered.

The aide picked up the glass of water sitting by the bedside and held the straw up to Helen's mouth.

"Doctor left orders saying we were supposed to check on you every couple of hours. Let you have what you wanted, within reason, of course, and to let you sleep. He's a good doctor. Always lets the ladies sleep awhile before he gets to working on them."

"Tha-ou," Helen said, aware she hadn't been able to say what she wanted to say. Everything seemed so hard. The room was cold. She wished she had another blanket but didn't ask for one because she was afraid the words would come out all wrong again and crazy. She turned her head away from the aide and closed her eyes and softly began crying.

Richard did not like the smell of hospitals. They smelled of blood and disinfectant and left an acrid lingering taste in your mouth of pain and death. He wished there had been somewhere else to take Helen: a cleaner place filled with light. He'd read once that people in places like Alaska and the Netherlands suffered from depression because they didn't get enough sunlight during the winter months. He wondered if Helen just needed a little more sunshine to make her better. He figured that was why she was always out in the garden. Maybe she had a vitamin D deficiency. He was pretty sure vitamin D was the sunshine vitamin. He wanted to ask the doctor if there might be some kind of vitamin D shot she could get that would make her better.

He made a mental note to mention it to the doctor the next time he talked to him on the phone. Richard had gone inside the hospital just once to sign the papers to have Helen committed, and he hadn't gone back inside since then. He did, however, go by the hospital every day and sit in his car in the back of the parking lot trying to figure out what he should do.

When he signed the papers, the doctor had told him he thought it would be best for Helen if Richard stayed away until she was in a better frame of mind. Even though Richard didn't like going inside the hospital, he didn't particularly care for the doctor telling him he couldn't or shouldn't see Helen.

He had been so anxious to get out of the hospital he had forgotten to ask the doctor if he knew why she left him. He wondered what Helen was telling him. He was afraid it was his fault. There were so many things he wished he'd done differently.

He wished his mother were alive. She'd be able to tell him what to do. She was a little like Helen: she got quiet sometimes. He didn't know anything about "woman" stuff. His mother had never told him about monthly woman things or the change. Maybe Helen was going through her change, and that's what was wrong with her. For all he knew, maybe even his mother had gone to the hospital when she went through her change.

He didn't tell Tommy or Linda their mother was in the hospital. He didn't know what to say to them, and he didn't know what it was he was supposed to do for them, so he just left them to be on their own. When he wasn't sleeping or pretending to sleep, he went to work.

Tommy avoided seeing Linda or his father by spending most of his waking hours with Mindy. Linda managed by going to school and working in the garden.

Although she was plenty angry with her mother, she took her mother's advice and didn't go out of her way to take care of either Tommy or her father. She did, however, cook dinner every day. If Tommy or Richard was there when the food was done they ate with her. If they weren't, she put the leftovers in the refrigerator for them to heat up and eat later. Sometimes she left a note on the counter telling them what she'd cooked, and sometimes she didn't. When things got overlooked in the refrigerator or went bad, she threw them out.

Greyjack had been right when he told Linda about people talking. Even though she tried not to listen, it was hard not to overhear what was being said. Linda knew by the way the people in the church and the town talked, they thought it was shameful her mother had left. Linda, however, was too angry to care one way or the other about what the people in town thought or said.

When her mother had painted the kitchen she had taken down all the curtains and curtain rods and didn't put them back. Linda found the curtains stuffed into a ragbag in the corner of the laundry room. She just left them there.

Without the curtains to block the view, Linda could see the driveway and the woods beside the drive from the kitchen window. In the evenings, she could watch raccoons and deer moving out from the woods looking for food: the raccoons in the garbage, the deer in the garden. Standing by the kitchen sink in the morning drinking tea, she could see blue jays and robins, squirrels and crows all scurrying from place-to-place looking for nesting materials or food. But, most importantly, when she sat at the kitchen table, she could look out the big double window by the kitchen table and see the garden.

A month after her mother left, her father had come into the kitchen and asked Linda if she knew where her mother had put the kitchen curtains. Linda lied and told him no. He didn't ask again and didn't go looking for the curtains either, so the window stayed the way her mother had left it. After her father had gone to bed, Linda went down to the pantry, found the old curtains, and stuffed them into the trash.

One morning when the morning light was just perfect in the kitchen and the orange walls were aglow with the warmth of color, Linda thought she could feel her mother sitting in the kitchen.

Linda walked cautiously into the room. She went to the stove and grabbed the teakettle. When she was sure she was the only one in the room, she filled the kettle and put it on the stove and stood by waiting for it to whistle.

She closed her eyes while she waited and let the warmth of the room fill her. She wasn't sure anymore she wanted her mother back into her life. Whether her mother came back or not, Linda was sure of one thing: painting the kitchen orange had been some outrageous act of courage on her mother's part.

It was like shouting in a house where other people only dared to whisper. When Linda came down early in the morning before Tommy or her father got up, she sat at the table drinking tea alone watching the sun creep up the bright orange walls like fire. It made her happy to think her mother's bold walls were something she forgot to pack up and take with her.

Linda loved having the kitchen all to herself and would stand every evening by the window washing dishes, poking both at the hurt her mother's leaving had made and the anger fueling the hurt she felt. Even though she was hurt and angry, she never stood in the kitchen without wondering why her mother left and whom she was with now.

The kitchen felt like a sacred place. Linda was careful to wipe down the counters and put everything away every evening before she turned off the light and went to bed. She scrubbed the floor when it got dirty and kept the windows washed.

Linda never talked about missing her mother and neither did Tommy and Richard. No one talked about Helen or wondered aloud where she had gone.

A couple months after Helen left, everyone quit pretending like they were waiting for her to return and started getting on with their lives. Richard began watching the evening news after dinner, and Tommy started coming home more often to eat with them. Everything seemed to be the same but different.

It was time to move on. One evening, after dinner was over, Linda pulled her mother's chair out from its place between the window and the table and pushed the table against the window frame. She got all the plants her mother had scattered around the house and repotted them together like a dish garden into the bottom half of an old enamel turkey roaster and put the planter in the middle of the table.

She didn't have any homework to do, and she wasn't tired enough to go to bed, so she decided she'd clean the cupboards and throw out everything she didn't like or anything she thought was too weird or too old to consider eating. This included two cans of hominy and an old tin of sardines. She couldn't stand the smell of sardines or how the oil got all over the counter when you opened the can, so she threw the sardines away. She also hated how the thick white lumps of hominy felt in her mouth when she was forced to eat them, so she threw those cans away as well.

Her father stuck his head into the kitchen after the news was over and asked her when she was going to bed. She told him she would when she finished. He didn't ask what she was doing or when she would be finished. He said goodnight to her. She kept working, and it felt good.

The next afternoon when she got home from school she

decided to make cookies. Linda remembered seeing a recipe on the oatmeal box the night before when she was cleaning out the cabinets. The first batch she made was overcooked, but her father and Tommy seemed to drift into the kitchen about the time she was taking them off the pan, and they ate them and said they were good.

Her mother always said the packaged cookies in the store were so cheap it didn't make sense to mess up the kitchen to bake. When there were school bake sales, she'd buy cookies, and Linda would take them out of the package and stack them in bundles of twos and wrap them in wax paper, twisting the top bits of paper shut.

It was always Linda's job to take the cookies to school and give them to the PTA ladies who ran the bake sales. Whenever Linda brought the carefully rewrapped store-bought cookies the other mothers would look at her, then look at each other and raise their eyebrows as if she were handing them a dead cat instead of cookies.

Linda decided she didn't care anymore what anyone thought. People were bound to talk about her mother leaving no matter whether she had ever baked cookies or not. None of that mattered anymore.

Linda went to school only because she had to. She continued to go to church, only because she didn't want her father to have to sit by himself. She went to church, but she didn't listen to anything either Reverend Jacobs or Joe Nathan said. She also refused to stand up when they said to stand up, or to kneel when they said to kneel or sing any of the hymns.

Unfortunately, not looking at Joe Nathan didn't stop her from hearing the ladies of the church gossip as she passed by. She knew, by the way they bent their heads together when she and her father walked down the aisle to their pew, they were talking about her mother leaving. Sometimes Linda could hear people whispering about her mother in her sleep. These whispers always sounded like a rainstorm or a roaring waterfall at the mouth of a long, cold canyon.

Linda built a wall around her when she went to school or in to town so she couldn't listen and she couldn't feel. But as hard as she tried not to hear what people were talking about, she knew Tommy was getting into trouble. Surprisingly, Mindy wasn't the center of his trouble, he was: he was drinking and skipping school. She'd even heard whispered stories about him drinking at school.

Tommy showed up for dinner most times, but then he'd leave and not say where he was going or when he might come home. Linda was aware of a faint yeasty beer-like smell to his body and breath. She didn't say anything because their father kept silent as though not asking meant nothing was happening, and therefore he didn't have to do anything about it.

Linda knew he and Mindy were sometimes skipping school together and driving out to Crystal Lake. Everyone at school was talking about Tommy and Mindy carrying on, and no one even tried to keep it a secret from Linda. Linda also knew Tommy wasn't doing any homework and was on the verge of failing all his classes. It made her feel sick.

"What do you think you're doing?" she asked him when he came home late one Sunday night smelling this time not like beer so much as like cheap liquor and cigarettes.

"Looking for something to eat," he said.

"I ought to tell Dad you're skipping school."

"Good idea," Tommy said, rummaging first through the refrigerator, then, when he didn't find anything there he wanted, through the pantry.

"Maybe a better idea would be for you to graduate."

"Yes, Mother," he mocked.

"Tommy, please."

"Please what?" he said, opening a jar of peanut butter and grabbing a spoon.

"Please graduate."

"So I can get into the Army?"

"So you can go to college."

"That's you," he said, tapping her on the chin with the tip of his spoon, "not me."

"There's plenty of money."

"That's yours, not mine. Besides, I don't want it."

Linda knew it was true.

"What about Mindy?" she asked.

"What about her?"

"Do you have plans?"

"My plan," he said, scraping another mouthful of peanut butter off the spoon with his front teeth, "is quite simple. I plan to love her." Then he took the jar of peanut butter and the spoon, and he went to his room and shut the door.

Linda's face burned with jealousy.

"Asshole," Linda screamed at the top of her lungs. The word flung itself out into the room like the angry snap of a whip.

Tommy didn't get up the next morning to go to school. Linda went into his room three times and tried to shake him and make him get up before she left. He told her he would get up and go when he was good and ready and not to get so twisted up about his life.

When she got to school her homeroom teacher handed her a note and told her Mr. Mankoff, the principal, wanted to see her in his office during first period.

"I understand," Mr. Mankoff said, motioning for Linda to sit down in the chair in front of his desk, "your brother Tommy has been skipping school."

By the way Mankoff nodded his head for her to sit down he made it clear that he had decided since their mother was gone that she was in charge and now responsible for Tommy's actions. Mankoff's presumption and his arrogance made Linda angry.

"I'm Tommy's sister, not his mother," she said with as much edge as she could muster. "Why don't you call Tommy's dad?"

Mr. Mankoff didn't say anything in return. He just looked at her the same way the ladies at the PTA used to look at her when she gave them the store-bought cookies she had bundled and twisted in waxed paper.

"Have you talked with him lately?" he asked, looking through some papers on his desk as though they were important.

"To my father?"

"No, Tommy."

"I talked to both of them just yesterday," she said, the anger inside of her pushing and bubbling against her throat. She tried her best to look at Mr. Mankoff hard like she was daring him to say anything else to her.

"Right now, your brother is failing all his classes."

"And I'm not," she snapped.

Without waiting for his reply, Linda got up and walked out. Once she was in the hallway she figured it was just as easy to leave school as it was to leave Mankoff's office, so she went out the front door and started walking home. No one tried to stop her so she kept walking.

It felt good to be walking down the road alone while everyone else was sitting in class, their heads bent close to their desks taking notes and listening to the teachers drone on and on about one stupid thing or another. She could see why Tommy liked skipping school. It was exciting. She picked up her pace. It was as if some string that had been holding her back before had been cut, and she was faster and lighter than she had ever felt before. She felt free of the world. It scared her.

When she got home it was almost noon. Tommy was gone and her father had left for work. The house felt cold and empty. She didn't want to be alone. She didn't know what to do so she called Greyjack.

"Want some lunch?" Greyjack asked, before she could even

tell him about being home and what happened. It was like he had been there and knew or maybe followed her home and was waiting for her to call.

"Lunch?"

"I was thinking about making some egg salad. Like egg salad?"

"Yes, but not much mayo. A little mustard and lots of salt and pepper."

"I like it that way too," he said. "Be there in a couple of minutes."

When she hung up the phone she decided to change into her gardening clothes. It didn't feel right being dressed for school and not be in school. It also felt weird being in the house on a school day without being sick, so she thought she should do something useful like work in the garden.

Linda heard Greyjack arrive just as she was bringing a wheel-barrow full of compost to the melon patch. Melons were heavy feeders and did better if she worked in some extra compost around the mounds. She didn't stop working.

Greyjack got out of the car and walked towards her. He held up the sack of sandwiches he had and the cold drinks and motioned for her to stop and join him. He sat down in the same spot they had eaten lunch in the first morning after her mother had left.

"I got called into the principal's office today because Tommy was skipping school. Because Tommy was skipping school, not me, Tommy. Like I was his mother or something."

Greyjack took the sandwiches out of the bag, handed one to her and took one. He unwrapped it, took one bite, chewed for a minute then spoke.

"Did you know he was skipping?"

"Didn't you?" Linda challenged.

"You ever talk to him?"

"Yeah, I said something to him." She unwrapped her

sandwich, lifted up one corner of the bread to make sure it didn't have too much mayo then took a bite.

"And?" Greyjack said, taking a sip from his drink.

"I don't think he cares."

"He cares. He just fell down the rabbit hole," Greyjack said, looking off into the garden like there was some answer out there she hadn't noticed before.

"The rabbit hole?"

"Like Alice. Too much is happening all too fast, and he can't find a way out. Skipping school is just about the only thing he can do right now to keep from going crazy."

Linda ate her sandwich and thought about what Greyjack had said. Greyjack reached into the bag and took out a third sandwich and offered her half. She took it, and they ate on in silence. When they finished eating, Greyjack picked up all the wax paper wrappers from their sandwiches, and balled them up into a tight wad and put them back into the sack. Then he rolled the sack closed like he was going to put it somewhere to save it. It was the same thing he had done when they had eaten together on Easter Sunday, and it made Linda realize it was probably one of the things her mother had liked about him. He had a way of tidying up and making the world feel orderly.

"Mankoff probably thought it would be easier for Tommy if whatever he had to say came from you, not your dad." When he spoke, Greyjack looked at Linda to make sure she understood what he was saying.

"But," he went on, "he was wrong to expect you to do anything about it. Which is why he didn't try to stop you. He knew he was wrong as soon as he said what he said. Probably would be fine with everyone if you just pretended like nothing happened. You haven't caused any trouble if that's what you're worried about."

Linda hadn't really thought at all about being in trouble or about going back, but what Greyjack said made some sense. She knew he was right. She would go back to school tomorrow like nothing happened. Her dad wouldn't be home until late, and Tommy didn't make a habit out of being home during the day, so no one but Greyjack and Mankoff would ever know she'd left school.

"I know you think Tommy shouldn't go into the Army," Greyjack continued, "but the service can give you some time to grow up. Tommy would do okay there. Right now he's restless. Thinks the world is his with Mindy for the taking, but he can't sit still to wait for the right time to take it. He thinks it has to happen now.

"I should have talked to Mankoff before now. The Army won't take Tommy unless he graduates. I've called the recruiter. He'll take care of Tommy and make sure he gets in a good place. Can I tell Mankoff we had lunch today?"

It was as much a statement as it was a question, but Greyjack waited for Linda to answer.

"Did you love her?" she asked.

"After her mother died, your mom spent a lot of time over at our house. She was like a sister."

"Do you love her now?"

Greyjack rolled the brown lunch sack back and forth in his hands like it was a lump of clay he was going to fashion into a thick coil.

"I don't love her in the way you might be thinking," he said. He stopped talking for a moment, but not long enough for Linda to ask or say anything else.

"You call me anytime," he said, getting up and walking to his car. "Anytime."

Chapter 13

Helen tried to keep her eyes focused on Dr. Abrams' mouth. He had a nice face. Smooth, freshly shaved. There was a faint smell of Bay Rum aftershave in the room. His hair was a lovely steely grey color. It was combed back with a crisp part cut straight and clean on the left-hand side. His eyes were a reddish brown. He wore small round tortoise shell glasses. He did not look like anyone she had ever known before. He looked like he had been to college.

She liked the sound of his voice. She could hear him talking, but she was having trouble making sense of his words.

"Can you tell me why you're here, Helen?"

Helen wondered if he had just asked her a question. She strained to hear if there might be an echo of what he said still in the room.

"You're here, because?" he prompted her, not so much because he wanted her to answer the question, but because he himself had begun to wonder if she really belonged in the hospital. He saw a lot of women like Helen, and lately he had begun to doubt they needed to be hospitalized or that the treatment they received at the hospital actually helped them. In truth, he thought they would be better served by a week away at some nice resort rather than being locked up in a psych ward. Most of them just wanted to talk, to rest, to have their hair washed, and to have someone else cook their meals for them. Most just wanted to be taken care of for a change.

He was feeling a bit uneasy about the evening attending physician continuing to sedate her. Dr. Abrams had mentioned it him, and they had a slight disagreement regarding Helen's care. Dr. Abrams believed using drugs to sedate agitation was a self-fulfilling prophecy of continued agitation and sedation.

It was clear it was becoming a pattern for Helen. She would

sleep off the effects of the sedation during the day, and in the evening become agitated and weepy and unable to sleep. The sleeplessness coupled with her crying would have the evening physician writing orders to sedate her once again in order to get her to settle down and sleep through the night.

It wasn't exactly the kind of medicine or psychotherapy Dr. Abrams believed in, and he was at odds with many of the other physicians on staff regarding the heavy use of sedation with patients like Helen.

Last night had been a rougher night than some of the others and it was noted in her chart that after she was given the first shot she continued to struggle with the doctor, and he made the decision to give her a second injection.

She seemed more out of it than Dr. Abrams would have expected, even with a second sedative. Most of the women who came to them had a rather high tolerance of drugs as a result of years of self-medication with alcohol not to mention the latest anti-depressants the family doctors dispensed to them so freely. It wasn't unusual for the women to have a rather high tolerance to the drugs used in the hospital and it often took more than one shot to knock someone out.

Dr. Abrams regretted Helen had been admitted to the psychiatric ward and wanted desperately to find a way to get her steady on her feet again and out of the hospital.

If he could talk to Helen he believed he could get her to accept responsibility for her actions and to think about her family. Perhaps the other doctors were right that she needed the shots when she became agitated and couldn't sleep, but he strongly believed she also needed to learn to cope a little better and go back to her family and get on with her life.

"Can you tell me why you're here, Helen?"

"Be-cause," Helen struggled with pushing the word out of her mouth. Her whole head felt like it was swaddled in thick bandages. She closed her eyes and tried to think. She really wasn't sure how she had gotten here.

The night when she left home and went to Greyjack she asked him to let her stay with him for a while. When he told her he didn't think it was a good idea. He also told her he thought she needed to see a doctor, to go to a hospital to get some help. She tried to run from him. He held onto her, and she couldn't get away. She was so exhausted from crying she couldn't fight him. She had not wanted to come to the hospital.

Ironically, she couldn't think about leaving the hospital now because she was so tired, so very tired. All she wanted to do was close her eyes and go to sleep again.

"You left your family, remember? Can you tell me your children's names, Helen?"

Helen shook her head. She knew their names, but she could not think about them being children. It was wrong to leave children. She didn't want to talk about them being children. Not today, she didn't want to think about anything today.

The doctor watched her and waited for a response. Helen then turned her face away from him.

"You do remember your children, don't you?" he shouted, hoping to break through the fog of the medicine.

Helen started to cry. She brushed her hand against her wet cheek. Her face felt raw. She wondered if they would take her back to her room now and give her another shot to stop her from crying. She struggled for a moment trying to form a sentence. It had been cold in her room last night. She hoped she would be able to find the words to ask for another blanket before they gave her the shot and she fell asleep again.

Greyjack was sitting in the parking lot of his office, the engine of his car idling. He had just come from having lunch with Linda. On his way back to the office he had driven by the hospital. It was the fifth time he had driven by there recently, hoping to see Helen standing by the fence or walking over the grounds. He just wanted to see her to know she was doing okay.

The night when she came to him and he held her while she cried, she felt so small and hurt in his arms. He wondered what had gone wrong with her and Richard. He often wondered what would have happened to all of them if Warren hadn't been killed in the war and they had all come home heroes.

Greyjack had known Richard all his life. They had grown up as best friends. But the war had changed Richard. When they came back from the war, Richard and he were still friends, but they were not as close and sometimes couldn't talk because Warren was gone.

When Richard married Helen, Greyjack felt pushed further away. Richard got angry quicker than he ever had before the war, and sometimes Greyjack felt as though Richard was jealous of his friendship with Helen.

Greyjack missed being friends with Helen. She was easy to be with. She was his connection to Warren and the childhood they shared before the war. When she came to him crying and he held her, he knew she needed help, help he couldn't give her, so he took her to the hospital. He didn't want to lose her.

But, the only way he could get Helen to go agree to check into the hospital was to promise he would look out for Linda and Tommy. It was an easy promise to make. He had always thought of Linda and Tommy as the children he didn't have. He had come to all their birthday parties, their school performances and ballgames.

He knew he should, but he did not want to tell Richard about what had happened at school. He knew Richard would be angry with Mankoff for trying to make Linda responsible for Tommy. Probably angrier than he would be when he learned Tommy had been skipping school.

Richard wasn't capable of taking charge of Tommy right now. Richard was lost without Helen and too angry and ashamed she had left him to see Tommy was in trouble and needed him.

Richard could barely get himself together enough to go to work and Greyjack knew it.

It was time, however, to talk to Richard about Tommy. Greyjack knew Richard and he needed to put whatever pressure they could on Tommy to graduate so he could join the Army and straighten out his life. But, before Greyjack talked to Richard, he decided he should give Mankoff a call.

He turned off the car, took the keys out of the ignition, then walked into his sheriff's office and closed his door.

"I followed up on the Nichols' girl who left school this morning," Greyjack said in his best official sheriff's voice.

"And?" Mankoff asked, waiting for an answer.

"She'll be back tomorrow morning."

"She left school today," Mankoff said, irritated.

"Can you blame her?" Greyjack said.

"Sometimes a sibling can bear more pressure than a parent."

"I hope Linda's not in any trouble," Greyjack pushed.

"She left school."

"With good cause, and she'll be back tomorrow, and I think it would be best if this is forgotten. Don't you agree?"

"What about the brother?"

"I'm in touch with the family. There's been some upset there recently. Tommy and I have talked about the possibility of him joining the Army after he graduates. Give him some time to grow up and have a little direction. The Army would be a good place for him, don't you agree?"

Greyjack knew Mankoff would agree. Mankoff had served in WWII with him and Richard. Mankoff, however, had already graduated from college when he enlisted and had been a captain. The rest of them, including Warren, enlisted straight out of high school and had been just privates. Both Greyjack and Richard had had the bad fortune to draw Mankoff as a captain during their training. He was a jackass then, Greyjack thought, and a jackass now: once a jackass, always a jackass.

"Could straighten him out."

"What needs to happen for him to graduate?"

"He'd have to make up the work he's missed. I can't erase his absences."

"Tommy's done some work for me."

"I've heard about your little juvenile work teams."

"Maybe there'd be something Tommy could do around the school to make up for his absences. Looks like there could be some landscaping that could improve the looks of the place. "

"I think that could be worked out."

"Thanks," Greyjack said, and he meant it.

Greyjack drove to the plant and waited by Richard's car in the parking lot until he finished his shift.

"Have you talked to her?" Richard asked, once he was close enough so he didn't have to shout.

"This is about Tommy." It pissed Greyjack off that Richard thought he had anything to do with Helen leaving him.

"What about him?" Richard said, the edge in his voice sharpening.

Greyjack waited a minute for Richard to cool.

"He's skipping school, but you knew that. Mankoff called Linda into the office about it today."

"Called Linda?"

"It was stupid on his part, but then again, Mankoff has always been stupid," he said, trying to throw off what Mankoff had done and get on with what he really needed to say.

"Why didn't he call me?"

"He said he thought Linda could put more pressure on Tommy about graduating. He said siblings are often stronger advocates in this sort of thing. Peer pressure, I guess."

Richard didn't say anything, and Greyjack could feel his anger building.

"The Army will take Tommy if we can get him to graduate,"

Greyjack offered.

"What's that going to take? His mother coming home? Some kind of miracle? What are we talking about here?"

"A few papers and a little landscaping work on weekends at the school. Nothing much. I can't claim to know how hard this is for you right now but I care about you and I care about Tommy."

"And Helen? Care about her, too?"

Greyjack wanted desperately to take a good solid swing and knock Richard on his ass. It had been a long time since the two of them had cleared the air, a long time since they'd had the courage to go at one another until neither one of them was left standing.

"Yes," Greyjack said, his teeth tight and his chin pushed out ready for a fight. There were too many things between them about Warren and the war and Helen that had gone unsaid for too long. "I care about Helen and I cared about Warren and I care about you. Do you know that, asshole? What happened to my brother happened. It wasn't your fault. It wasn't my fault. It just happened, and there's nothing you or I can do about it."

Richard took the first swing. He swung wide and high and clipped Greyjack hard on the ear, knocking his sheriff's hat to the ground. Greyjack threw a punch in Richard's stomach, hoping to knock the wind out of him. Richard started swinging wildly.

Greyjack swung back hard, not realizing the anger he was carrying. His fist hit hard into Richard's mouth. He saw blood on his hand and knew he'd busted Richard's lip. Greyjack wasn't sorry about Richard's lip. In fact, Greyjack wanted to beat the crap out of Richard for losing Helen. He wanted to slap his face and tell him to get himself together. He wanted to hurt him.

Richard was swinging blindly, his eyes closed and his face down as though he might decide to ram Greyjack in the chest with his head. Greyjack stepped back in order to get a good swing, but reconsidered.

"You're the asshole," Richard said, sucking on his bloody lip.

"Come on and hit me again. I dare you. Hit me."

Greyjack shook his head.

Richard started to take another swing and instead punched his hand into his fist. He didn't want to fight.

"Why'd she leave?" Richard asked, his voice barely a whisper.

"I don't know," Greyjack answered.

"Did she say anything?"

"No."

"Is she coming back?"

"Right now you've got to think about Tommy."

"She always said he was so wild she couldn't manage him and I never did anything about it. Hell, we were wild."

"Mankoff says he'll see to it Tommy graduates. He has to make-up the work he's missed and also put in some time on the weekends at school cleaning the grounds and planting a few trees. He needs to graduate. Tommy also needs to get away from Mindy so he can figure out if he's dealing with love or just a growing itch in his pants."

"You think he should go to into the Army?"

"What do you think?" Greyjack asked, hoping Richard would make the decision his.

"I'll talk to him."

"I'll talk to the recruiter, see what I can do."

"Thanks, Greyjack."

Greyjack picked up his hat and dusted it off before putting it on. "You've still got some fight in you," he said.

"The stuff with Helen makes me crazy."

"We're just friends," Greyjack offered.

"I know," Richard said.

"I don't want to lose her."

"Neither do I."

Tommy was not surprised by either his father's ultimatum he buckle down and do the school work he'd missed or move out, or

Greyjack's proposal he do some supervised grounds keeping work to make up for the school he'd skipped. He didn't exactly like either offer, but he grudgingly accepted them both.

He loved Mindy but didn't know what to do with his feelings. His love for her had a desperate edge to it. It scared him. Sometimes when he looked at her he felt like he had to look at her hard, real hard, in order to burn her image into his mind because he was afraid all the time he was going to lose her. Her hands. God, her hands were so beautiful he felt like he could look at them forever.

The taste of her mouth drove him crazy. He wanted to have sex with her. He wanted to tear off her clothes and ram his body into hers so forcefully he would drive himself deep inside of her, so deep he would never be able to let go, and she would never be able to run away.

His mother ran away. Late at night after he took Mindy home he often drove around looking for his mother. Sometimes he wove his way up one street and down another through town. Other nights he drove as fast as he could on the dirt roads out in the county. He didn't know what he'd do if he found her. Once, late at night, he thought he saw her standing on a corner near the bank, but when he pulled up to get a good look he realized it wasn't her. He started banging on the steering wheel with his fists. He beat the steering wheel until his hands were numb and he didn't have the strength to hit it again.

If he went into the Army maybe he and Mindy could get married. He'd heard the Army gave you a good living allowance if you were married. They had places on base where you could live with your wife. He'd like that. If they got married, he'd be able to get Mindy away from her freaky father. He hadn't asked her yet, but he thought she'd say yes.

Right now he wanted more than anything to get away from home.

Chapter 14

Helen didn't like the rough cotton dressing gown the hospital made her wear whenever she left her room. It was dappled with coffee stains and so big it hung nearly to her ankles. One of the belt loops was torn off, and the other had obviously been torn off at some other time and then sewn back on in the wrong place, so it was down around her hip rather than up at her waist. In order to tie the belt she had to bunch up the robe around her middle then cinch the belt tight and knot it twice so it would keep the thing from slipping loose and flapping around her knees when she walked.

"You need to put your robe on," the aide was shouting at her. They always shouted at her whenever they wanted her to do something as though she were a stubborn child or a dumb animal that couldn't understand what they were saying.

"The doctor says he wants you to go outside today. Says you've been cooped up here too long. The sunshine will do you good. Come on now," she said, holding the gown up so Helen could see it. "You haven't been outside since you've been here. Be a good girl and put your arms in."

Helen closed her eyes hoping to make the aide disappear. She didn't want to go outside. Someone might see her.

"Gonna be a hot summer. Hot already and it's only June."

June. Helen had forgotten or maybe didn't know anymore that it was June. She'd been in the hospital a very long time. Sometimes she couldn't remember being anywhere else. The doctor often asked her if she wanted to leave, and she always told him no.

The doctor had said something about June just the other day. They were talking about Tommy, and she was trying to remember what it had been like when Tommy was little. She had told the doctor it always felt like she was the one, not Tommy, who was in danger whenever he ran away into the woods, or threw stones at snakes or climbed too far up a tree or jumped to the ground from the roof of the garage. Whenever Tommy got into trouble at school it felt like she was the one in trouble.

The doctor asked her if she thought Tommy was a part of her she kept hidden from everyone, even herself.

The question made Helen turn her head away from the doctor. Sometimes it did feel like she was Tommy or Tommy was some how inside of her, deep inside of her and she was afraid to let him out. Maybe she was afraid to let him go because if she let him go she would have to let herself go. Linda was inside of her too, but that part of her felt familiar. She saw herself in Linda and wondered if Linda saw herself in her mother.

"Tommy graduated from high school yesterday," Dr. Abrams said, watching her face for some reaction.

"That's good." Helen was glad she hadn't been there. She wouldn't have known what to say to Tommy about why she left or what to tell him about what he should do with his life.

"I asked you if you wanted to go, but you said no. You missed your son's high school graduation."

She drew in a big breath and sat very straight and upright in her chair. She didn't want to cry. The doctor cleared his throat and went on.

"I talked with your husband. I think he would like to see you. Would you like to talk to him, to Richard?"

"No," Helen managed.

"He told me Tommy has joined the Army. He leaves next week. Richard and I thought you might want to go home to say goodbye to Tommy before he leaves. Would you like to go home?"

"No."

"It'd be a nice thing to see Tommy, say goodbye to him. Reconnect with your family."

"Richard was in the Army."

"Yes."

"A long time ago," Helen said, realizing it really did seem like a lifetime ago. Like something she read about rather than lived.

"Did Richard ever talk about what happened when he was in the Army?" Dr. Abrams prodded, hoping to get Helen to talk a little more.

"Some terrible things."

There were six boys from Tommy's class of 1964 who signed up right after graduation to go into the Army. All six, including Tommy, hadn't even tried to get into college. None of them had any interest in working in the factories with their fathers. Tommy had played baseball with two of them, and the other three were guys he knew but didn't hang with much. The recruiter made a big deal over them signing up together and arranged for them to leave together and go to the same boot camp. They were scheduled to leave the week after school was out, so they decided to throw a combination graduation/enlistment party the weekend after graduation.

Mankoff got wind of the plans and called Greyjack.

"Your little ward and his new Army buddies are planning a rather large blowout. Seems the whole school is invited. The whole school, that is, except me."

Greyjack was tempted to ask Mankoff if he had called in the hopes of getting an invitation but held his tongue.

"Tommy told me," Greyjack said, not offering any further commentary or invitations for Mankoff to attend.

"What do you plan to do about it?"

"I promised Tommy I'd drop by."

There were times when Greyjack hated his job and times when he loved it and often they were the same. This was one of those times. Mankoff irritated him.

When Greyjack and Warren were kids and ran wild in the

woods beside their parents' home, they would play a crazy game they called "Good Guy, Bad Guy." It was sort of like a game of Tag, and Hide and Seek all twisted up together with a plot. Warren always laid out the plot.

"Okay, Francis," he'd say, pulling on Greyjack's shirt sleeve so he'd get close enough to listen carefully. Warren was the only person in the world except his mother who called him Francis. His father always called him Hank as though he hadn't been consulted when his mother decided to name him. Everyone else just called him Greyjack.

"Yes," Greyjack would respond anxiously, hoping this time he would get to be the bad guy.

"I've just robbed a bank."

"Anyone shot?" Greyjack would ask.

"No, just an old couple tied up. They're harmless. I locked the bank president inside the vault."

"What about the alarm?"

"Cut it."

Warren always thought about everything: cutting the alarm and phone wires, bringing rope along in his pocket to tie up people, a full tank of gas in the getaway car, everything. He rarely shot anyone, and if he had to shoot he was careful just to wing the person just enough to stop them.

"Where was I when you were robbing the bank?"

By this time Greyjack knew he would be the cop. He was always the cop and as the cop he always had to chase Warren and capture him. Warren was good at hiding and sometimes Greyjack couldn't find him, and Warren "got away" by running into the house before Greyjack could tag him. Greyjack was never sure whether the object was for Warren to get away or for Greyjack to catch Warren and bring him in, but whatever the outcome, the game occupied most of their time growing up.

"You were on the other side of town. You got a call earlier about a disturbance at the little convenience grocery mart at the edge of town."

"You made the call, didn't you?" Greyjack just knew he'd made the call. Warren always thought of everything.

"Yes, but you didn't know it so you went to check it out because you're a good cop and good cops always follow through."

Greyjack was the good cop. He always followed through. He did what he said he would do. He did what he knew he should do and he took care of his business.

He would talk to Tommy and tell him if his friends were going to be drinking at the party, they better plan on not driving or doing anything that could get them into trouble. He'd even go out to the lake and make his presence known, say goodbye to the fellows who were leaving for the Army and just be there so everything would be smooth and easy.

When the party was over, Greyjack would dutifully report back to Mankoff.

God, how he missed Warren. Sometimes, when he stood at the edge of the woods near his house, and the sun was just starting to fall against the horizon, he could almost feel Warren hiding out there in the trees waiting to be found.

Linda made a big bowl of potato salad and bought three big bags of chips and a case of soft drinks to take to the party. Tommy and the other boys all chipped in money for a keg of beer and a bunch of hot dogs and buns. Greyjack came by the house to talk to Tommy about the party and suggested they invite a few parents just to make it easier for all of them to celebrate without getting into trouble. Tommy didn't care much about the suggestion but knew he didn't have much choice. Greyjack gave him a twenty and told him to use it to buy beer. He told him that if they were going to drink he preferred they had good beer to drink. It went without saying if he helped pay for the beer there better not be any hard stuff or drugs floating around, or he'd have to take notice.

Word got out Greyjack would show up and some parents would be there but there would still be beer and somehow, as though Greyjack's twenty held some magic, the parents were fine with the drinking.

Richard came out early and helped Tommy stack the wood for the bonfire and brought out an old door and some saw horses to make a table for the food. He also fixed the tap on the keg, and he and Tommy shared the first foamy beer. He stayed around for an hour or so after people began showing up then begged off saying he had to go to work.

Richard felt awkward being at the party and kept shoving his hands in his pockets and taking them out again as though he wasn't quite sure why he had hands. Tommy was glad his father had come by even though he had a kind of scared look on his face similar to the one he had on the morning their mother left.

"Thanks for coming, Dad," Tommy said, throwing his arm around his father's thick shoulders.

"I'm sorry your mother couldn't be here."

"She left. You're here, that's what matters," Tommy said, but the words choked him a little because it was the first time they had ever talked about her leaving, and he knew he hated her for it. He hated the way it had hurt them all.

"I've got to go to work," Richard said not wanting to talk about Helen.

"I know," Tommy said. "Thanks."

Shortly after Richard left, Joe Nathan and a few of the other parents came out to check on things claiming they wanted to say goodbye to all the guys going into the service. A couple of them had a beer and a hot dog. The rest of the parents just hung around and talked. It was kind of nice and the evening felt easy.

Joe Nathan worked the crowd a little, shaking hands and laughing like he was the reason the earth spun around. The way he strutted around greeting everyone it looked like he was there to bless the food or to start preaching. No one seemed to pay him much mind. For the most part the kids were polite but ignored him and didn't bother to try to hide the fact they were drinking a beer.

Greyjack showed up at 10 p.m. and made the rounds talking with some parents as well as the new recruits as though he was making a social call, not an official visit. He made a point of finding Tommy in order to let him know he'd been there and to make sure Tommy understood as far as Greyjack was concerned, Tommy was in charge.

Linda spent most of the evening roasting hot dogs for people, dishing out food and picking up trash. She was happy to have something to do because it was a whole lot easier than standing around drinking. She felt like she couldn't drink, because somehow she needed to be sober in case things went wrong. She did, however, have one small paper cup of beer just to spite Joe Nathan. She even walked over and asked Mindy if she wanted one, but Mindy turned her down. She said she wanted one but knew if she took one sip in front of her daddy he would start preaching and acting like a fool. She said it was easier to drink her soda than to have him embarrass her to death.

Joe Nathan stayed around until there wasn't any food left to eat, beer to drink, or wood to throw onto the bonfire. When the fire at last burned down, people started leaving. They were all kissing and hugging and wishing each other good luck and telling Tommy and the others it had been a great party.

Mindy pitched in and started helping Linda pick up the empty cups and trash. By then it felt to Linda like the party was not only over but also something important in their lives was over, and it made her feel cold and empty.

Just about the time they finished picking up, Larry came to her and offered help. He had drunk a righteous amount of beer in the evening and probably a little liquor, and when Linda walked by him on the way to their car, Larry grabbed her. He threw his arm around her and tried to kiss her, but she turned her face.

"You're drunk," Linda said, pushing him away. "Give me your keys."

"Whatever you say, Mother Priscilla," Larry said, tossing her his keys.

Linda knew Tommy had raised her "Priscilla" status to "Mother Priscilla" recently, and she let the comment slide. Motherhood, she figured was the best protection she could get from Larry at the moment.

"Get in," Linda told Larry, giving him a gentle push towards his car. "Give me a minute to find Tommy. Then I'm driving you home."

Larry started to protest, then stumbled forward and started puking his guts out. Linda stood by patiently waiting for him to finish before helping him into the back seat.

When she went looking for Tommy she found him lying on the sand down by the edge of the lake with Mindy.

"I'm giving Larry a ride home," she called out, not wanting to come any closer because she really didn't want to know what was going on.

Tommy lifted his head for a moment, smiled then waved her on.

Chapter 15

Helen stood by the fence. It was hot. She was wearing her heavy hospital bathrobe and could feel the sweat rolling down the backs of her legs. The aide had tried to make her get dressed, but she had refused the mismatched clothing they brought for her to wear. They were not her clothes and she did not want to wear them. She asked about the jeans and the shirt she had worn the day she came into the hospital. She also asked about her earrings. They had taken them away from her when she was admitted and she wanted them back. The aide mumbled something about getting everything back when she was ready to go home. Helen didn't believe her.

"Looking for someone or something?" the doctor said, coming up behind her.

She had never stood so close to the doctor before and was surprised to see the doctor was not much taller than she was and that he was slight. She could smell his aftershave. She wanted to touch his face with her hands. She shoved her hands in her pockets and turned her head away.

For the last half hour she had been trying to remember the dream she'd had last night. The dream had felt important as though it held some message for her about what she was supposed to do next or who she was or why she felt so empty and afraid of going back home.

"What are you looking at?"

"Just looking."

"You're looking good today. How are you feeling?"

"I washed my hair."

"Would you like to go home so you can say goodbye to Tommy before he leaves for the Army?"

"I can't." She didn't want to go back right now. She was sleeping better. There was something comforting about knowing that when she slept, someone was watching over her. The hospital was a safe place for her.

She missed Tommy, but she didn't know what she would say to him or Linda about where she'd been and what she'd been doing while she was gone. She didn't know what it would be like to sleep with Richard again.

"Why?"

"I left."

"I think you're getting better. You don't cry as much any more."

"The last time I cried they threw me into the shower."

"I was sorry we had to do that." He meant it. He only used the shower because he didn't want to use the drugs anymore. The drugs didn't seem to help.

"What happened?" Helen asked.

"When?"

"In the shower."

"You eventually stopped crying, and we carried you to your room, and you slept."

On Sunday morning, everyone who came to the party Friday night went to the bus station to say their final goodbyes to Tommy and the other boys. There was a lot of kissing and crying, and Linda thought Mindy acted like a lovesick fool.

After the bus pulled away from the station, people stood on the sidewalk for a long time just talking. Mindy and some of the other girlfriends huddled together on the long wooden bus-terminal benches crying and consoling each other. Richard left for work and Linda went home alone. She was angry. She couldn't believe her mother had not even come home to say goodbye to Tommy.

The house had felt torn apart after her mother ran away. It was terrible, but it felt like they could survive. Going home alone after Tommy left felt worse. It was like stepping into the wreckage after a bombing where there were no survivors.

A part of their lives had disappeared when Tommy got on the bus. He'd left an awful silence. Now, the only sound in the house was the loud lonely ticking of the grandfather clock.

When she was little she found the incessant heartbeat of the clock comforting. Whenever she had bad dreams she would go down into the living room to sleep by the clock, letting its deep predictable tick drag her back to sleep again. After her mother left, the familiar sound of the clock made her feel safe and secure.

With Tommy gone the ticking of the clock was a hammer beating against her chest. She went up to her room and brought down her clock radio and put it on the kitchen counter and turned it on to drown out the sound.

She listened to the morning news while she washed the breakfast dishes. She had gotten up early and made bacon and fried eggs and a heap of buttered toast. Tommy had made a sandwich with his eggs and toast and ate the bacon with his fingers. Her father picked at his food and chatted nervously telling Tommy what it had been like when he went away to boot camp. Tommy had listened quietly and periodically answered with a stiff but respectful "Yes, sir."

Tommy had never called their father "sir" before. The first time he did it Linda wanted to punch him in the arm and ask him what he was thinking, but she didn't. Instead, she sat there drinking her tea listening to Tommy and her father talking about the Army and thinking this moment was different than any time she could ever remember. She felt very grown-up as though she was Tommy's mother rather than his little sister. Tommy, however, seemed too old to have a mother anymore. They all seemed older and quieter and more careful with each other.

The newscaster on the radio was chattering on and on about the possible escalation of the war in Vietnam. Thinking about Tommy going to Vietnam made Linda's skin crawl. She fiddled with the dial until she found a music station. She wished her mother had come home to see Tommy off. She wondered where her mother was and if she was ever coming back.

The DJ put on Dusty Springfield's new song: "I Just Don't Know What To Do With Myself."

"Boy, is that right," Linda said to the empty room.

She turned the music up as loud as she could get it. The radio buzzed a little but she didn't mind.

"I…just…don't know…what to-do…with my-self," she sang, swaying her hips to the music while washing the dishes.

"Don't know just…what to-do…with my-self." She wiped her hands on the dishtowel and started dancing around the room. She closed her eyes and twirled around in the empty room until it spun and she felt sick. The clock in the living room ticked on.

When the song was over she turned off the radio and went out into the garden to get away from the huge dead feeling of the house.

Richard started working overtime to avoid being home. He didn't like being in the empty house, and it made him nervous when Linda was around. He didn't know what to say to her. He had found it easier to be with Tommy. They had things like baseball and football to talk about. He really didn't know anything about Linda or the garden.

The garden and Linda were Helen's world, not his. He had always felt shut out of their world and he didn't know how to be part of it. Before Helen left he sometimes stood by the kitchen window watching them working their way down the rows of the garden talking and laughing. Sometimes he would go out to the backyard and ask them what they were talking about, and they always said, "Nothing."

He had never tossed ball with Linda or helped her with batting practice or sat in the bleachers and watched her play a game the way he had done with Tommy. Linda didn't seem to be interested in cars or sports or any of the things he was interested in that he could so easily talk about with Tommy.

Richard missed Helen. He didn't understand why she couldn't come home to say goodbye to Tommy. He'd talked to the doctor, asking him if she might come home and the doctor said he'd see what he could do. Richard was so sure Helen wouldn't let Tommy leave without seeing him, he even let it slip to Linda that he thought Helen might come home before Tommy left, to say goodbye to him.

Richard didn't know how to take care of Linda. He didn't know what he was supposed to do. He really didn't know much about women in general. He didn't know why Helen had left him or what made her crazy. He didn't like to think about her being crazy. He worried it was something he had done. It frightened him and made him afraid to spend time with Linda, because he didn't want her to become crazy too.

When he was at work at the plant, the sound of the machinery and the line was so loud it drowned out his feelings and his fear. When he was there he could relax. He felt safe. Being at work was easier than being at home, and if he worked a long shift he would be tired enough when he came home to sleep.

Every night he dreamt of Warren being shot and the blood in the water and all the bodies of his friends floating around their boats like stunned fish. He knew he called out to Warren in his sleep, telling him to get down, underwater, where the bullets couldn't get him. If Warren had only gone underwater so they couldn't see him he would have been safe. If he had just swum to the shore instead of moving in the water with his big leaping stride to the front of the group, to lead them, to take them straight into the fire, Warren might be alive. Richard often wondered if he could have done something to save Warren's life.

He knew his fitful sleep and bad dreams kept Helen awake and worried. He wished he had told her how much it mattered to him that she was there. Now, when he woke in the middle of the night, the bodies floating in the room, in the dark swirling places of his mind, the room cold and empty: there was no one there to talk him back to sleep.

He didn't like being alone, and he worried about Linda being home alone all the time. He knew he should be there, but he really couldn't. He told Linda he was sorry he had to work late some nights. She understood. He asked Greyjack to check on Linda in the afternoons when he couldn't be there. Richard didn't know how to keep her safe.

Linda spent the early morning hours in the garden picking, weeding and watering. After lunch she'd wash what she'd picked in the morning then arrange it on her stand out in front of the house by the road. She felt restless. She didn't like the way the stand looked anymore so she took the leftover paint from the kitchen and painted her little wooden stand the same burning pumpkin her mother had painted the kitchen. It was a glorious color, and she loved the way it soaked up the sunshine and just glowed. Once the stand was painted, it felt fancier and seemed to demand something more polished than just piles of picked vegetables strewn about willy-nilly.

She decided to use their Easter baskets for the tomatoes and the cucumbers. She found an old brown leather suitcase in the attic and heaped it full with cantaloupes and put it on the ground by the side of the stand. She filled their largest china platter with green beans and her grandmother's cut-glass punchbowl with peppers. She filled a dozen small vases with flowers and put them about the vegetables as though she was decorating for a fancy party.

Ever since her mother left, she didn't feel content enough to just sit and read. They had always spent the afternoon together in the shade of the stand, reading and waiting for customers to come. Linda found she couldn't sit still now, so she mowed the front lawn or fussed with stacking the vegetables while she waited. She dug a circle around the post of their mailbox and planted it with morning glories. Sitting made her jumpy.

Greyjack came by every now and then to check on her. Mostly he'd come by in the late afternoons when she was getting ready to close up the stand for the night. By then, Linda would only have a few things to sell, and Greyjack would usually buy a little bit of whatever she had left, taking his time to decide on whether he wanted cucumbers or corn for dinner. Linda knew he had his own garden and didn't really need or want what she had to sell. She knew he came by only because he wanted to check on her.

Greyjack would buy a few things or hang around talking. He'd talk a bit, but, mostly, he'd listen. Greyjack had a way of standing still when he listened that made people want to talk to him. Linda would tell him about the book she was reading or about the garden. Greyjack would ask if she'd heard from Tommy and Linda would tell him what Tommy wrote. One time, she even read one of Tommy's letters out loud to him. She quit asking Greyjack about her mother.

Mindy started coming around after work to hang out with her. Before Tommy left Linda didn't really consider Mindy a close friend, or any friend at all. Linda half knew Mindy came by in the afternoons to see her because she wanted to talk about Tommy, not because she really wanted to talk to her. But, Linda looked forward to seeing her anyway. At least Mindy was someone to talk to.

Mindy had a summer job working at the mini-mart about a mile from their house and sometimes she'd stop by on her way to work. Mostly she'd talk about Tommy and how she'd gotten a letter from him or a phone call. Tommy wasn't much of a correspondent, so Linda was grateful for the information, if not for Mindy's company. After awhile, Linda began to watch for Mindy and hope she'd stop by.

Mindy had changed since Tommy left. She didn't seem so aloof or look so beautiful or grown-up anymore. She just looked like some high school kid with a boring summer job who wanted someone to talk to. Linda and she would laugh about the dumpy blue smock she had to wear at the mini-mart. They called it the ugly schmock, like the sound you might make on a countertop if your hand was wet and you smacked it flat against it.

The smock was a shade of blue that looked deadly on anyone but particularly bad on Mindy with her pale skin and light blond hair. It made her look washed-out and tired, and Linda had jokingly told her Tommy sure didn't have to worry about anyone wanting to try to pick Mindy up at the mini-mart if she had to wear that blue schmock.

Mindy had laughed, but Linda had known as soon as she said it she shouldn't have because Mindy really hadn't looked good since Tommy left. She didn't seem to be too interested in doing anything fancy with her hair or make-up. With her hair pulled back and no makeup, Mindy had a tendency to look plain and tired.

"If they're going to make you wear that ugly thing," Linda said, trying to smooth over what she had said, "you ought to at least wear a little make-up."

"People who frequent the mini-mart," Mindy drawled in her sassiest Southern joking way, "are not the kind of people I want to encourage. Besides, I'm saving myself for Tommy."

Linda would have laughed, but she knew Mindy meant it.

"I don't wear make-up either," Linda said. "My mother always wore lipstick and her garnet earrings, even when she was wearing jeans and working in the garden. I always thought it made her look like she was expecting something good to happen."

"Hmmm," Mindy said twisting her head a little to the side and looking at Linda with one eye as though she was trying to figure out what kind of nose she should have instead of the one she presently wore perched on her face.

"You'd look good in ruby tones. Perhaps a touch of blue in the red would give you an air of mystery. Midnight in Cairo might just be perfect."

Mindy rummaged through the bottom of her purse and produced a lipstick.

"Midnight in Cairo," she announced, "here's a mirror. Give it a try."

Linda took the mirror and the tube of lipstick. She smoothed her lips over her teeth, then opened her mouth just enough to let the lipstick glide onto both her top and bottom lips at the same time, the way her mother had shown her.

"It might look a little softer," Mindy said, taking the lipstick from Linda, "if you did your lips like this."

Mindy pushed her lips out softly like a kiss and opened her mouth slightly in order to draw the lipstick smoothly from side to side. She then took the tip of one finger and cleaned up the corners of her mouth and marked the bow of her lips in front with a little flicking motion.

"Here, you try," she said, handing the lipstick back to Linda.

Linda pushed her lips out a bit too far. Mindy mirrored the action for her again so she could see how to push out her lips just far enough.

"Smoothly, from side to side. Right. Now, touch up the corners. Great. Now, take a look."

"I love the color," Linda said, pleased for the moment with what she saw in the mirror.

"It's you," Mindy said. "Keep the lipstick. I've got another one. Besides, I don't need it anymore."

Chapter 16

"Let's talk about the going home," the doctor said, speaking sternly while still measuring his words very carefully. Nearly ten weeks had passed, and although Helen wasn't any worse, she hadn't made the kind of progress he had hoped for. He wanted to get some reading on her to determine if it was safe to think about sending her home. It was time for her to move on and go back to living.

Helen didn't speak. The doctor never talked to her about going any place besides home. When he talked about going home she felt a storm-like rage burn through her body.

"Can I paint the living room yellow?" she challenged.

"You'd have to discuss that with your husband."

"He didn't like it when I painted the kitchen orange. I won't go back unless I can paint the living room yellow. Bright yellow."

"Your husband called today to say Tommy was coming home this weekend. Wouldn't you like to go home to see Tommy?"

Helen sat very still. The anger in her body numbed her hands and caused a kind of buzzing sound in her ears. Tommy? If she sat very still and kept her eyes on the doctor, not really on him, but looking through him as though she were capable of seeing through his body, through the wall, through the garden, past the gate to the road then down beyond to some other place, she didn't scream or cry. She rather liked looking at people this way as though they were invisible. Her ability to make other people invisible made her feel infinitely more visible.

She was not sure she wanted to see Tommy. At least, not yet. But she did want to talk to the doctor about Tommy. Sometimes, when she looked into the mirror, what she saw was Tommy: Tommy's wild eyes, his restless spirit, and his defiant mouth. Then there were the tiny lines around her own mouth which were the many fights she had had with him because he ran away or didn't do his homework or didn't listen to anyone, or because he drove recklessly and sometimes came home drunk.

Tommy was out of control. She didn't want to be out of control. Out of control was dark and turbulent and frightening. What if she got so out of control she could never come back and find herself again? She knew now that she wanted to find herself. She needed to find herself. She needed to find her house, her life, and her own face in the mirror. She wanted to find a new place she could call home.

She leaned forward in her chair and let her fingers run through her hair. It had been nearly three months since she cut her hair. It had grown out now over her ears and the bangs flopped into her eyes. If she twisted it with her fingers and wet it she could force it behind her ears. It looked sloppy. She wanted to go back to her room and wash her hair. She wanted to ask the nurses if they would give her a pair of scissors so she could cut her hair. She felt pretty when her hair was short and her wild lose curls framed her face.

"I need a haircut," she said.

"There's no one here who can cut your hair. If you went home, you could get it done. Why don't you go home?"

What if she did go home and Tommy fought with her? What if he came home drunk? What if he ran away with Mindy? What would she do? What could she do? What if she lost control of everything?

She had been feeling better lately, even a little hopeful. She was thinking a lot about the house and what, if she did go back, she wanted to do there. She wanted to paint the living room. She wanted to buy bookcases and real hardback books. She wanted to buy a new chair for herself and a reading lamp. She wanted to throw the old brown couch into the ditch.

"Did you hear what I said?" the doctor raised his voice. He wasn't losing patience as much as he wanted to shock her into responding.

"Hmm," Helen managed, her fingers twisting a long lock of hair at the nape of her neck.

"If you went home you could get your hair cut. Besides, a mother's place is with her children, her family. You've had a good rest."

Helen blinked. She had not understood that what she was doing here was resting. She was exhausted from thinking about leaving, thinking about Tommy and Linda, thinking about why she painted the kitchen orange, and why it had made Richard so angry.

She was pretty sure she had loved Richard: he was a good man, a kind man, he didn't cheat on her, he didn't get drunk every Friday night, he worked hard, he was careful to make sure they had what they needed. She had once believed life with Richard would be filled with adventures.

She did not like the way the doctor was talking to her. He sounded like Richard when he was angry or when he'd had a bad dream and shouted at her in his sleep.

Richard was often angry with her. So angry she was afraid to move the furniture or touch anything without asking permission. It was Richard's house, not hers. Sometimes she was angry with Richard when he wouldn't let her fix things.

"It was just paint."

"What was?" The doctor asked.

"Paint," Helen said, the word slurring slightly. Suddenly the room felt very hot and close. Helen let her eyelids close to keep from fainting. She couldn't see the doctor anymore, and she couldn't hear him.

"Open your eyes," the doctor shouted. But it was too late. Helen was gone. The warm dark wave of sleep she had come to rely on to keep her safe had once again let her escape.

"Tommy's coming home!" Mindy shouted from her car window as she slowed to a stop in front of Linda's vegetable stand.

"Home for the weekend."

"That's wonderful," Linda said, feigning she didn't know even though she did. Tommy had called the night before and told her he would be heading home on Thursday afternoon after his basic training graduation ceremony. He and the other guys would be taking the bus. They'd arrive sometime late Friday evening. He'd have to leave again on Monday morning to get to his new assignment at Fort Eustice in Virginia.

"I told Tommy you'd come to the bus station with me to pick him up."

"Thanks," Linda smiled weakly. "Dad and I thought we'd both be there to greet him."

On Friday evening, Mindy, Richard and Linda went to the bus station to get Tommy. There were more parents and friends there as well to greet the other new soldiers. Linda thought it felt like a special occasion, but kind of dream-like. When Tommy got off of the bus in his dress uniform it was wrinkled a little because he'd slept in it. When he stepped through the doorway of the bus, right before he took the first step down to the sidewalk, he smoothed the front of his shirt and tucked it in neatly across the front of his trousers then he brushed his hair back with his hand and his face filled with a smile.

He was tan, dark tan like he had been out working in the fields without a hat on, and his hair was short, and bristly with hair cream brushed through it so it stood up in front. The sun glistened against his hair cream, and Linda had to look twice to see what color his hair really was because it looked darker than she had remembered.

Tommy was thinner than he was when he left. His body looked tight and muscular. Linda could see where he'd tucked his shirt into his pants that his stomach was now flat and well-defined. His arms felt thick and strong when he hugged her. His hands were rough and calloused like he'd been bailing hay without gloves on. He was handsome like a man. His face was more angular, more grown as though he hadn't been gone eight weeks, but eight years.

He looked like a stranger, but more like Tommy than he ever had in his life. She wondered who he was now and how he had changed. Linda wished their mother could see him.

Mindy went rushing up to him. She was crying. Richard stood back from the crowd the way he always did when Tommy won some big baseball game. Linda noticed, how just like Tommy was more himself than he had ever been before, her father looked like himself again as he stood apart from Tommy, loving him.

It annoyed Linda that Mindy was crying as though Tommy had returned from the war instead of just from boot camp. By the way Mindy was carrying on, Linda knew for certain she and her father wouldn't see much of Tommy over the weekend, but then again, she never really expected they would.

Despite the expectation they wouldn't see him, she had prepared a kind of homecoming meal for him. Linda had never been involved in a homecoming before so she wasn't sure what she was supposed to do, but she'd had this sense from novels she'd read that when someone came home, you cooked. So, she cooked.

She started with oatmeal cookies and moved from there to a recipe she'd seen on the back of the cornflakes box for oven baked fried chicken. She had some really beautiful butter beans from the garden to cook. She also had an abundance of cucumbers and peppers she could slice and toss with vinegar and salt and pepper like she'd seen her mother do.

Linda also decided they should have fresh baked bread to eat. She didn't really know how to make bread so she settled on biscuits popped out of one of those refrigerator tubes. They didn't taste particularly good, especially once they got cold, but they filled the house with a good yeasty smell.

Tommy wasn't home much during the weekend. They never

got a chance to sit down to dinner together. She and her father had dinner before he left for work the next day, then the leftovers went into the refrigerator. She threw the biscuits away.

On Monday morning, Linda got up early to make breakfast for Tommy. She let her father sleep. He had worked the midnight shift in the hopes he would get to see Tommy in the afternoon, and he did, briefly when Tommy came by with Mindy. Her father told Linda to wake him so he could say goodbye. She said she would.

When she came down to the kitchen to put the kettle on, Tommy pulled up in the driveway. He had been out all night with Mindy.

"Looks like you've been doing some serious drinking," Linda said as she made him a cup of instant coffee.

"Easier here than having a good time on other things," Tommy responded, opening the refrigerator door with one hand while he picked up a piece of chicken with the other.

"Easier than what?" Linda asked sarcastically.

"The Army is full of surprises. A real traveling pharmacy. Uppers, downers, poppers, weed. You want it, they've got it. Did my basic training."

"Hmmm," said Linda, trying not to be shocked. She felt like a parent. She didn't want to feel like a parent. She wanted to feel like his sister, and he wasn't going to let her. It made her angry.

"Tried them all, Priscilla, so you don't need to. Do you hear?"

Now it was Tommy's turn to parent. He looked Linda straight in the eye to be sure she understood what he was talking about. Linda watched him take a bite of the cold chicken leg in his hand. He looked older, more cautious or anxious or just uncomfortable like he had somehow made a wrong turn and landed in a place he didn't care for much.

"You're going to school," he said, shaking the chicken bone at her.

"Anything else?" Linda spit out the words. She did not want

to fight, not now, not this morning before he left. She wanted him to be close to her. She felt suddenly afraid of him going away.

"Don't let anything stop you."

"Like what?" Linda challenged.

"Anything."

Then he began talking softly about basic training as though he needed to whisper so they wouldn't wake up their father. He told her about the guys in the barracks and how they could get all these drugs and things to get high on when they weren't so dogged tired they just collapsed. He said high was better than thinking about getting killed. He talked about the possibility of being shipped out. He talked about what he'd heard was going on in Vietnam and Korea. He said they were bad things: snipers dressed like women, hidden traps everywhere, if they were captured rumor was you were kept alive so they could torture you day after day. Scary shit. Things he didn't want her to know about.

When Linda asked about Mindy, he got edgy.

"I know you don't like her," Tommy said.

"I like her," Linda protested.

"Just talk to her. Okay. She's lonely. She thinks you're too smart to want to be around her."

"I like it when she comes by. Really, I do."

"It would mean a lot to me if you would be friends with her. I feel like someone needs to take care of her. Her old man is a mean son-of-a-bitch even if he is a preacher. I think about her all the time. She's so beautiful. I really love her."

"She's been coming around on her way to work. It's nice. We talk. She's really sweet."

"Thanks," he said. Then he came over to Linda and put his arms around her and kissed her hair.

"Go to school," he said again. "No matter what happens. You go. Promise me."

"I promise," she said, and tears were streaming down her

face.

"I gotta shower."

"I'll wake Dad."

"Promise."

"Promise."

By the time they got to the bus station Mindy and Joe Nathan were there waiting for them along with Larry and some other kids from school. There were too many people at the bus station for Linda to have a chance to talk to Tommy alone again.

When it was time to go, Tommy came over and shook his father's hand and hugged him, then he came over to Linda and kissed her goodbye. After he kissed her, he put his hands on her shoulders and looked at her straight on.

"Remember what I said."

"I'm going," she assured him.

"It's not your fault Mom ran away, and it isn't your job to take care of me or Dad. And, it's not your job to take care of Mindy, but I hope you'll be friends with her. You need a friend too, Priscilla."

The way he said it made Linda feel like he could look right through her and see everything there was to see inside of her.

"No matter what," he said again, "you go to college."

Linda shook her head and kissed him on the cheek. He was the last to board the bus and when the doors shut, the bus pulled out of the station. He was gone.

Mindy stood on the corner for a long time crying after the bus was out of sight. Joe Nathan didn't seem to notice, but stood around talking to Richard like there was nothing else in the world going on. Linda went over and put her arms around Mindy, and held her while she cried. It sent a shiver through Linda's spine. Mindy felt tiny and scared in her arms the way a lost child might feel if you caught them and held them. Linda didn't say anything. She just held her and stroked her hair.

"I'm really tired," she said at last, pulling away from Linda, "tell Daddy I'm going to lie down in the car. Would you?"

Linda did not exactly consider herself on speaking terms with Joe Nathan, but told Mindy she would. She knew if she didn't say something to him he would stand on the corner talking until hell froze over. So, she went over to him.

"Mindy's tired," she told him, "she went to the car to lie down. She wants to go home."

"Mindy's always tired these days," Joe Nathan replied without bothering to look up and see who was talking to him. "She can just wait."

Linda looked over to the Nathan's car and couldn't see Mindy so she knew Mindy was lying down in the back seat. Linda was feeling kind of tired herself so she slid her hand under her father's arm and told him she wanted to go home.

Nothing changed after Tommy left. Linda got up early every morning and picked what there was to pick from her garden. Afterwards, she'd wash the stuff she'd picked and put it out on the stand and if she didn't have anything else to do, she'd sit out there in the shade with a book, reading until a customer came along.

Mindy usually came by in the afternoon on her way to work, and they'd talk. She'd tell Linda what had happened at work the day before, which wasn't much, and they'd talk about what they'd heard from Tommy.

Three weeks after Tommy left for Fort Eustace, Greyjack came by in the middle of the afternoon. He parked his car in the driveway and walked slowly to the vegetable stand. His sheriff's hat was tucked under his arm the way you might hold a newspaper you were trying to keep out of the rain, and Linda could tell by the careful way he walked that he'd come to tell her Tommy was dead.

Chapter 17

The aide opened the door to Helen's room and turned on the light.

"The doctor wants to see you," she told her. When Helen rolled over and opened her eyes she could see the aide was holding the big floppy bathrobe for her to put on. The doctor wanted to see her now, not later.

"It's nighttime," Helen said, swinging her legs over the edge of the bed and offering up her arms to the robe. She couldn't remember ever being woken up before in the evening to see the doctor. She wondered if she'd overslept.

"What time is it?"

"Eight."

"In the morning?"

"At night. Get up. They told me to come get you."

"Why does the doctor want to see me now?"

"They just tell me what to do around here, not why."

"I don't want to see him now. I haven't showered. My hair is dirty. Can I brush my teeth?"

"Brush your teeth, but make it snappy. I've got things to do."

Helen went to her sink and brushed her teeth as quickly as she could. She also washed her face and pushed her fingers through her wild tangle of hair. She desperately wanted a haircut. She would have liked to have her father's razor with her so she could do it herself, but in order to get it she would have to talk to Richard, and she didn't want to talk to him, at least, not yet. Even if she asked him to bring it to her they wouldn't let her have it.

They wouldn't even give her a pair of blunt school scissors. She had asked for a pair last week to cut out a picture of a flower garden she had seen in a magazine. They had asked her why she wanted the scissors, and she showed them the picture and told them she wanted to cut it out. One of the nurses took the magazine from her and tore the picture from the magazine and gave it to her. Helen didn't like how the flower garden in the picture now had a ragged ripped edge. It ruined it for her. When she left the nurses station, she threw it away.

"Is it because I asked for a pair of scissors?"

"All they told me I was supposed to walk you down there. Make sure you get there."

"I can walk by myself."

"Apparently they don't think you can."

"I've never tried to run away."

"I'd say," the aide roared with laughter. "It's pretty hard to run away when you never get out of bed."

Helen felt slapped by her words. Stung, but not hurt, suddenly awakened to the realization what she said was true: she didn't get out of bed very much. In fact, she slept all the time. Sleeping was a wonderful warm refuge from thinking. Sometimes she slept just because she wanted to sleep, and other times, when she'd been crying, she slept because they gave her drugs to make her sleep.

She told the doctor she didn't like the drugs. They gave her terrible nightmares. The doctor had promised her there would be no more drugs if she would talk to him.

It had been a long time since she had anyone to talk to. Once she began to talk she felt better. Before the aide had woken her up she had been dreaming about being in her garden. She missed her garden. She wondered what Linda had planted after she left. She wanted to ask the doctor if he could find out. She wanted to tell him about her mother dying when she was little and how she tried to plant a garden just like the one her mother-in-law used to have. Helen told him she learned to cook all her mother-in-law's recipes for her father-in-law. Most importantly, Helen told him about finding Lillian's beautiful embroidery hidden in the back of the closet, and how it made her realize she didn't want to die and never have a day in her life that was special enough to use the beautiful pillowcases.

Helen had been dreaming about those pillowcases when the aide woke her up. She wanted to sit down for a moment in her room before she went to the doctor's office so she could sort out her thinking a little, so she could have a good conversation with him about the pillowcases and how Richard had taken them off and thrown them onto the floor when he found them on their bed.

"Let's go. The doctor is waiting."

"You don't have to take me. I can go by myself."

"I do what they tell me to do and if they say I need to take you to see the doctor, then I take you to see the doctor. Now let's go."

Helen pulled the bulk of the big robe around her waist so she could tie the sash tightly and keep the whole thing from falling off of her. When she stepped out into the hallway the other aides, who were sitting at the desk doing their chart work, looked up as she walked past. Helen hated the way they always watched the patients as if they were wild animals ready to snap and tear the place to pieces.

When the nurses saw her they turned their heads away. Helen tightened the sash on her robe and held her head up as she walked down the hallway. She had a sense something was wrong, and they knew what it was but weren't going to tell her. She had an urge to go up to them and slap them for being so smug, but she kept walking.

She tried her best to walk straight down the middle of the hallway without looking at them. When she got to the doctor's office his door was ajar.

"Come in, Helen," he said a little too quickly, his voice soft and warm.

"They woke me up," she said, running her hands through her unwashed hair. The doctor's friendly tone made her feel uncomfortable. She wasn't properly dressed.

"Sit down," the doctor said, pointing to the chair across from his desk.

There was a filled syringe sitting on the edge of his desk.

"I thought we agreed there would be no drugs."

"That's right, as long as we talk."

"I'd like to talk. I was having a dream when the aide came. A dream about those embroidered pillowcases I told you about, except they were bigger in the dream, like umbrellas or maybe parachutes, or those fancy things you see on canopy beds. I've always wanted to sleep under a canopy bed."

"Would you like to sit down?"

"Yes," Helen said.

It was the same chair she had sat in a dozen times before when he talked to her. It was wooden. The seat of the chair was rubbed smooth with wear. Whenever she sat in it she had a sensation of floating for a moment while she slid from the front to the back of the chair. She closed her eyes to steady herself.

"There's been an accident," he said.

"With the pillowcases?"

She didn't know what he was talking about and shook her head.

"An accident," he said again, only this time louder. "And your son was killed."

Helen pushed her feet against the dark polished wood of the floor in order to stay anchored in the room. She was a balloon floating up to the ceiling. She gripped the cool smooth arms of the chair. She could see the doctor's face, his mouth was opening and closing, but she couldn't hear what he was saying because there was a loud ringing in her ears and a strange drumming sound like her heart pumping inside her head. She felt dizzy and faint.

"Do you understand?"

The doctor was standing over her now, bending over her in such a way she could see the whiskers on his face. She smelled the soap on his skin. She wanted to reach out and touch the roughness of his face just to know for sure she wasn't dreaming. She felt his hand on her shoulder. Her own hand was gripping the arm of her chair so tightly her arm was beginning to shake.

Someone or something was pulling at her arm. She struggled to pull away. She was terribly frightened. She tried to get up from the chair to run from the room.

The doctor grabbed her other arm and pulled her up from her chair. He grabbed both of her hands and pinned them down at her sides. His arms were strong. Helen struggled to get away from him, but she couldn't. He was talking to her, not talking as much as singing. The singing sounded like a little song he made up to help her sleep.

"You're okay," he crooned, "it's okay."

A nurse came in. The doctor nodded towards the syringe on his desk. The nurse picked it up and pinched the back of Helen's arm. Helen could feel the nurse's cool fingers on her skin. She could feel the pinch and the sudden jab of the needle. Very quickly afterwards she began to fall. The room was dark and dizzy and warm and all she could hear was the sound of the doctor singing, singing his song about how she would sleep for now then wake up later and be fine.

The call had come late in the afternoon to the recruiter's office. Before the recruiter placed the call to Richard, he decided to call Greyjack. He knew Greyjack and Richard were friends. He'd heard Helen had recently left Richard. He needed to know how to get in touch with Helen, and he didn't want to ask Richard. He hoped Greyjack knew.

"I've got to make the call, to both of the parents. Do you happen to know where Helen is?"

"She's in the psychiatric unit of the State Hospital. Dr. Corbin is the one who is taking care of her. No one knows. I'd appreciate it if you kept it quiet and didn't share this information with anyone else. The kids don't even know."

"I've got to call both of them."

"I think you should call Dr. Corbin. It would be better if he told Helen."

"Thought you might be able to help, maybe drive out to the plant to be with Richard when he finds out."

"Yep," said Greyjack, putting on his best sheriff's face, the calm one: the one he had learned to use when there were accidents, when things went wrong, terribly wrong.

When Greyjack hung up, he called the plant, told the supervisor Tommy had been in an accident and the recruiter would be calling to talk with Richard.

"I want to be there when he finds out," Greyjack told the supervisor.

The drive to the factory was the longest drive he could ever remember making. He was uncomfortably aware it had been his idea for Tommy to go into the Army. The decision was a weight on Greyjack's shoulders he couldn't seem to shift and he was afraid he wouldn't be able to live with. It had been a stupid idea. Tommy wasn't ready to die.

Richard was standing by the back door of the factory, his hands folded, eyes closed, leaning against the building when Greyjack pulled up.

Greyjack got out of his car and closed the door as quietly as he could.

"I don't know what to say," Greyjack started talking softly as he approached his friend. "I should have never pushed him into the Army. I thought he'd grow up. Thought he'd come back to us."

Richard moved from the wall and took one step forward and wrapped his arms around Greyjack, and they stood there, wrapped so tightly in each other's arms they looked like a rock.

"It's not your fault," Richard whispered, while Greyjack held him. "It's no one's fault."

"I thought he'd come back."

"I can't go home right now. I can't tell Linda. I just can't."

"I'll go. I'll tell her," Greyjack said. "The recruiter asked about Helen. I had to tell him she was in the hospital. He has to call her."

"Should I go to the hospital?"

"Let's wait to see what the doctor says."

"I need her."

"Of course," Greyjack said, pulling back to look closely at his friend's face. "This may set her back. She'll need some time. You have to give her time."

"They were on a training mission," Greyjack said, speaking softly and slowly, not wanting to repeat any of the details. Linda stood very still listening. He wanted to, but was afraid to reach out and touch her.

"It was Tommy's job to drive. They were carrying a load of explosives. They were on their way to practice blowing up a bridge, and Tommy lost control and their vehicle rolled down the embankment and burst into flames. There were three other people in the jeep. Everyone was killed.

"Your father asked me to come and tell you. He'll be home soon. Let me help you put things away."

"Mindy?" Linda managed.

"I can tell her if you'd like."

Linda could feel her mind tearing loose from her body. Greyjack had taken his hat from under his arm and put it on top of the box of tomatoes. He was staring at the green beans scattered on the ground. He stooped to pick them up.

Linda was surprised to see the beans were scattered across the counter and onto the ground, like someone had pushed the basket away and it had spilled out, spoiling her lovely arrangement. There were green beans everywhere.

"It's okay, I'll get them, it's okay," Greyjack kept saying over and over again.

Linda realized he was saying she had pushed the basket and spilled the beans and he was going to pick them up.

"I won't cry," Linda said calmly. Her fists were clinched so tightly her nails dug into the palms of her hands. She wasn't going to be like her mother. No, she wasn't. She wasn't going to cry or run away or anything else. She was going to be there when her father needed her.

"Had he been drinking?" she asked, slowly bending down to help pick up one of the beans and put it back into the basket.

Greyjack looked away for a moment before he answered her.

"Yes," he said.

That evening Tommy's supervisor from the Army base called to offer his condolences and to explain the details regarding the transport of Tommy's body: it would come with an escort by plane early the next morning, and once someone from the family identified the body the escort would release it to them. Once the body was released, all other arrangements would have to be made by the family. This included transporting the body from the airport to the funeral home. When she hung up the phone, Linda called Greyjack and asked him to call the funeral home. Greyjack asked about her father. She told him he was sleeping. Greyjack asked if she wanted him to come along in the morning to help. Linda told him no. She felt she and her father should look after the details.

Linda drove to the airport the next morning. Her father sat on the passenger side staring out the window. He didn't speak. In fact, they had hardly spoken to each other since they learned about Tommy. There was nothing to say. When they got to the terminal, they were directed by the security guard to drive to a hangar out beyond the regular terminal. Linda parked the car. Before she could get out and go around to open her father's door a security guard came to the car and offered to take them to a special baggage area. The military escort was waiting for them. A soldier in dress uniform saluted as they approached.

As they entered the hangar, one of the guards reached over the large table in front of him and carefully unzipped the top of the bag. Tommy's face had been badly burned along one side of his head, but it was still his face. He looked like he was sleeping.

As soon as Linda saw him with his quiet closed eyes and calm mouth she had trouble keeping her mind from pulling away like it had when Greyjack came to tell her about Tommy. Her mind struggled to abandon her body and hurl itself a safe distance away so she could watch without having to feel anything. She didn't want to feel anything. She could hear her father crying.

"Can you identify this soldier?" the uniformed escort asked quietly.

Neither she nor her father spoke.

"I'm sorry, sir," he said, bowing his head slightly in Richard's direction, "you have to tell me if this is your son."

Richard nodded his head. The escort looked at Linda. Linda nodded. The escort quickly zipped the bag closed again and took a clipboard from beneath Tommy's body and made a notation.

"I have to ask you to sign the papers," he said softly, holding the clipboard out to Richard. He didn't move. "Please, sir," the escort said, "I can't release the body until someone signs."

Linda reached for the clipboard.

"I can sign," she said.

"You are?"

"His sister."

"I'm sorry."

Linda had trouble holding the pen and keeping her letters from looping out of control and cutting through the text. The pen seemed to have a will of its own and wanted to make a wild scribbling patch across the whole of the paper instead of a careful tight signature. She took her time working out the neat letters of her name and breathed as deeply and as evenly as she could while she worked to make her signature. She wasn't going to cry in front of the soldier. She held the pen tightly and forced her hand to shape her name. When she finished she knew it didn't look good. She retraced the capital L of her first name, hoping to reshape it enough to look like an adult had written it.

"Thank you," the escort said, taking the papers from Linda and offering Richard a salute. When he turned to step away from the table, Linda noticed two men in dark suits standing off to the side of the building. She realized they must have been standing off to the side the whole time. She hadn't seen them when she walked in.

Her father was crying. His shoulder brushed against hers. Linda was frightened by how sad and broken he looked. She was afraid to reach over and take his hand. The escort looked over to where the hearse from the funeral home was parked. The two men came forward with a kind of cart on wheels to move the body. The soldier snapped to attention as they lifted the body from the table to the cart then ended his salute when they pushed Tommy's body toward the waiting hearse.

Linda stood still and stiff next to her father while they put Tommy's body into the back of the car and collapsed the cart. The building they were standing in was wide and rambling and made of tin. There were fans as big as airplane propellers at either end of the building blowing air in order to keep the place from being suffocating. The noise of the fans vibrated against their bodies and filled their heads so they didn't have to think about anything but the noise. Linda had no desire to leave.

"They're taking the body to the funeral parlor," the escort said softly. "You're to follow them."

Richard lifted his head a little then slowly saluted the escort. The escort saluted back and handed him a folded flag.

"Let's go," Linda said, carefully reaching out to touch the edge of her father's elbow. She guided him to their car and opened the passenger side door for him. He sat down as though he was crippled and had to ease himself into the seat in order to maintain his balance, then he swung his legs in one at a time. He looked old and broken.

When they got to the funeral home, the director was waiting for them by the door.

"He's here," he announced in a whisper, as though Tommy had somehow mischievously snuck into the back of the building and was waiting to surprise them. "Shall we take a minute to consider the arrangements?"

"Yes," Linda managed, although she had no idea what arrangements he was talking about or what they had to consider. Her father remained silent.

They followed the man into a showroom of caskets. The funeral director kept a close but respectful distance as they walked. His pace was even and measured as he moved, pointing from one casket to the next. As they looked at each possibility, he began a low soft patter of talk, a sales pitch of sorts. He neither walked nor talked too fast, and it was easy to keep up with him as they went from coffin to coffin. It felt oddly comforting and Linda was aware of how gracefully her body moved along with him through the rows. Her mind had pulled away from her body and was watching.

The funeral director asked a few questions about Tommy, their religious affiliation, their thoughts on eternity, and their wishes. Linda had not quite considered the real possibility of eternity before and had to stifle a giggle when she realized they were supposed to pick out the coffin they thought Tommy would like the most. She couldn't imagine Tommy would have liked any of them. None of them looked big enough for him nor did they look particularly comfortable. Tommy always slept sprawled across the bed from corner to corner as though he were diving to stretch for home plate or just wanted to make sure no one else could enter his space.

When the funeral director realized they were unable to either discuss the choice or to make a decision, he suggested they settle on something dignified in dark wood.

"I want the casket closed," Richard said, turning his head away from the dark walnut box.

"Of course," the funeral director answered as though there was no other decent or civilized thing to do.

When they finished at the funeral home and had signed all the papers, the funeral director asked if they would like to see Tommy again.

"No," Richard said quietly, shaking his head.

Linda had wanted to see him but didn't speak up. She couldn't believe this was happening and wanted to make sure he was okay and his eyes were closed and his face calm. She had also wanted to kiss his forehead or to touch him and know he was there, really there, not just pretending to be there.

After she drove home, she walked her father to his room and sat him on his bed. She unlaced his shoes and slipped them off and covered him when he lay down. She knew he wouldn't sleep much but hoped he'd sleep some.

She then went into Tommy's room and lay on his bed. She breathed in the smell of Tommy's hair and his skin that was still on the pillows. He had thrown the shirt he had worn the last night he was home over the back of his desk chair. She picked it up and slipped her arms into its long sleeves. She buttoned all the buttons and let the collar rub against her neck. Everything smelled like Tommy. She wondered if she should give the shirt to Mindy or keep it for herself. She wondered how long his smell would last.

She didn't want to leave Tommy's room. She couldn't think about working in the garden because she was afraid to leave her father in the house alone. She could hear him crying. She lay back down on Tommy's bed and pretended to sleep.

The funeral was at the church. Before the service started, Greyjack came up to Linda and hugged her, then hugged her father. Greyjack and her father held each other for a long, long time. Both of them were crying. She stood close to her father. When Greyjack let go of him and moved to the back of the church, she reached over and took her father's hand and led him up to the front where they were to sit.

Reverend Jacobs conducted the service. Joe Nathan sat up front with his hands folded in his lap. Linda couldn't hear what Reverend Jacobs was saying because there was a buzzing sound in her ears like grasshoppers or crickets rubbing their legs together on a hot summer's night. When she closed her eyes the sound got bigger, not louder, but bigger like the big fans blowing in the baggage area of the hangar where they had identified Tommy's body.

Eventually, Reverend Jacobs stopped talking and then some of Tommy's friends came forward, picked up the casket and carried it down the aisle of the church. Linda could hear Mindy crying. The sound of the crickets in Linda's head got louder. She closed her eyes again. A few minutes later she felt someone standing in front of her. It was Reverend Jacobs. He put out a hand to help her get up. He told her she was to ride with her father in the funeral car to the cemetery and the others would follow them.

They drove slowly through the middle of town with the windows rolled up tight. Her father sat beside her in the back seat. The crickets in her head had gotten louder again, so loud it made her head hurt. When they got to the gravesite, Tommy's friends carried his casket from the hearse to the open grave. As they did, Reverend Jacobs held his hands up high like he was going to catch a ball or maybe try to fly. His eyes were squeezed shut and he was praying. Linda watched as he prayed and thought how funny he looked talking with his eyes closed.

After he finished praying, they lowered Tommy's coffin into the ground. They then got back into the limousine to drive to the funeral home. When her father slipped into the seat next to her, he suddenly stopped crying and slumped over in his seat as if he was dead. Linda let him sleep.

When they pulled into the funeral home parking lot she touched his shoulder and shook him, but he didn't wake, so she just sat there. The funeral director came over to the car and opened her door.

"This happens sometimes," he said, carefully opening her door and taking her hand. "The ones who are left, especially when a child has died. They sleep," he continued, helping her out of the car, "until they find a place where they have the courage to make a decision to come back again. Right now he needs time to decide to come back. Don't worry," he said, resting his hand ever so gently and reassuringly on Linda's shoulder, "they always come back."

He nodded to the driver to get her car.

"Robert will drive you home. There will be friends and neighbors coming by the house, bringing food and offering their condolences, and you need to be there to greet them."

Linda could feel herself moving to the car. She could see herself walking from the big black limo to their small car. She saw the man open the door. She felt herself slip into the hot car and hand the driver her keys. She worried she shouldn't leave her father, but the funeral director seemed so sure of himself she thought it would be all right. She wished Greyjack were there to drive her home. She wondered where he was.

"It's a kind of healing process," the funeral director said as if it was the most natural and easy thing in the world, "and the food and all the people are part of it. You need to go home," he continued, "and right now your father needs to sleep.

"I'll stay here with him while he sleeps. When he wakes up, I'll bring him to the house. It won't take long," he reassured her as he closed her car door. "They usually don't sleep more than an hour or two, just long enough to get them started healing."

He told her she shouldn't expect him to talk very much or do much but sleep over the next week or so.

"By then," he said, his hands softly clapping together as if he were executing an easy magic trick, "he'll be coming back."

Coming back. Her father had gone far away and at some point would have to decide to turn around and come back. She thought maybe it was a little like when she got up and left school the day Mankoff called her into his office and how each step she took towards home took her farther and farther away from her life at school.

She was glad she hadn't let herself cry or, worse, hadn't let herself go into some sleep-laden depression like her father had done. She wasn't sure she would know how to come back.

When the driver from the funeral home pulled up to her house people had already arrived with their arms heavy with food, waiting to unload their burdens and offer their sympathy.

She had never been to someone's home after a funeral and didn't know what she should do. She went into the kitchen. One of the women from church came in behind Linda. The woman put her casserole onto the kitchen table. Another woman brought a stack of paper plates and cups and plastic forks and spoons. The one who had brought the casserole picked up the turkey roaster Linda had so carefully planted with African violets and took it into the laundry room and sat it on the washing machine. She seemed to be in control, so Linda left.

She didn't want these women in her mother's beautiful pumpkin-colored kitchen. She was afraid they would look into the cupboards and snoop inside the refrigerator. She didn't want them to see the three half-eaten opened jars of jelly or the cold roast beef she had forgotten to cover last night and the crisper full of rotting cucumbers and beans. Linda didn't want the women from the church knowing what was wrong with their lives.

Linda was afraid they would find the container of soured milk she had shoved back into the corner. She wanted to run into the kitchen and lock the refrigerator door so they couldn't find the stick of butter where her knife had scraped a deep rut across the top for her toast instead of slicing a pat neatly off the end. She didn't want them to think she and her father were abandoned and living dangerously. She felt like a child caught in a horrible lie. Linda wanted to run away.

Linda could see the women turning to each other, nodding their heads, whispering to each other as though they could see beyond the closed cupboards and the leftover food in the refrigerator to something else they suspected was there. They laughed and chatted as they uncovered their casseroles, opened the drawers to find serving spoons, and laid out the paper plates and napkins. One of their husbands dragged in a large cooler and filled it with ice for drinks. They pushed and shoved and made room for everything they had brought. They laid out cookies and cakes and talked about where they should set up the coffee and whether or not they should use the Styrofoam they'd brought or the china cups from the cupboard they'd found. They made the kitchen theirs.

The anger Linda felt over their invasion made her forget for a moment about Tommy dying. She could feel her hands moving into tight angry balls of fists. She imagined her body moving across the room, her fists hitting the woman who was taking her mother's beautiful china cups out of the cupboard and lining them along the counter top.

She could feel her mouth opening and the sound of a gurgling roll of words gushing out from somewhere deep inside of her. She started to step towards the women, and just she did, Greyjack came into the kitchen, put his arms around her and gently moved her into the living room.

"Sit down," he whispered in her ear, "there is nothing you can do here to stop what's happening. The women don't have anything better to do with their grief but talk. They have to have something to talk about so they can forget it could have been their son who died. It will be over soon, but right now there's nothing you can do to stop it."

The way Greyjack talked about the women reminded Linda of what her mother had said about Tommy when they had eaten lunch at Kresge's when they went shopping for her Easter dress. What's happening with Tommy, she had said, was what was going to happen, and there was nothing she or anyone could do to stop it.

With her body sitting in a chair and her mind flying about the room, Linda didn't have the strength to do anything, so she did as Greyjack said: she sat still. She didn't talk much, just listened as people chattered on and on about how good Tommy was and what a loss they all suffered. Over and over again, like some ancient chant, they kept saying: "It was an accident, a horrible tragic accident." Even though Linda knew they believed otherwise.

Everyone in town knew the truth: Tommy was reckless. He had probably been drinking. But no one would say it. Instead, they all lied and the little lie of the comforting words was like music. The nodding of the heads, the hands placed on arms, the hugs, and the movement of the whispers through the crowd all looked like a dance to Linda.

At some point, Joe Nathan came walking into the house with his arm around Mindy. Her face looked puffy from crying. She stiffened, as she made ready to meet the people who were waiting there to comfort her. Linda watched as Mindy worked her way slowly across the room. Mindy looked like herself, like the way she had looked before Tommy had left, but thinner and older. Her hair was washed and curled, her clothes perfectly pressed. She held her head high in order to ward off anyone who might not want to carry the lie of Tommy's tragic death to her. She was not open to the truth. She looked like a brave young widow who knew the crowd expected a show. She understood her role better than Linda understood her own and she was there to make Tommy proud. Her dress was black and tight.

After Mindy worked the crowd with her father by her side,

going from one person to the next, accepting hugs and support, she came into the living room and sat down next to Linda.

"Hello," Linda said, and when she did, Mindy slipped her hand into hers and held on tightly. Mindy didn't say anything, just sat holding Linda's hand. When visitors came into the house they came over to present the food they'd brought and to offer their condolences. They stood in front of their chairs and said kind things to Linda and Mindy.

All the talk and the whispered false truths of "I'm so sorry," sounded like bees buzzing. The gentle droning sound filled the house. It was not an entirely unpleasant sound. Linda closed her eyes from time to time to listen.

One of the ladies from the church carried plates of food to Mindy and Linda and told them to eat. The offering startled Linda, and when she looked up she realized everyone who had come from the funeral was eating and talking. It was like a big party. Linda wanted to laugh: they had never had a party in their house before.

Greyjack was sitting on the couch with her father. She didn't know when he had come into the room. Her father's shoulders were slumped and his head was tilted to one side like he was trying his best to be attentive. All the crying had gone out of him. His body looked dry and withered.

Linda tasted the food. It was rich and warm and somehow a connection to the real world again, a way out of the bad dream of the last few days. She couldn't remember the last time she had eaten hot food. While she ate, she looked around the room and tried to catch snatches of conversation. It was like watching a movie or sitting in the middle of a stage during a play.

Except for Greyjack, Larry and Mindy, no one else who was there had ever been in their house before. Linda could see the people looking around at the clock, her grandmother's Blue Willow china in the hutch, and the dark old furniture crowding together in the living room like a den of sleeping bears. She saw their shocked faces as they caught the first glimpse of her mother's glowing pumpkin walls. She saw them look up the tall narrow staircase to the rooms upstairs and knew if they could they would go up those stairs and look into their bedrooms and their closets.

Tommy's trophies for baseball and track were lined up on the fireplace mantel. His senior picture, still unframed, and the folded flag the Army escort had given them. It was a kind of makeshift shrine she had put together this morning before they had gone to the church. People were clustered around whispering about some big game or amazing hit or throw Tommy had made. Larry sat in the corner alone. Tommy was a hero.

Linda wasn't hungry, but she ate because suddenly she wanted to fill herself up with anything but Tommy's death. She wanted to be stuffed with ham and biscuits, scalloped potatoes, cucumber salad, and sticky sweet coconut cake. She wanted to eat until her eyes fell out. The house was filled with people, and she wanted her body filled with food because she was afraid to feel empty.

She tried to get Mindy to eat, but she said she couldn't. She tightened her grasp on Linda's arm and pulled herself closer to her. Mindy said ever since she heard Tommy had died she hadn't been able to eat. She said even the smell of food made her feel sick.

People stayed until it got dark outside. Some ladies from the church stayed to clean up the kitchen and package up the leftover food and put it in the refrigerator, dumping the soured milk and throwing away the dried out roast beef they'd found there as they did. Mindy clung to Linda the whole time letting go of her only to pick at this little bit of biscuit or that little pinch of the sticky sweet coconut cake.

After most of the people had left, Richard went upstairs and shut his bedroom door. Greyjack told Linda he'd stay until everyone else had gone. He said he'd make sure the kitchen was cleaned up and things put away.

Joe Nathan hung around. Linda noticed he seemed to have a rather good appetite. He kept his plate filled, and when he heard the ladies putting things away he scurried in for another slice of cake and a brownie. His wife was with the ladies in the kitchen cleaning up. Neither of them seemed to notice Mindy sitting by Linda's side.

Mindy asked Linda if she could stay the night in Tommy's room. Linda said she didn't mind, in fact, she'd like the company. The house all of a sudden felt big and empty and sad.

Greyjack stood by the side of the room waiting for Joe Nathan and the ladies to leave. Mindy went into the kitchen to ask if she could stay. Joe Nathan said he didn't care.

"I'd like to wash up," Mindy said to Linda.

"There's fresh towels under the sink and there's even new toothbrushes and stuff in the top drawer. Mom always kept a stash in case we ever had company."

Mindy squeezed Linda's hand and thanked her. When she went upstairs she found the towels in the cabinet and the extra toothbrushes in the vanity drawer. There, jumbled with the hairpins, lipstick tubes and toothbrushes, was Tommy's straight razor.

Mindy picked it up and marveled at its weight in her hand. It was heavier than she imagined. She slipped it from its leather case and touched the smooth pearl handle.

Tommy had touched this handle. He had opened this blade and shaved his face.

She had said something the night of the party at the lake about how she loved kissing the smoothness of his cheek after he shaved. It was cool against her lips. She loved how shaving made his face dreamy with the smell of soap and water and aftershave.

Tommy told her about the pearl-handled straight razor, and how his mother, not his father, had taught him to shave with it.

He said his mother gave him the razor on his 16th birthday. He told Mindy about how his mother would shave his grandfather every morning with the razor.

She opened the razor. There was a fleck of soap and dark whisker stuck to the edge of the blade. She flicked the soap speck with her fingernail, catching the small dark hair that had once been part of Tommy in her hand. She held her hand up to her face and breathed in the smell that had once been Tommy.

Mindy closed the razor, put it back into its soft leather case and slide it into her pocket.

After everyone had left, and Mindy had gone upstairs to the bathroom to wash her face, Greyjack came into the kitchen to speak to Linda.

"I talked with your mother yesterday. She would have been here today with you if she could have," he said, as though he was trying to tell her something without telling her everything, like he was talking in code. "If she could, but she can't. Not right now, and she's very sorry. She loved Tommy very much, and she loves you too. She hopes some day you'll be able to understand."

Chapter 18

Helen was afraid to sleep. She did not ever want to dream again. As long as she was awake she could drive the voices in her head out by pounding her ears with the flat bruised palms of her hands. By slapping herself, she could shut out the horrifying picture she imagined of Tommy's dead body. By singing or shouting she could stop herself from crying. When she was too tired to sing she paced the edges of her room until her legs felt leaden and wobbly.

Sometimes, much against her will, she fell into sleep and found herself slumped in a corner. When she did she picked herself up and started hitting her head again. She could not dare let herself get caught by sleep. As long as she was awake she could make herself forget. When she slept, she lost control, and everything she was afraid of came rushing at her through the dark.

She had left her children and now her most difficult child, the one she sometimes worried she loved the most, was dead. Tommy was dead. If only she had been stronger Tommy would be alive. If she could have made him behave when he was little he might be safe at home now, waiting for her to come love him again.

If only she had gone home to say goodbye.

The nurses strapped her arms in a straight jacket to keep her from hitting herself. They tied her into the bed to keep her from pacing. They threatened to tape her mouth if she didn't stop shouting. She heard what they said, and she would have stopped shouting if she could have stopped shouting, but she couldn't. When all else failed, the nurses called the doctor and told him they couldn't control her.

"I'm not going to let them tape your mouth," he told Helen, as though he was suddenly on her side. He had let them tape the mouths of some of the patients before, but never with someone who was as far gone as Helen. In the agitated state she was in she could struggle so hard against the taping she might vomit and choke to death. He couldn't take the chance.

Helen struggled to pull away from this awful man who had lied to her about not giving her any more drugs. She never wanted to sleep again. She wanted Tommy's death to destroy her. She twisted and flailed in the bed until she could feel her breath coming in hot swooping streaks from her lungs to her mouth and through her dry lips. She wanted a drink of water. Her throat was raw and burning.

"Drink," she screamed.

The doctor held the straw up to her mouth so she could drink.

"Would you like to have something to eat?"

Helen shut her eyes and shook her head violently from side to side.

"It's been three days since you've had anything to eat. If you don't eat tonight I'll be forced to put a tube into your stomach to feed you. You wouldn't like that, now would you? It would be better if you ate something on your own. Wouldn't it?"

Helen opened her eyes to consider the question. She felt like lying. She wanted to say she would eat, even though she had no intention of eating, just to make the doctor go away. She had an urge to spit in the doctor's face. She closed her eyes again.

"Listen to me, Helen," the doctor said, anger creeping into his voice. "We can't let you starve."

"Tommy," Helen managed, not really knowing what she wanted to say about Tommy. That he was dead. That she missed him. That she was somehow responsible for what happened. That she had tried but couldn't be responsible for him anymore. That he was always more than she could manage. That she didn't know how or even if she wanted to be a mother or a wife. That she didn't know who she was anymore. That when she held Tommy when he was little, it felt like she was wrestling with her soul. That she loved him but hated him sometimes. That she had always been afraid he would die and perhaps that is why she left.

Richard had come to see her. He had touched her face and tried to hold her hand. She had shut her eyes so she couldn't see him. She had screamed so she couldn't hear what he was saying to her. Although she fought and screamed, in truth, what she really wanted was for him to hold her. Not talk. Just hold her until she could fall asleep without dreaming.

As much as she wanted to, she didn't ask him to hold her. She was afraid if he touched her, her skin would crack and bleed and her heart would break.

Greyjack came sometime later, but by then they had given her so much sedation, she didn't even bother to try to shut him out. She let him talk, but she didn't listen. When she got tired of hearing his voice, she closed her eyes and turned her head away.

"I'm so sorry Tommy is dead," Greyjack had whispered in her ear, his breath warm against her face.

"Tommy," Helen said. Then she closed her eyes and pretended to go to sleep.

Mindy had wanted to sleep in Tommy's bed. Linda couldn't think of any reason not to let her sleep there, so she gave her a nightgown and said good night.

She lay on her bed listening to Mindy washing up in the bathroom. She wondered if Mindy noticed the dirty sink or the bits of hair and fuzz around the toilet base. She wondered if she should have told her father Mindy was sleeping in Tommy's bed. She got up to check on her father. When she opened the door a crack she could see his large body lying perfectly still to one side of the bed, as though he wanted to leave room for her mother to crawl in beside him if she came home to comfort them. She decided not to wake him. She closed the door and let him sleep.

When Mindy was finished in the bathroom Linda went in to

brush her teeth. She felt jittery and exhausted. She searched the medicine cabinet for her father's sleeping pills. She knew he took them. She could hear him sometimes, roaming the house late at night after he'd been in rummaging through the medicine chest, looking for the little prescription bottle. She'd hear him take the sleeping pills, then pace the house for half an hour or more before the medicine kicked in and he could at last sleep.

When she couldn't find the pills, she took a couple of aspirin hoping to make whatever hurt inside of her quit hurting so she could sleep.

She listened to Mindy crying softly in Tommy's room. She heard her father snoring and the wind in the garden whistling a little as it blew and rocked through the resting leaves of the bean and cucumber vines.

When she finally slept she dreamed about her mother. In her dream Linda could see her mother walking at the end of the grocery store aisle, but every time she pushed her cart down the aisle to talk to her, her mother would disappear. Later, in her dream, Linda would see her mother sitting in her car with a book propped up on the steering wheel, reading, waiting for her. Again, when Linda got close, her mother would disappear.

Then Linda dreamed of Tommy's funeral and saw her mother sitting in the last pew at the back of the church. Tommy was sitting up in his casket laughing, and their mother was staring at him in the tight-lipped way she always stared at him when she knew it wouldn't do any good to talk to him. In the dream, Linda tried to show her father their mother was there and Tommy was alive, but her father pretended he didn't understand what she was trying to tell him. It was then in her dream she realized no one else could see her or hear Tommy, and when she tried to cry out Tommy was alive and they shouldn't bury him she woke up with a start, the words strangling in her throat.

She looked at the clock. It was 5 a.m. The sun was coming up. She lay in bed and thought about why their mother had left.

Greyjack had said yesterday their mother loved them. Linda really wanted it to be true, but if it was true then she didn't understand why she could leave them. She bit the inside of her cheek. She wasn't going to cry, not again, not ever, even when no one was looking.

"Fucking mother," she said to the empty room.

Linda closed her eyes and ran a litany of foul words through her head and her whispering lips. It felt good. She could feel the anger seeping through her skin. She wanted to shout, to beat the walls, but instead she lay there and cursed and swore and said every foul thing she could think of until she began to realize her mother hadn't left them, she had left their father.

The cursing broke free an image of her parents as fish in an aquarium: swimming from side to side, yet never touching. Linda was startled by the realization she could never recall ever seeing her parents touching or even accidentally bumping into each other. They didn't seem to need or bother each other. They just swam from side to side, through their lives with their heads hardly turning as they passed each other to see what the other was doing. When they swam past each other, it was like they had magnets in their bodies so whenever they accidentally got close the magnets pushed them away from each other. But Linda knew it was more than magnets. Their bodies held some invisible force powerful enough to keep others away as well. They had kept Tommy away, and they had also kept her away.

Their family didn't talk. They also never laughed the way you saw people laugh together in movies or read about them talking together in books. Their house was a silent house.

She wanted to lash out at her father. She wanted to burn the house down. She wanted to run away like her mother had done, but she couldn't run away because she couldn't leave her father. If she did, he might die like Tommy had died and then she would have no one. She hated her mother for leaving.

Her parents had fought the night her mother had painted the

kitchen. Linda heard them through her closed door. When they fought that night, it had felt like a terrible fight although no one threw anything or screamed or called each other names. It was just a fight, but it tore the house apart.

She didn't understand their fight. She couldn't put her finger on what was so wrong about her mother painting the kitchen, but even though she couldn't explain what she felt, she knew something was terribly wrong about those brilliant burning pumpkin walls. She knew painting the kitchen was more than painting a kitchen the way an iceberg is more than what you see out above water.

Linda liked the kitchen. She didn't understand why painting it had made her father so angry. She had never thought about him this much before and in thinking about him she realized she really didn't know him. She had thought she knew her mother. But she was wrong.

"Crazy bitch," Linda spit. The kids are school were right to laugh at her mother.

The words felt raw and angry against her lips. They made her teeth feel sharp. She was angry with her mother, not her father. Her mother had left him and now Linda knew she had to take care of him. She felt as though an arm had been ripped off or a door slammed in her face. She felt different. Old. Cornered. Responsible.

She had always thought her father was a quiet but kind man. Linda knew he loved her and he also loved Tommy, and she believed he had loved their mother. If her mother were in the room right now, she would hit her. Yes, she would ball up her fists and punch her in the face. She would spit and scream at her and tell her she was a whore.

Linda didn't know what to say to her father. He was lost for the moment in his private dark world he occasionally fell into. But always before when he fell into this private world of his, their mother was there to pretend it wasn't happening. They all pretended.

When her mother pretended, she would talk a little too much, plant another row of flowers, make too big of a roast or too many mashed potatoes for dinner in order to fill the empty spaces plaguing their house.

It had been three days since Linda had worked in the garden. Three days since Greyjack had come by to tell her Tommy was dead. She got up from bed and looked out the window. She could see the vines were heavy with cucumbers. It had rained a couple of nights and the days had been so hot the cucumbers had blown up like big green footballs.

She pulled on her jeans, put on a shirt and carried her shoes downstairs so she wouldn't wake anyone. She got a bushel basket from the garage and went out to pick whatever hadn't rotted since Tommy died. What had rotted, she pulled from the vines and threw into a heap at the edge of the garden in the hopes the rabbits and deer would come and eat those instead of what was good and still growing.

She filled the basket with swollen cucumbers, some of them nearly a foot long, and another basket with ripening tomatoes. She pinched the suckers so the remaining tomatoes would grow large and juicy.

The kitchen was still full of food from the funeral. When she took everything inside there was no place to put the tomatoes out on the counter or the table so they could to ripen. She put them on the back porch hoping she could sell them to someone who either had the patience to wait for them to ripen or liked fried green tomatoes. She wondered when it would seem right for her to open her stand again. She made a mental note to call Greyjack and ask.

She knew the cucumbers were too big and overblown to sell. The thought of just throwing them out on the compost made her sick with waste.

She decided she'd make pickles. Her mother always made

pickles with the cucumbers they couldn't sell. Linda had helped her make them a dozen times or more. The recipe was on a little leaflet in the Ball Jar Lid box. She got out the big canner and the jars and lids and started boiling water, then she began cutting and seeding the cucumbers. They were full of big seeds so she split them down the middle and dug the seeds out with a teaspoon. She cut them into bite-sized chunks and put them in a pan of ice water to help them crisp before she pickled them.

She washed the jars her mother had left stacked at the bottom of the pantry and, just like she had seen her mother do, had poured boiling water over them. Once rinsed, she began packing the jars with the cut cucumbers. When the jars were all filled, she boiled up the pickling juice adding an extra dash of hot peppers. She liked them hot and tangy.

She was pouring the hot liquid on the pickles and putting the lids on the jars when Mindy came down for breakfast.

"You're up awfully early," she said.

"Cucumbers needed picking."

"Looks like they needed more than that," Mindy said, pointing to the mess of seeds she'd scraped from them.

"I still need to screw the rings down tight and put the pickles in a hot water bath to seal and process them. You want to scramble some eggs for breakfast?"

"I think the smell of cooking eggs would make me puke."

"I don't like eggs either. I usually just have cookies and tea these days."

"Joe Nathan would think that's the breakfast of the Devil," Mindy said, picking up the wooden spoon Linda had used to stir the pickling juice and waving it in the air like she was striking at the Devil as he flew through the room.

"Joe Nathan's not here," Linda said, holding the hot jar with a kitchen towel while she tightened down the lid. "And neither is my mother. I eat whatever I want. In fact, I'm out of cookies right now, and I was thinking about having some of the leftover cake the good church ladies baked for us." She pointed to the collection of pies and cakes presently covering the kitchen table. "They've left an amazing assortment of goodies."

"They do look righteous," Mindy said, pulling a chair from the table in order to sit down near where Linda was working, "there's no arguing about that."

"As soon as I slide these jars into their hot water bath, I'll put on the kettle for tea and get some forks and plates so we can sample what we want."

"I think I'll start with a piece of coconut custard pie."

"I prefer a slice of pound cake, myself," Linda countered.

"Sounds like a perfect division of labor," Mindy giggled.

Linda laughed. The laughter felt good. She was surprised at what laughter sounded like in their kitchen.

"A perfect division," she echoed.

Although she and Mindy had talked together when she would come by her stand in the afternoons, they had never laughed or joked and she was sorry they hadn't. The laughter made her feel whole.

"Tommy said you were nice. He said I'd like you if I only gave you a chance. He was right. I do like you," Linda said, before she could stop herself from mentioning Tommy.

"Thanks," Mindy said, getting off the stool and reaching for the kettle. "I'll get the tea."

Mindy started with a thin slice of coconut custard pie. Linda took a hunk of lemon pound cake. They sliced and sampled and talked.

Linda narrowed her eyes and watched Mindy eat. There was something light and easy about the way she sat in the chair, as though her skin was comfortable. Linda never felt like her skin fit. She could see how her mother had thought Tommy and Mindy were alike. The world was easy to them. They didn't worry about what other people thought.

Tommy and Mindy didn't seem to care about anyone or

anything except each other. Linda thought it was amazing, how unlike her parents, Tommy and Mindy were not afraid to love each other. They could touch. They were not afraid of themselves. Tommy and Mindy knew how to love. Linda could see why Tommy liked her.

Linda sat with Mindy for an hour or more eating cake and talking about the ladies in the church and how they went through the house looking for things to gossip about all the time they pretended to be serving food at Tommy's funeral. Mindy joked and fanned around the room and did wicked impersonations of this church lady and that church lady, her pinky held high in the air, her voice shrill and haughty. Linda laughed. Mindy made another funny face then she flopped into her chair and started talking about Joe Nathan.

"Sometimes, he gets up in the middle of the night and starts prancing around the house in his bathrobe preaching to the walls just to hear himself preach."

"And, what do you do?" Linda asked, cutting a thin sliver of chocolate cake for herself.

"Nothing. Just pretend we're sleeping so he won't start preaching to us."

"Want some?" Linda asked, holding the knife, ready to cut more.

Mindy shook her head no.

"I knew Tommy was the one for me the first time I met him," she said quietly.

Linda knew she meant it and believed it was probably true. She could also see how Mindy's life, more than her own or her father's or even her mother's was changed when Tommy died. Mindy started to cry. Linda just sat there looking at her cry and how the warm light of the morning sun was now moving across the table.

"I'm so sorry," Linda managed, pushing her plate away.

Linda slid her hand across the table until her fingertips

touched the soft warm skin of Mindy's arm. Mindy turned her hand over so Linda could hold it. When Mindy stopped crying, Linda got up and started fussing with the dishes.

"Let me help you."

"I need to take the pickles out of the bath and get their lids screwed down."

Mindy got up and started to clear the table. Linda pulled the hot jars from the big canning pot one by one and lined them up along the counter. Mindy draped a kitchen towel over her hands and held each of the jars steady while Linda screwed down the rings a second time. They waited quietly to hear the lids pop and seal as the jars cooled.

Then Mindy went upstairs to get dressed. When she came down she was wearing one of Tommy's old shirts. It startled Linda at first, seeing her wearing her dead brother's shirt. Mindy giggled a little and swung her body back and forth like a small child who wanted something.

"Would you mind if I took this?" she asked.

Linda could tell Mindy just wanted something with Tommy's smell and warmth still in it.

"Take what you want," she told her.

"This was my favorite," Mindy said, running her thin hands down the front of the shirt like she was pressing Tommy's warmth in it against her body. Then she danced over and hugged Linda. Linda pulled back at first then let her head fall onto Mindy's small shoulder.

"I can drive you home," Linda said, breaking free of Mindy's arms.

"Thanks for letting me sleep here," she said, picking up the handbag she had dropped into the corner of the room when she had come yesterday after the funeral. "And for the breakfast."

"It wasn't much."

"It was what I needed."

"Thanks," said Linda.

When she returned from taking Mindy home, Linda showered and changed and cleaned up the kitchen. She didn't know what to do with all the leftover food. There were casseroles and salads all jammed into the refrigerator. Cakes and cookies were scattered across the kitchen table. The amount of food was overwhelming.

She took what she thought would freeze well then threw the rest of it away. It was weird having so much food around. She didn't want to have to face it day after day, watching it rot and spoil until it wouldn't be fit to eat.

She wrapped up most of the cakes and put them into the big locker freezer her mother kept on the back porch for frozen packs of okra, beans and corn they'd eat on all winter. She didn't want to throw the cakes away. She left the lemon pound cake out as well as the chocolate layer cake just in case her father wanted something sweet to eat when he woke up. What he didn't want, she'd have a slice at a time for breakfast or whenever Mindy came by to see her. When those were gone, she'd get a couple others from the freezer to take their place.

After she finished putting away all the food she did something she hadn't done since her mother had disappeared: she packed a lunch for her father to take to work.

One of the women had brought a big spiral cut ham, so she pulled off some meat and made him a thick ham sandwich. She filled a container with potato salad and sliced off a big piece of chocolate cake. She thought for sure her father would go to work. There was nothing for him to do at home.

She decided she needed to get her vegetable stand set up today. She decided she didn't need to call Greyjack to get his permission. She didn't know how long she should wait before opening it, and she didn't care what people thought. She had no intention of staying inside all day and didn't really have anywhere else to go.

She had green beans to sell as well as a few cantaloupes, the bushel of near-ripe tomatoes and a few decent cucumbers someone could use in a salad. When she had left her father sleeping in the funeral car yesterday, the funeral director had given her a pack of "Thank You" cards and a list of all the people who had sent flowers. He told her she should acknowledge the people who had given flowers and the ones who had brought the food to the house.

"You need to do this," he had said, pressing them into her hands when he gave them to her, "people expect to hear from you. It's part of what's expected of you when someone dies."

Linda had thought the way he had said it was kind of funny, like there were rules, and if you didn't follow them everyone would know you didn't know how to play the game of dying. She had wanted to ask him why he didn't give them to her father.

After she got the vegetables laid out, she went into the house to get the cards. She opened the package. There was already some verse inside thanking people for whatever they had done or said, and all she really needed to do was to sign the cards and address the envelopes. She decided she wouldn't bother her father with them and she'd just go ahead and sign his name. She didn't want to sign hers. For a moment she thought she might sign her mother's name as well, but felt funny about it. In the end she decided to sign just her father's name. She was glad she had something to do.

Linda didn't imagine many customers would come by because they would probably think it was too close to the funeral. She didn't care. She didn't want to be sitting in the house waiting for her father to get up or something to happen to remind her of Tommy's dying. She wondered if most people would find it easier to get their vegetables somewhere else then to have to suffer through some awkward thing of saying they were sorry Tommy had died. Linda also knew it wouldn't be long before everyone in town would know Tommy had been drunk when he had the accident. Some things were hard to keep a secret.

Her father got up around 2 p.m. to go to work. When he came downstairs and didn't find Linda in the kitchen he went to the front door to look for her. He saw her sitting at her stand. He opened the door and stepped out onto the porch. He didn't come any further, just stood on the porch as though the porch was a safe distance and anything closer wasn't. He kept far back but leaned forward to show he could be polite and not be so far away he would have to yell in order for her to hear him.

Linda was glad he stayed where he was because she was afraid if he moved any closer she'd start crying and would never be able to stop. Writing the thank you notes had made the numbness start to leave her hands and arms, and she was beginning to feel the emptiness of their house creeping into her mind.

"I thought I might go to work," he said. "You going to be all right by yourself?"

"I made you some lunch: a ham sandwich and some cake and some other stuff from yesterday. It's on the counter by the stove."

"Thanks," he said. He went back into the house. A few minutes later, he came out to the car and got in. When he backed down the driveway to ease out onto the road, he rolled down the window and waved. She waved back.

Not too many people came by, and those who did didn't say much except they were sorry. Sorry was okay because it seemed to make people buy more than normal. Most of the beans sold, as did the cucumbers, even the bigger ones that were a bit iffy. There were only a couple of melons. Everyone touched them, but no one bought them. Linda suspected they thought there wasn't enough of them and to buy one would leave her stand looking skimpy.

She usually closed around 6 p.m. figuring most people were home cooking dinner by then, but she didn't feel like going into the empty house. She kept the stand open until way after dark.

She didn't bother to get up to turn the porch light on or anything, just sat there in the dark.

She heard Greyjack's car coming down the road before she saw it.

"Thought I'd come by and help you close," he said, leaning out his car window.

"Not much left," she said, not sure she wanted Greyjack's company. She had been enjoying the coolness of the evening and thought she just might stay there all night until her father came home from work.

Greyjack parked his car in the driveway then came up to her stand.

"I see the beans are gone. Heard you had some nice green tomatoes. I've been thinking for some time about cooking up a platter of fried green tomatoes. Maybe make a cucumber salad to go with them," he said picking up the last cucumber. "That, and a cantaloupe. Looks like a good one."

Linda didn't move to help him.

Greyjack kept talking about tomatoes and cucumbers while he first filled a bag with green tomatoes and another with the lone cucumber and the cantaloupe. He put some money in her box and took his things to the car. When he came back he started stacking up the empty baskets and folding up the cloth she had laid out across the counter before she'd put out the vegetables. When he finished he carried the baskets around the house to the back porch, all the while talking in this easy kind of way you might talk to a spooked horse. Linda was listening to him talk but she couldn't move. The night air felt good on her face. She was tired.

"Had anything to eat?" he asked, once he'd put his vegetables into the backseat of his car and closed her cash box.

"Had cake with Mindy for breakfast," Linda managed.

"Sounds good," Greyjack said. He started talking about cake and how his mother used to make this wonderful coconut cake every year for his birthday. As he talked about how she made the cake the day before and then soaked it in coconut juice overnight before she frosted it, he started walking to the house. Linda followed him.

Greyjack saw the cakes sitting on the kitchen table and the pickles lined up across the counter.

"I see you got breakfast covered here with the cakes and those pickles. Looks like the cake might last you six, eight days...one slice at a time, if that's all you plan to eat. How about a sandwich?"

Greyjack pulled the ham out of the refrigerator. Linda handed him a loaf of bread.

"Mustard or mayonnaise?"

"Both." All of a sudden Linda felt hungry and tired.

"Living dangerously, heh?" he kidded. "How about some lettuce?"

"Lettuce sounds good."

Greyjack doctored the bread with a good smear of mayonnaise and mustard. He stacked his creation with a thick slice of ham and a chunk of iceberg lettuce, cutting the sandwich from corner to corner to make two fat triangles. He put the sandwich on a plate, put the plate on the table, looked in the refrigerator and pulled out a cold bottle of cola.

Linda ate in silence. When she finished, she asked him if he would make her another one. The sandwiches tasted salty and better than any other sandwiches Linda could ever remember.

"I'm really tired," she said when the second sandwich was gone.

"I'll clean up," Greyjack offered.

Linda went upstairs without thanking him. She felt jittery and didn't think she could trust herself to speak. She didn't want to cry.

She lay in bed for a long time in the dark listening to Greyjack clean up in the kitchen. He washed the dishes by letting the water run while he wiped things clean with a rag. She wondered if he didn't know where the soap was or why he didn't fill the sink with water.

After he turned off the water and put the dried dishes away in the cupboard she heard him turn on the television. He kept the sound low. It was a lovely soft hum. She closed her eyes. She did not hear him drive away two hours later, or her father come home from work, walk down the hallway and open her door to check on her.

Chapter 19

Helen was standing by the fence. Her robe was untied and the front of it hung open carelessly. The robe felt heavy and her arms and legs felt like thin dried sticks. Her skin hurt.

She had told the doctor just this morning she didn't believe God existed. She also told him her skin hurt. Her teeth hurt too. She could feel her lips when they brushed against her teeth when she swallowed or chewed. Her face twitched and tingled. She was a toaster oven with a frayed cord.

"It's the treatments. The shock treatments," he had shouted at her over his desk. "It will go away in time. It's nothing to be worried about."

It had been two weeks since Tommy had died, and they had given her the shock treatments. She was beginning to worry. She still had trouble remembering things and thinking. She could feel the skin hanging on her bones and her nerves dancing at the ends of her fingers.

"Helen," the aide called as she approached her. "You've got company."

Helen tried to shape the word company against her lips but failed.

"Get yourself tied up there and come on in," the aide cajoled, grabbing at the ties of the robe and bringing everything securely closed around Helen's thin waist. "That preacher man is here to see you. Do you good to see someone."

The aide took Helen's hand and led her back to the building. Helen was trying hard to remember what preacher. She hoped it wasn't that idiot Joe Nathan. The last time he came he had tried to put his hands on her head to pray for her, and she had tried to bite him. She didn't want to be touched, especially not by him.

"Whaa pre-sure?" Helen asked, the thick words crawling in her mouth.

"The same one who came last time. You tried to bite him, remember?"

She remembered.

"No," she shouted.

"Oh, yes. The doctor said to bring you. Said the visit might do you good. Stir things up. Bring back some of the memory they tried to fry out of you a couple weeks ago."

Helen tried to struggle but succeeded only in shaking her head from side to side a little and slowing down their progress. The aide pressed on.

"Going to take you to the visitor's room. Got a window in it so we can keep an eye on what's happening. Want to make sure you do all right. You tried to bite him last time. Doctor says we need to keep an eye on you."

Helen went down the hallway past her room to the visitor's room. The aide opened the door. Helen could see Joe Nathan sitting in a chair at the table waiting for her.

"Here she is," the aide said, pushing Helen's shoulders a little so she would move toward the chair and sit down. "We'll be outside if you need anything."

Helen tried to talk, but couldn't. She closed her eyes hoping Joe Nathan would disappear.

"You going to be all right?" the aide asked, looking first at Helen then at Joe Nathan.

Joe Nathan nodded his head. The aide nodded back then left the room, shutting the door behind her. Joe Nathan got up from his chair and reached into his pocket for his handkerchief.

Joe Nathan took a step back from his chair. He leaned his thin body back like he was trying to get Helen into focus. He wiped his face with his handkerchief the way someone who had just come in from working in the fields might wipe his face. All of a sudden, his body started swaying. A low humming sound filled the room. The louder the sound got, the faster Joe Nathan moved, until he was strutting around the room, circling Helen like she was some kind of wild animal he was trying to tame.

Helen had opened her eyes when she heard the humming sound. She watched Joe Nathan weave and bob, turning in her chair from side to side as he pranced and danced around her. The droning singing sound of his voice filled her with dread.

His voice was getting louder and louder. She could feel the heat in the room crowding in on her. Her skin crawled and tingled with a kind of excited fear. She wasn't scared as much as anxious, and she kept watching him weave from side to side and around her. It felt like a dream.

She noticed his handkerchief was gone, and he had something else in his hand. It was big and black. Maybe it was a book or maybe it was a rock. She tried to keep her eye on it to figure it out. She worried he might hit her with the rock. She brought her hands up to cover her face.

"Je-sus," Joe Nathan shouted, striking his opened hand with his Bible, "Sweet Je-sus, save this Jezebel."

Helen saw the big black rock hit the palm of Joe Nathan's open hand. She felt the crack of the rock against his hand as if it had hit her face.

"Heal this harlot woman, this mother of the Devil," Joe Nathan shouted and danced, fanning the big black Bible in the air. "Strike the whore from her heart," he roared, and as he did, he slapped the Bible against his hand a second time. "Bring her back to her family where she belongs."

Helen's heart pounded in her chest. She kept her eyes on the black thing in Joe Nathan's hand. The black thing could kill her. She could feel the weight of it in the room. Her bones felt like brittle sticks, her robe a thin protection against her skin. She bent over in her chair and covered her head with her hands. She could feel Joe Nathan coming closer. She looked up and saw him raise his hand, the one holding the big black rock. She moved to get out of the way, and as she did she remembered she was sitting in a chair.

She wrapped her hands around a chair leg. Joe Nathan was shouting. She couldn't understand what he was saying. She saw his face coming closer to her, and as it did, she quickly stood up still holding on to the chair leg. She swung with all her might and knocked the black thing from his hand and him to the floor. Before she could raise the chair to hit him again, the aide came flying into the room and grabbed her.

Linda went down to the kitchen to make some breakfast for herself. It had been a more than a month since Tommy's funeral and she couldn't stop thinking about how hard the first week was, then the second, and now the first month. His birthday was in the first day of October. That would be hard, as would Thanksgiving and Christmas. Then Easter would come again, and she knew she would have to live through their mother leaving without him as well.

She rummaged through the kitchen looking for something to eat. All the cakes and pies the ladies had brought to the house after the funeral were gone. She looked in the cupboard for some oatmeal to make a batch of cookies. The phone rang. The sound startled her. It wasn't yet 6 a.m. Not the usual time for someone to call. Her heart raced with the hope it was mother.

"Hello," Linda said.

"Do you remember that night after Tommy's funeral when I stayed over and we were eating cake for breakfast," Mindy said, "and I told you how sometimes Daddy starts prancing and preaching in the middle of the night?"

Mindy was talking fast in order to keep tears from tumbling out between words. Linda didn't know quite what to say, so she didn't say anything. She just kept listening and nodding her head.

"Do you?" Mindy shouted. "Do you remember?"

"Yes," Linda said, anxious to give Mindy space to talk.

"Okay," Mindy said more calmly.

Linda could imagine her pushing her hair back from her face and wetting her lips a little with her tongue the way she always did when she said, "okay," as though she was getting ready to tell you a secret.

"I didn't tell you everything. One time he got to preaching about Lot's wife and how she was turned to a pillar of salt because she didn't do what God had told her to do, and he was prancing around the house and his voice was singing, and he grabbed me and pulled me by my hair. He dragged me to the kitchen, and he filled his hand with salt and he tried to make me eat it. He pushed his hand into my face, and he held it there. He was holding me so tight I could barely breathe. The salt got in my nose and my eyes and I got so scared I couldn't fight him."

"Are you hurt?"

"My mother screamed at him. He grabbed her too, and she told him she'd eat the salt in his hand and all the salt in the house if he would just let go of me."

"Mindy," Linda shouted afraid Mindy couldn't hear her, "are you hurt?"

"He always lets me go and then he says we need to pray. So we pray. And then it's over."

"Did he hurt you, Mindy?"

"My mom was over to see her sister. When I got home from work it was late. Daddy was sitting by himself at the kitchen table. It was like he'd been waiting for me all day. He threw his Bible at me and called me a whore."

"Why would he do that?"

"I'd been to see the doctor yesterday and found out I was pregnant with Tommy's child. I told Momma."

"You're pregnant?"

"It's God's way of letting me keep Tommy with me. I'm sure of it."

"Did Tommy know?"

"No. I wasn't sure when he was home the last time. But I'm

sure now. Doctor said I was three, maybe four months."

"What'd your mother say?"

"I told Momma because I wanted her to tell Daddy. It's hard to tell Daddy anything. I plan on keeping the baby."

Linda could hear the sound of cars driving by and knew Mindy was calling from a payphone outside somewhere.

"You're going to have a baby."

"I told Daddy this was my baby, not something that was handed down at some church bazaar. It was mine, all mine and Tommy's and I was going to keep it."

"Where are you?"

"I was gonna come by your house on my way to work today and tell you about the baby. I think it's a boy. When I told Daddy I thought it was God's way of letting me keep Tommy close to me Daddy told me Tommy was the Devil and any child of Tommy's was the Devil's work."

"Mindy, can you tell me where you are?"

"The doctor pressed my hand against the side of my belly then he pushed on the other side. I could feel the baby move a little. It felt like a flutter of a small bird's wing. That's when he told me I was three months, maybe four, and then he asked me if I knew when I got pregnant and who the father was. Of course I know. It's Tommy's baby. If I have to, I'll run away to have it."

"That's good," Linda told her calmly. She didn't want Mindy to do anything stupid. "Tommy would be happy. I bet you're right. I bet it is a boy. Tell me where you are Mindy, and I'll come get you. We'll have some breakfast, and you can tell me all about the baby."

"Daddy might follow you. He was acting pretty crazy."

"I'll make sure he won't follow me. We won't even come back here. We'll go someplace else. I'll call Greyjack. We can to his house."

"I'm not feeling so good," Mindy said, "I'm tired. Really tired and my stomach is cramping up a bit and my legs hurt."

"Did he hurt you?"

"He never means to hurt me. He doesn't hit me hard, and he always stops so we can pray. He never means it. I know he doesn't mean it, but I think he hurt my baby."

Linda tried to think about all the places where Mindy could be calling from a payphone. There were payphones at all the gas stations and on most of the corners in town. She couldn't imagine Mindy was downtown. Downtown wasn't a good place to hide and it wasn't the kind of place you'd go to at 6 a.m. in the morning.

"Tell me where you are, and I'll come get you."

"I got a ride from a truck driver last night. I waited until everyone was asleep, then I left. I had the money I'd been saving from my job so we could get married. I took the money and a few things, and I started walking. When I got to the highway this truck driver pulled off the road and offered me a ride."

"Where'd he take you?" Linda asked, hoping Mindy knew.

"He kept asking me if I wanted to go home. He told me he'd take me home, but I told him I didn't want to go home."

"Where are you?"

"He was a real nice man. He had a soft way of talking. He told me he had a daughter about my age, and if she left in the middle of the night he wished someone like him would bring her home. I told him about the baby. He said he bet it was going to be a beautiful baby. I told him what my Daddy had said and what he had done throwing his Bible at me. He said he was sorry. He said some men get scared and don't do right. Daddy just got scared."

"Tell me where you are and I'll come get you, okay?"

"I don't know how far we went, but it seemed pretty far and then he pulled into this truck stop. It's a nice place, real clean. It has a motel in it. The man gave me some money for a room. He told me to get some sleep. He said the baby and I needed sleep. He kept asking if I was hurt. I told him I was fine. He was nice. He kept telling me I should get some sleep. He said I looked awfully tired, and I needed to rest so the baby would be healthy. I've tried to sleep, but the baby keeps waking me up. I think he's hurt. Do you think Tommy's in heaven?"

"Sure he's in heaven," Linda said.

"I don't know what I'll do if our baby's hurt."

"Maybe you should see a doctor. I can come get you. It won't take long, then we can go to the doctor and we'll know everything's fine."

"I need to get some sleep. The man was right. If I get some sleep, the baby will be fine."

Mindy's voice sounded scary and far away. Linda had a bad feeling everything was going to fall apart, and she wouldn't be able to stop it.

"I love you, Mindy," she said.

"I love you, too," Mindy said. Before she hung up she added, "I just know Tommy's in heaven."

Linda had heard about heaven all her life, but she was started when Mindy said the word heaven: it was the first time heaven ever sounded to Linda like a place you could get to on your own. She believed in heaven, but she always thought it was just a warm spot in your imagination, like a special dream. The way Mindy said the word heaven made it sound like it was someplace you could get to if you only knew which bus to ride or which road to turn down. Mindy also made it sound as though once you got to heaven, you'd be fine.

When Mindy hung up, Linda called Greyjack. She told him everything she knew, including the baby and how Joe Nathan had done something to Mindy but she didn't know what. Linda could hear Greyjack draw in a breath when she told him about Joe Nathan calling Mindy a whore.

"There's only half a dozen or so truck stops with motels within a couple hundred miles of here. She's not far. We'll find her. You go and open your stand. If Joe Nathan comes by to ask you about Mindy, don't tell him about the call. Is your dad working today?"

"Going to work is about all he does," Linda said with a bit of edge.

"He's a good man."

"Better than Joe Nathan, I guess."

"He's been through a lot. You tell him what you want about this, but I'm not sure I'd tell him about Joe Nathan maybe hurting the baby. At least not yet."

While Greyjack was talking, all Linda could think about was how Mindy was going to have Tommy's baby. Tommy was dead, but the baby was alive. Some new life she hadn't counted on was going to come to them. Her stomach wobbled like a bowl of warm Jell-o. Mindy was right, she thought, having Tommy's baby was like having a way for Tommy to come back to them.

"She said she couldn't sleep because the baby was keeping her awake. She said she thought the baby might be hurt."

"I'll come by as soon as I know anything. I promise."

The cantaloupes in her garden were just starting to come in. They were big as footballs and sweet. There had been a lot of rain and hot weather since Tommy had died. She picked a bushel of cantaloupes and another of yellow crookneck squash. She had a peck of tomatoes and some red and green peppers and just about a bushel of snap beans. It took a couple of hours to pick everything get them washed up and ready to sell.

By ten o'clock she had everything nicely displayed and her father's lunch made. She took a book out with her to the stand and sat in the shade reading, waiting for customers to come by. Everyone who stopped bought one of the melons and said they'd call their neighbors to tell them how pretty they were and that they should come by too.

Her father got up around eleven and came out to say he was going to work. He said he'd heard the phone ring earlier and asked who had called. Linda had been afraid he'd ask, but she'd had time to think about what it was she was going to say, so she just said it was Mindy, and it seemed like she and Joe Nathan had had some kind of misunderstanding and Mindy had run away.

"You talk to Joe Nathan?" he asked.

"No. I called Greyjack."

"That's good. Greyjack'll find her. They're working overtime at the plant right now. I'll be home late, but if you need me, you can call and ask for the foreman. He'll come get me. I'll let him know you might be calling."

Linda nodded her head. Her father looked down at his shoes. Then, without saying anything, he walked out into the yard where she was sitting. He bent down and kissed the top of her head and put his hand there like he was trying to make sure the kiss didn't slide away.

"She's going to be all right," he said, like he knew about the baby and about what Joe Nathan had done.

She told him she had fixed a lunch for him.

"Thanks," he said again, and went back in the house.

After her father left, Linda felt jittery and jumpy. I had been hours since she talked to Greyjack. Hours. She couldn't concentrate on her book and she couldn't sit still waiting for someone to come along to buy something. She left her book on her chair and went around the back of the house to the shed to get the lawnmower.

Tommy was the one who taught her how to mow the lawn, first going one way then cutting across a second time at an angle so the yard looked like the outfield of a ballpark. That's the way he liked it. And, for the first few days after he cut it, when you drove by the house, you could see the light dance off the last angled cutting. It made the grass glint like diamonds, and it made you feel like there was something exciting about to happen right there in your own front yard.

Once she cut the first direction, she raked the grass. When she finished raking, she cut across on the diagonal and raked again. It had been weeks since she had last mowed. The grass was thick and deep. It took her all afternoon to cut the lawn because she had to stop every few minutes to wait on someone who wanted to buy from her stand.

The sun was just beginning to set when she finished. She turned on the porch light. She didn't want to go in the house and sit there alone. She pushed the lawnmower around the house to the shed to put it away. When she opened the shed door, she saw the hedge clippers. She couldn't remember the last time either she or her mother had trimmed the hedges. She pulled on a pair of gloves and threw the clippers into the wheelbarrow and went out to the front again.

The privet hedges lining the front of the house had gone a bit wild and made the place look like it had slipped into trailer trash. Linda stepped back to figure out how she would prune.

She reached into the thick of the bushes and started clipping. She could hear her mother, the mother she had in her head now, say you must cut from the inside, staggering the cuts to keep the bush full and lush with leaves. The branches scratched Linda's bare arms. She went into the house and found an old shirt of Tommy's in the laundry room and pulled it on.

The bushes were so thick and tall she couldn't really see what she was doing. She'd stop ever few snips, stepping back to survey her progress. She and her mother had usually done the pruning together: one could clip while the other looked on giving directions.

Linda remembered seeing pictures of Disneyland where they had trimmed the privets to look like cones and spirals and even animals. She thought how funny it would be to trim the bushes into a chorus line of elephants linked trunk to tail circling their house.

She stepped back from her work and squinted her eyes and tried to imagine which end of the bushes would be the head and which one the tail. How wonderful it would be to cut a circus of dancing elephants prancing across the front of their house. The idea delighted her, but she stopped herself because making the bushes look like a parade of elephants was a little crazy, like her mother splashing orange paint on the kitchen walls. She quickly pushed the elephant idea aside and kept clipping, bringing the bushes into a tidy row of green hitting right below the edge of the living room window.

She decided, however, as she went along, not to make them square like a boxcar like they had always been but softer and rounder, more like bushes. A little like fat-rumped elephants. The more she cut away at the bushes' sharp edges, the more she liked the roundness of them. When she finished, what she had was not a row of linked elephants but a rolling swell of bubble-shaped bushes.

Five or six more customers came by while she was pruning and they all looked over at her work and twisted their heads this way and that while they picked out their tomatoes and cucumbers. They all said the bushes looked good. She could tell, however, by the way they said it they thought she was going to catch h-e-double-l in eternity from her grandmother for not cutting them square like they had always been cut before.

It was dark when she put her tools in the shed. Her stand was just about empty. After she took the few beans and melons into the house she started raking up the clippings and putting them into the wheelbarrow to throw away. There was a small clearing out near the edge of the woods where they put grass clippings and branches. Eventually the pile would get big, winter would come and the snow would pack it down. By spring the pile would be small again, and they'd start adding new clippings to it. When the pile began to resemble a squat mound of earth and it was too lumpy to push a wheelbarrow up over it, they'd start a new pile.

Linda was walking back from the woods when she heard

Greyjack's squad car coming down the road. It was moving slow and sad, and she knew when Greyjack pulled into the drive and rolled his window up before he got out, that the news was bad.

"I got there too late," he said quietly as he got out of his car.

Linda froze.

Greyjack took a step forward and tried to reach out to grab Linda by the shoulder but he didn't move fast enough. Before Linda could step into his arms, her knees buckled and she dropped to the ground.

She felt like her heart had burst. She bunched her knees up under her chin and wrapped her arms around them as tightly as she could. She rocked back and forth making a soft sad sound.

Greyjack crouched low to the ground and moved close to Linda but didn't touch her. He wished Warren were here. Warren would know what to do. He had always known what to do. He could feel Linda's hurt and anger creeping up the sunburned skin of his arm like a cold shadow.

"She'd cut her wrists with a straight razor. There was a lot of blood. Looks like she might have had a miscarriage."

Greyjack didn't know how much more he could or should tell Linda. She knew more than any of them.

"She said she was worried the baby was hurt. Joe Nathan hurt the baby."

Linda's voice was flat and heavy and distant as though she was giving a report over the telephone. She fell silent for a moment then began rocking back and forth on her heels, her arms hugging her knees, pulling her into a tight protected ball. She began to hum as she rocked. The humming became staccato then broke into a deep ripping animal-like sound.

Greyjack waited. He didn't move any closer than he had to. Eventually Linda rocked back and forth, back and forth, hard and silent as though she was trying to rock herself into a safe place deep in the earth.

"She's found Tommy," Linda said at last. Then she reached out so Greyjack would take her into his arms.

Safely there, she buried her face into his shoulder and cried. She cried because her mother wasn't there. She cried because Tommy had died and now Mindy and his baby were dead.

And, she cried because she now understood that, unlike Mindy, she didn't know how to get to heaven. Not knowing made her feel lost.

Chapter 20

When Helen hit Joe Nathan, and the aide came running into the room and tore the chair from her hands, a large wooden splinter got wedged into the palm of her hand. Without thinking, she quickly pulled it out with her teeth. She could taste the blood. She lunged out at Joe Nathan and smeared the blood across his face. She wanted to hurt him.

He pushed her and her bloody hand away and started hitting his hand with the big black thing again and shouting about Tommy and a Devil baby. Her heart had caught on fire.

"I am here to drive the Devil out of YOU!" Joe Nathan shouted, his face close to hers, so close she could smell his soured breath.

She spit in his face.

The black thing hit his hand with a loud crack.

"I am a Devil hunter, and I am here to drive him out!"

Joe Nathan was the Devil. Helen was sure of it. The other aides and nurses came, pushed Helen out of his way and Joe Nathan out of the room. Good, she thought. They can see it too. Her heart and her head quit racing.

They knew what he had said and how he tried to hit her with that big black thing. They were throwing him out. She began to relax.

"Relax, Helen, just relax," the nurse was saying, circling around in front of her, inching her way one step at a time closer.

"Blanket," the aide yelled.

Helen turned to see what was happening, and when she did the nurse who had been talking to her grabbed her from behind and pinned her arms to her sides. Another came into the room with a blanket. They pushed her to the floor and rolled her into the blanket while a third nurse prepared a shot.

Helen didn't fight back. She had been wrapped in the blanket before, and she liked it. She felt warm and tired. She could feel the needle as it broke the skin in her arm and the sting of the medicine as it pushed its way to her brain.

Greyjack was standing out by his car in the driveway the next morning when Linda got up. He was holding the morning paper. Linda came outside and looked down at the porch and realized it was their paper he was holding. She went out to the car. Greyjack stood by his squad car without saying anything while she read the article.

The headline on the front page proclaimed: Minister's Daughter Commits Suicide. The article had Mindy's yearbook picture next to a picture of the motel room where she was found. In the picture of the room you could see the crumpled bedspread and where the blood had spilled out from the bed onto the floor where she had bled to death.

The reporter had interviewed the truck driver who had taken Mindy to the motel and paid for her room. Greyjack had picked up the man and held him briefly for questioning. No charges were made: there was no physical evidence linking the truck driver to Mindy's death, and no sign of struggle or foul play. The article did not mention Mindy's phone call to Linda or what Linda had told Greyjack. The truck driver was released.

"I knew she was running away from something," the man was quoted in the article as saying. "I gave her money for the motel and some money to call her parents to come get her. I did what I hoped someone would do for my daughter if she ever ran away. She was a pretty girl. I don't know why she killed herself."

The article talked about Mindy's slashed wrists, the pearl-handled razor they found on the floor, the bag of clothes she had with her, and the $200 the police found in her wallet. It also mentioned Mindy had been Tommy's girlfriend and told how Tommy was recently killed during a routine training exercise in the Army. The article did not mention the bruises all over

Mindy's body or her miscarriage.

"Are you going to arrest Joe Nathan for killing her?" Linda asked Greyjack when she finished.

Greyjack looked away for a minute and pulled his shoulders up around his neck and twisted his head a little from side to side the way someone who was getting ready to go into a ring to fight would do.

"I can't," he said. He pushed his balled-up fists into his pants pockets and let his body slump into his clothes. "The coroner's report is clear. The cause of death was suicide. I have no legitimate reason to go after Joe Nathan."

"I want to see the coroner's report," Linda demanded.

"Did Mindy say Joe Nathan hit her?"

Linda closed her eyes and tried to summon Mindy's voice. She wanted to hear Mindy tell her that he had hit her, but Mindy hadn't. She knew, no matter how much she hated Joe Nathan and no matter how much she wanted to hurt him, Mindy had not said he hit her.

"No," she breathed. "She just said she thought Joe Nathan had hurt her baby, but she didn't say he hit her. But you know he did. Joe Nathan killed Tommy's baby, and he killed Mindy. When she lost the baby she had nothing else to live for and nothing left to do but kill herself so she could be with Tommy."

"I can't arrest Joe Nathan," Greyjack said quietly, "on what someone believes might be true. We have no proof he hit her. The only evidence we have is the coroner's report, and it says Mindy died because she cut her wrists."

"I want to read the coroner's report." She would not take no for an answer.

"It isn't pretty."

"I want to see for myself what it says."

"I talked to your father. We've decided you deserve to see it, but you can't tell anyone I showed it to you."

"There's no one left for me to tell."

"Do you want me to stay while you read it?" He asked, as he reached into his car and brought out a copy of the report.

"No."

"I'm sorry I didn't get there on time."

"You couldn't have done anything," Linda said, folding the report in half and slipping it into the newspaper. "My mother was right: what was going to happen, happened."

Linda waited until she could hear Greyjack's car moving down the gravel road away from their house before she took the newspaper and the report into the garden and sat down under the shade tree. The coroner's report listed the cause of death as hemorrhaging. It identified two different hemorrhaging sites: Mindy's womb and her wrists. The excessive bleeding from her womb came from an apparent miscarriage. The fetus, the report noted, was male and dead before being aborted. The bleeding from the wrists was caused by several long cuts made diagonally across the wrists with a straight razor. The wounds were thought to be self-inflicted. There was a pearl-handled razor covered with Mindy's fingerprints found on the floor beside her body.

Linda knew the razor had belonged to Tommy.

The report noted the location of various bruises on the victim's face and shoulders. The bottom rib on the left side of the ribcage was cracked, and there were several large bruises across the front of her abdomen. The coroner noted the bruises on her abdomen most likely happened before the miscarriage and could have possibly come from a self-attempt to induce a miscarriage. The bruises and the cracked rib were not listed as contributing factors in the cause of death. There was nothing said about the possibility she might have been hit.

The report was clear. Mindy had cut her own wrists and bled to death. But, real truth lay beneath the bruises.

The coroner's report failed to even hint at the possibility Mindy's suicide was the result of some other injury, real or imagined, psychological, spiritual or physical. It never mentioned the possibility Mindy could have died of grief over the loss of her child or from Tommy's death or as a reaction to her father's cruelty.

Linda had hoped the report would put her mind to rest. Instead, it pulled a blanket of exhaustion over her body. She wanted to close her eyes and make Mindy's death disappear. But, she was afraid of sleep. She had seen what sleep had done to her father, how it had snatched him from living and driven him into a dark cold well of silence.

She tore up the report into tiny pieces and pushed it into the cool loamy soil of the garden, poking her finger with each tiny piece as though she were planting seeds. She pushed fresh dirt over the holes and tore the newspaper in long strips and threw them on the mulch pile. She went to the shed and got out her wheelbarrow and her pitchfork and the baskets for gathering vegetables for her stand. When she picked what was ripe, she washed the produce, put it in baskets and carried everything to her stand. Afterwards, she went back to the garden and worked the mulch with the pitchfork burying the newspaper with each flip of the handle.

When she finished, she washed her hands, washed her face, packed her father's lunch, and went out to the stand.

She knew people would come by. Knew they wouldn't be able to stay away, and she wanted to be at the stand waiting for them. She wanted to hear what they had to say.

It was amazing what people said to her while they looked at her vegetables and decided what to cook for dinner. They said Mindy flirted shamelessly with everyone who came by the Mini-Mart. They said she had a reputation. Some were even so bold as to say once Tommy died, Mindy threw herself at any boy who came along. And now they said Mindy committed suicide because she had realized what kind of a girl she'd become and she knew she had no place to go but to hell.

Linda didn't respond. She just listened and pushed their vegetables into bags and took their money. She didn't tell anyone about Mindy's phone call. She didn't tell them about the bruises or the baby. She didn't tell them she'd read the coroner's report. She didn't tell them Joe Nathan had killed Mindy.

She despised them. They were shallow and small and cruel. They talked about Mindy because they were afraid for their own daughters. They gossiped because they were jealous. They told secrets behind their wrinkled hands because they thought they were better than everyone else and would live forever because they were good Christians.

She hated them all.

The funeral was scheduled for Saturday morning.

"You need to go," her father said, standing in the doorway of Linda's bedroom, his church hat in his hands. "You need to say goodbye."

"She's already gone," Linda responded. "Leave me alone."

"I'll wait for you downstairs. Greyjack thought we should ride together."

Greyjack came by the house to pick them up. Richard sat in the front with Greyjack. Linda sat in the back seat alone. They didn't speak on the way to the church. It wasn't an uncomfortable silence, but more a silence of respect for the distance they needed to maintain in order to survive together.

When they got to the church, her father came around and opened the door for her and offered his hand to help her out. She refused his help, and once in the sanctuary, she refused to sit with either her father or Greyjack. Instead, she sat on a far corner of the last pew by herself.

Linda watched her father walk by himself to the front and take a seat on the aisle, three pews up in order to make room for Mindy's family. Linda saw his shoulders slump forward when he sat down, and she knew he was holding his hat in his hands and was flipping it lightly against his knees. He did the same thing when he sat at the top of the bleachers watching Tommy play baseball. Linda knew he was praying. She knew he was thinking about Tommy. Greyjack stayed back and stood by himself, leaning against the wall near the back door. He almost never sat down anywhere he went.

Mindy's casket, like Tommy's, was closed. But, unlike Tommy's coffin, hers wasn't big or fancy. It was small, barely big enough to fit a twelve-year-old child, and plain. Linda recognized it as the cheapest one the funeral home sold.

When the pallbearers lifted her tiny coffin at the close of the service and carried it to the hearse, they seemed to do so without hesitation or strain. The coffin looked empty in its easy sway down through the aisle of the church and it made it seem like Mindy and Tommy's baby had vanished without a trace. When the coffin passed by her, Linda felt for a moment like she was caught in one of those floating dreams, or worse, like her mind and her body were about to part ways again and would never find their way back together.

They went to the gravesite service then drove home without stopping at Joe Nathan's to pay their respects.

On Sunday morning, her father came to her room and woke her up to go to church.

"I don't want to go," Linda said, pulling the covers up over her shoulders and turning her back to the door. "I can't stand to hear them talk about her and Tommy anymore. I'm sick of it."

"They'll talk less if we're there," he said, then flipped on the light and closed the door.

Linda really didn't want to go but knew her father was right so she took a quick shower and got dressed. She decided she would go, but she wouldn't listen to what Joe Nathan had to say. She would just go and sit there and try to talk with Mindy and Tommy in church the same way they always say you can talk to

God in church.

When they got to the church Linda slid into the back pew and let her father go up to sit in the front alone. She closed her eyes and tried to think of how tanned and handsome Tommy looked getting off the bus the day he came home from basic training. She thought about the first time she met Mindy and how her hair was perfect and fell to her shoulders and curled up just so like the way you always saw it in magazines, not at all like hair looked like in real life.

She bowed her head when they got to praying and closed her eyes and let Mindy and Tommy look their best while they held hands and walked with their baby through a meadow smelling of roses and sunshine and freshly mowed grass. It was, she thought, the heaven Mindy imagined.

When the singing and praying was over and the offering had been collected and it was time to go, Linda kept sitting there thinking of Tommy and Mindy. She was daydreaming about what their little boy would have been like when Mindy's mother came up the aisle and looked at Linda as if she needed to tell her something important.

She looked at Linda for just a second and their eyes caught. In that brief moment Linda could see Mindy's mother had a smear of thick make-up across her left cheek. Underneath her make-up was a large purple bruise. Mrs. Nathan quickly looked away and brought the Bible she was carrying in her left hand up toward her face. She ducked her head as though she was trying to hide more than just the bruise.

Once Mrs. Nathan had passed and the church was emptying, Linda picked up her purse and went out and sat in the car waiting for her father.

They got halfway home before she thought she couldn't hold it in any longer.

"He hit her," she said through gritted teeth. She knew her father had also seen the bruise on Mrs. Nathan's cheek.

He kept driving like he heard her but didn't want to hear her, like he had to think about what he was going to say before he responded.

"Sometimes we see things we might not understand," he said at last.

"You saw it too," Linda snarled. "You understand it as well as I do."

Her father kept silent.

Linda had never spoken to her father this way before, but seeing Mindy's mother's bruised face lit a dangerous burning anger in her. Her heart raced. She could feel her face flush with rage. Once this rage was unleashed, she couldn't stop it.

"You know he hit Mindy too. I told Greyjack, Joe Nathan killed Mindy's baby and he killed her, too. I told him and he didn't do anything, and now he's hit his wife."

Richard held tight to the steering wheel and kept driving.

"You didn't do anything either," she shouted at him.

He turned his face away as though he'd been slapped.

"I'm sorry. I didn't mean that," she said.

Her father didn't say anything. He didn't even look at her. He just kept driving and when they got to the house, he turned off the car, got out, and went up to his room and shut the door.

Linda went inside and changed her clothes. She came down and puttered in the kitchen. She made lunch for herself and sat at the table alone, eating. She cleaned up the dishes and made a sandwich for her father to take to work.

She sat at the table waiting for him to come down to talk to her. When he didn't come, she went outside to work in the garden. She weeded between the rows of corn and mulched the melon patch. She was careful to once again bury the strips of newspaper she'd put in the mulch pile with leaves and grass clippings. She did not want to think about what happened. She pinched back the suckers on the tomatoes and tied up the cucumber vines onto their fencing. She did everything she could think of doing and worked until it was dark.

She heard her father drive off to work.

After she finished in the garden, she was too tired to do anything else but wash her face and crawl into bed.

Chapter 21

Richard stopped at a gas station about a mile from Joe Nathan's house in order to call Greyjack and tell him he was going to have a talk with Joe Nathan.

"Talk?" Greyjack asked.

"He's hurt too many people."

"We can't prove he hurt Mindy."

"The hospital called. He's tried to hurt Helen."

"Is she okay?"

"She hit him."

"With?"

"A chair."

"Should I come with you or wait until I need to be there?"

"You might want to think about stopping in about a half hour from now or so. See how the conversation has gone."

"Officially or as a friend?"

"Whatever you think you need to be depending on what's happened."

Greyjack hung up the phone and shuffled through some papers on his desk, wondering what Warren would have done about Joe Nathan. Without a doubt, Warren would have seen through the coroner's report, just as Linda had, and known for certain Joe Nathan was responsible. He wondered if Warren would have arrested Joe Nathan and pressed charges or if he would have, like Richard, decided to go "talk" to Joe Nathan.

For sure, Warren would not have ignored the evidence. Warren would have understood from the get-go Joe Nathan had hurt Mindy and her baby and was the one who had caused their deaths. He would have also been quick to see the bruise on Mrs. Nathan's face and would have stepped up to defend her.

Warren would not have let Joe Nathan go near Helen.

Greyjack sat at his desk watching the clock on the wall,

waiting for the thirty minutes to pass. He hated being the good cop all the time, and Sweet Jesus, how he missed Warren.

Richard cut the engine and coasted to a stop in front of Joe Nathan's house. Joe Nathan's beat-up old Chevy was in the driveway and the lights were on in the kitchen and the family room in the back of the house. For a moment Richard wasn't sure why he was there or exactly what he was going to say, but he knew he had to come. Linda was right: something had to be said or done. Joe Nathan had hurt Mindy, and in hurting Mindy he'd killed Tommy's child. Then there was the incident at the hospital with Helen. What if the nurses hadn't rushed in and he had hit Helen? What if he had come by their house and hit Linda?

He looked at his watch. He'd told Greyjack to give him thirty minutes. Richard hoped Greyjack would show up on time. Richard believed thirty minutes would give him plenty of time to get into a deep discussion with Joe Nathan.

Richard waited a few more minutes. He got out of his car and walked up the driveway to the front porch. He went over in his head what he wanted to say to Joe Nathan.

He wanted to know what Joe Nathan did to Mindy and also what he had said to Helen to make her feel so threatened she had to strike out at him and hit him with a chair. The doctor had told Richard Joe Nathan must have said something or raised his hand to Helen or threatened her in some way. It wasn't like Helen to be violent.

He rang the doorbell and waited. He heard a muffled television turned up full blast in some back room. No one came to the door. He rang the doorbell a second time.

Mrs. Nathan came to the door. Richard noticed her face was freshly washed. She looked like she'd been crying. A large purplish bruise covered her left cheek. Her eye was swollen.

"Where is he?" Richard demanded.

She covered her mouth, as though she was afraid to speak. He reached out and touched her cheek.

"Did your husband do this to you?" he asked softly.

She closed her eyes and nodded her head.

"And Mindy?"

"The baby," she whispered, tears streaming down her face, "I was at my sister's. He'd sent me there. Told me not to come home until he called. I couldn't stop him."

"I promise you, he won't ever hurt you again. Where is he?"

She pointed toward the back of the house into the family room.

He saw the flicker of lights across the screen of a television in the room. He pointed toward the back room. She nodded her head.

He reached into his pocket and pulled out his car keys. He pressed the keys into her hand.

"Do you have someplace safe you can go?"

"I could go to Reverend Jacobs' house."

"Does he know?"

She turned her head toward the room where Joe Nathan was sitting.

"He doesn't know about the baby."

"He'll never hurt you again, I promise."

"Linda was so nice to Mindy. Real nice."

"Linda misses her a lot."

"Mindy was just a child," she said, closing her eyes to keep from crying.

"What's taking you so long? Who's at the door?" Joe Nathan yelled out angrily.

"Go." Richard commanded.

Mrs. Nathan stepped out of the house and ran down the sidewalk to Richard's car. She never looked back.

Joe Nathan came into the living room as Richard stepped into the house.

"What did you do to Helen?" he demanded.

Joe Nathan took one step forward, leaned towards the coffee table and swung his long arm out to grab his big black Bible. Before Richard knew what was happening, Joe Nathan was moving towards him, slapping the Bible against the palm of his other hand.

"Hell is full of Jezebel's whose husbands could not tame them." Joe Nathan called out, waving the Bible as though he was preaching.

Richard stepped back at first, shifted his weight and moved up into Joe Nathan's face. Richard could smell alcohol on Joe Nathan's breath.

"Full of Jezebels," Joe Nathan hissed, then swung out with the Bible as though he intended to knock Richard over with it. Richard grabbed Joe Nathan by the front of his shirt and held him for a minute. Then, with his free hand, he swung hard and hit Joe Nathan. Joe Nathan stumbled back. Richard held tight to Joe Nathan's shirt. He steadied himself and hit Joe Nathan again.

Blood spurted from Joe Nathan's nose. Joe Nathan swung with the Bible and kicked at Richard to get free. Richard moved to get out of the way, and Joe Nathan surprised him with a head butt in the chest, hard, ripping his shirt pocket. Richard let go of Joe Nathan. Joe Nathan grabbed his Bible with both of his hands, raised it up over his head and brought it down fast, catching Richard across the face.

Richard fell back and caught his balance. He rushed toward Joe Nathan, roaring.

"You killed Mindy." He swung wildly. "And you killed her baby."

"She was your son's whore," Joe Nathan spat. "Whore!"

Richard heard a noise in his head. It whooshed like a big wave breaking free and rushing toward the shore, tearing everything within its reach loose from its roots. He could hear these screaming noises filling the room. He felt his fists, hot from pain, slamming into Joe Nathan's stomach.

"You...will...never...hurt...anyone...again..." the words came out in staccato bursts, his breath ripping through his chest as he hit Joe Nathan again and again and again with each word. The knuckles of Richard's fist were torn and bleeding.

"Richard, stop," Greyjack said softly, putting his hand on Richard's shoulder.

"I had to do something," Richard cried, tears running down his face. "I had to stop him."

"Well, you did a good job of it."

"Arrest him," Joe Nathan screamed backing away from Richard. "He's crazy just like his wife."

Greyjack gently pushed Richard aside so he wouldn't hit Joe Nathan again.

"Arrest Richard? It's a damn lucky thing he came after you instead of my brother Warren."

"He tried to kill me," Joe Nathan shouted.

Greyjack picked up the bloodied Bible. He grabbed Joe Nathan by the wrist and snapped on a pair of handcuffs. "You're lucky Richard came to talk to you. Warren wouldn't have bothered calling me until he had killed you."

And then the two of them, Richard and Greyjack, started laughing as they dragged Joe Nathan from his house.

Chapter 22

When Linda got up the next morning, she realized her father had not come home from work during the night. She got up, showered, went downstairs and made a cup of tea for herself. She scrounged in the freezer for something to eat, taking her time, hoping her father would come home. It wasn't unusual for him to work a second shift, so she told herself she shouldn't worry. Greyjack would know if something bad had happened and would call her.

The phone rang. It was Greyjack.

"Is Dad okay?" she asked before Greyjack could even say hello.

"Something came up. He and I are going to go out to get little breakfast. He'll be home in a bit. He wanted me to call and tell you not to worry."

"Tell him I love him."

"He knows."

Linda hung up the phone and walked through the house. She touched the barren walls. She knew her mother loved art and always wondered why they were no pictures in the house.

The only pictures they had were Tommy's baseball team pictures and his high school graduation picture, but right now she didn't want any pictures of Tommy hanging on the walls. She didn't want to be reminded that he was gone.

She walked around the house talking out loud, trying to decide what kind of pictures she would hang on each wall and what else she would like to change. When she grew tired of dreaming, she went to the garden to pick vegetables for her stand.

She was sitting at her stand reading a book and drinking a glass of iced tea when her father pulled up. It was a little before noon. There was blood on his clothes and his shirt pocket was torn like he'd been in a fight and someone had grabbed him by the pocket. She looked up from her book but didn't say anything.

She could see he was going to go into the house without speaking. When he got to the door, he turned and walked across the lawn and stood in the shade of her stand.

"I suspect Joe Nathan will be moving on soon. You won't have to worry about him anymore. He knows we believe he killed Mindy and the baby. He won't come by to bother you."

"Thank you," she said, hoping he might come closer to her and put her arms around her.

"I've got to be to work by 4 p.m. Wake me in time to take a shower."

"Sure," she said watching as he walked to the door and went into the house.

She didn't have many people come by during the afternoon, but those who did seemed to step a little carefully around the stand when they saw her father's car sitting in the driveway. She knew gossip traveled as fast as burning gasoline on water. Whatever happened between her father and Joe Nathan had probably blown like wildfire through the town then back out to the county before a second cup of coffee had been poured that morning.

Around 3 p.m. she went in and called up the stairs to wake her father. She went into the kitchen and made him a sandwich. She got a fresh lunch bag from the drawer and put in some cookies she had made the morning Mindy had called and some fruit. She brewed a thermos of hot tea for him and put it next to his lunch on the counter. When she finished she toasted two slices of bread and buttered them. She put them on a plate by his lunch sack.

Before she went back outside Linda stood at the bottom of the stairs just listening to her father move from the closet to the chair by his bed getting dressed. She called up to him to tell him she'd made him some toast and something to take to work.

When he came outside, his hair was wet and combed back like he was going to a dance or something. He stood on the front stoop a long time looking at her. She thought he might come out and say something. When he started across the lawn she put down her book so he'd know she was listening and wanted to hear what he had to say.

"There was nothing I could do to help Mindy and not much I could do to keep Tommy from getting into trouble," he said, the cuff of his lunch sack rolled up in his hands, his big thermos tucked under his arm. "And, I guess there was nothing I could do at the time to keep your mother from leaving."

She could feel the cold lump rolling up through her throat begin to choke her. She couldn't say anything, so she nodded her head. She wanted him to know she understood.

"Nothing I could do," he said again, and then he turned away from her and walked to his car. "But I wanted to tell you I love you."

Greyjack came by around 6 p.m. She had been thinking about putting things away before then but was pretty sure he'd come by to check on her, so she just sat and waited. She didn't feel much like cleaning up and eating supper alone. It had been a long lonely day.

Greyjack got out of the car. He had a sack in his hand.

"Brought chili burgers and fries. Thought you might like a hot meal for a change. Your father tells me you haven't had time to cook much lately."

"I heard there was a fight," she said, guessing, hoping Greyjack would tell her what happened.

"I brought cokes too," he said, reaching into the sack. "I prefer cokes with chili burgers. Malts with cheeseburgers, but cokes with chili burgers. How about you?"

"My father said Joe Nathan is thinking about moving on."

"Sounds about right."

"He says Joe Nathan knows that we know the truth."

"Whatever the truth is," Greyjack said, handing one of the sandwiches to her along with a small crumpled bag of fries.

"You know the truth," she said, feeling very bold for the moment.

"The truth is you have both a mother and a father who love you."

"The truth about Joe Nathan," she said, not wanting to hear right then about her mother loving her.

"Here's the truth. Any man who hits a woman is afraid of something in himself."

"He's a preacher."

"He's a man and there are lots of men like Joe Nathan in this world. That's just the way it is, and your father got angry because he didn't know who Joe Nathan was before it was too late. He was angry Mindy lost her baby and killed herself, and he was angry Tommy was foolish enough to get drunk and was dead. He was also angry because he knew Joe Nathan had hurt you when he hurt Mindy and when he hit his wife."

"Did you arrest him?"

"Who?"

"My father?"

"Joe Nathan wanted me to arrest him, but I didn't. Only had one pair of handcuffs and used those on Joe Nathan."

"Will Joe Nathan go to jail?"

"No, but it's clear to him now that if he doesn't leave town he will be in jail. I've talked with Mrs. Nathan. She's willing to press charges if he stays."

"I didn't mean to hurt my father," she said.

"Your father knows what it's like to be afraid. He knows you didn't mean what you said, but he knows there's truth in what you said as well. Truth is a hard, hard thing. Eat your sandwich," he said, taking one for himself out of the sack, "before it gets cold."

Chapter 23

"I'd like to talk to Helen alone. I want to tell her something," Richard said. He was walking with the doctor on their way down the corridor to the visitors' room.

The doctor stopped, took off his glasses and polished them with a clean white handkerchief he had taken from his jacket pocket. He rubbed the lenses slowly and deliberately, taking his time to get them cleaned before he walked on.

"We've made some progress," he said. He put his glasses back on again.

"You told me to stay away, but I've been coming by everyday since she's been here, sitting in the parking lot. Saw her standing by the fence once."

Sometimes he'd come before he went to work. But, most often, he would come after the shift was over, in the middle of the night, and just sit in his car at the back of the parking lot, wondering what he did to make her want to leave him and what he could possibly do or say to convince her to come home.

"It was good you stayed away. Gave her time to think. She's done a lot of thinking since she's been here. A lot of hard work. It's hard work, you know."

"Yes," Richard answered even though he wasn't sure what the doctor was talking about. He wondered if Helen was still acting crazy.

"I'm sure she'll seem quite different than what you remember. When patients have treatments like your wife has had to have they always seem a bit older and slower than they were before. Less agitated. She's much less agitated."

Richard hadn't remembered Helen as being agitated. She was sometimes edgy or distracted, but never agitated. Right before she left, everything she touched seemed explosive or dangerous. It scared him when he came home and saw her slapping bright orange paint across the kitchen walls.

"I have something important to say to her," Richard said, confronting the doctor.

"I don't think she's prepared to hear any more bad news," the doctor said in an irritated kind of way.

"It's not bad news, at least not for her. I think it will make her feel better."

The doctor stopped walking and shoved his hands deep into his pockets before he spoke.

"As her doctor, I want to know what you're going to tell her before I take you any further. When that preacher, Joe Nathan, came to see Helen, there was trouble. I called you about that incident."

"You did."

"I need to know what you're going to say to her. We don't want her to become agitated."

Richard thought about it for a moment. He didn't think it was the doctor's business. He didn't think it was anyone's business but his and Helen's.

"I can't do that."

"Can't, or won't," the doctor pressed.

"Won't."

"When she learned about Tommy, we had to sedate her afterwards. Later, when we couldn't get her to stop crying, we had to do shock treatments. You don't want us to do that again, I assure you."

"You won't have to," Richard said, standing his ground. He had talked the whole thing over with Greyjack. Greyjack had agreed Helen should know about his fight with Joe Nathan. He thought it would help Helen.

Greyjack had also told Richard he could see Helen alone anytime he wanted to. Anytime. It was his right as her husband. Greyjack had offered to come with Richard to talk with the doctor. Richard declined, saying he wanted to do this on his own.

He felt he owed that much to Helen.

"Under those circumstances I feel as though I should be there when you talk with her," the doctor insisted.

"What I have to say to her is private."

The doctor didn't want to argue with him, but he didn't want to have to wrestle Helen to the floor again and restrain her. She had made so much progress in the last few days. Real progress. She was talking again, about Tommy and Linda and the house and how she wanted to change things. She seemed to have gained the strength to resolve any conflicts she had about being a mother and a wife in order to get well enough to go home. He didn't want anything to upset her.

"There are security issues. I'm afraid I'm going to have to be with you when you talk to her," the doctor insisted.

"She's my wife. Sheriff Greyjack told me I have a right to see her alone."

The doctor opened the door to the visitor's room and motioned for Richard to go in by himself, then made a big show of pulling the door closed and standing by the window in order to keep a close watch on what was going on.

Helen was sitting in a chair at the other end of a long wooden table. The table had scribbles of crayon marks, ink stains, paint splotches and rings of dark watermarks covering the surface. Everything in the room felt a bit too used and shabby. He didn't recognize the dress Helen was wearing. Richard didn't think it was one of hers. It seemed much too large for Helen, and had a big safety pin in the front where one button was missing. She had slippers on her feet. Her hair was longer and brushed back away from her face as though someone had just combed it for her.

"Hello," Richard said.

"Long time, no see," Helen attempted, the words slurring slightly. She tipped her head back a little and closed her eyes as though the effort to speak had been exhausting. It had been. Words still felt thick in her mouth and foreign.

She looked very frail and small. Richard had wanted to put his arms around her and say he missed her but wasn't sure it would be the right thing to do at the moment. He was sorry he hadn't come in to see her before. He really wanted her to come home.

"They told you about Mindy."

"Yes," Helen answered. She tried to push her lips into some kind of a smile so he would see she wasn't angry with him. She wanted him to know she was happy to see him and was much better than she had been when she left.

He wondered if she knew about the baby. He guessed she didn't.

"It was a terrible thing."

"Yes," Helen said again.

"Joe Nathan isn't a good man. I think he hit Mindy, and maybe him hitting her had something to do with her committing suicide. I believe he hit his wife as well."

Helen closed her eyes and nodded.

"They told me Joe Nathan came to see you."

"I hit him," Helen said softly.

"He hurt a lot of people. I was glad when I heard you hit him with a chair. That must have been something to see."

Helen closed her eyes. Her mouth tasted salty. Like tears. She swallowed and rocked gently back and forth to keep herself from crying.

"I don't believe he was really a preacher," Richard added.

Helen nodded her head, tears welling up in her eyes.

"I had a little fight with Joe Nathan myself the other night."

"A fight?"

"Something happened. I can't explain. I just had to do something, anything, to make things right again. There was evidence," he started then stopped. "We, Greyjack and I, we think Joe Nathan hit Mindy and that's why she killed herself."

Helen closed her eyes and turned her head to the side as though Joe Nathan too had just hit her.

"Tommy loved her," she said.

Richard sat down across the table from Helen. He moved his chair forward and leaned across the table so he could be closer to her.

"Yes," he said, wanting to reach out and touch her face. "Tommy loved her. Mindy was pregnant when she died. Pregnant with Tommy's baby."

"A baby," Helen whispered, her breath coming in short soft bursts, "Tommy's baby?"

She was breathing hard, rocking a little in her chair as though the rocking would settle her heart and help her to stay with him.

"It looked like Mindy had miscarried before she killed herself. There were bruises on her ribs and her stomach, like she'd been beaten up. Mrs. Nathan was willing to sign a statement saying Joe Nathan had not only hit her and her daughter occasionally but he had had a fight with Mindy and he'd hit her the day before she died."

"She needed Tommy, didn't she? She couldn't get away from Joe Nathan without him."

"I think that's right. They needed each other."

"What's going to happen?"

"Greyjack came, came when we were having the fight, and arrested Joe Nathan. I guess you could say I went to fight with Joe Nathan in order to give Greyjack a reason to arrest Joe Nathan. In any case, I did what I did, and Greyjack did what he could do according to the law. We got Mrs. Nathan into a safe place and she was able to help us keep him locked up for a little while."

"Will he go to prison?"

"It'd be hard to prove his beating up Mindy killed her, but we scared him pretty bad. Greyjack wrote him up and gave him an option to leave town and stay away from his wife, or get a lawyer."

"And he left?"

"That's why I came. I wanted you to know Joe Nathan was leaving. That he won't be by to bother you anymore."

"Thank you," she said.

"Linda misses you. I don't think she's doing so well. None of us are."

"The garden," Helen closed her eyes, struggling to conjure an image of her garden.

"Linda put in an extra mound of melons. There's been some rain and good weather. The melons have been great. The corn is good too, some of the best. Cucumbers got a bit big when it was so hot. Linda painted the stand with some of the orange paint that was left over from the kitchen. The color looks really nice. I think you'll like it. She's using the Easter baskets for the beans and some of my mother's big china platters for the tomatoes and such."

"Nice," Helen smiled.

"Puts all the flowers in vases now instead of tin cans. You should come see it."

"Hmmm." Helen put her hand out on the table as though she needed to do so in order to steady herself.

Richard looked at her hand. He had forgotten how small her hands were and how beautiful her fingers were with their soft white moons at the base of each fingernail. He had always loved her hands.

He moved his hand closer to hers.

"I saw you once, standing by the fence," he said.

"No, you didn't," she smiled, opening her eyes. "In my big white bathrobe?"

"I came every day."

"Here?"

"Not exactly here," he said, looking around the room, "but to the hospital. Hoping to see you. Mostly I would just sit in the car at the back of the parking lot."

"Why didn't you come in to see me?"

"The doctor told me you needed time."

"The time helped."

"It helped me to," Richard said, cautiously moving his hand until it touched hers, "to think about things."

"What kinds of things?"

"The kitchen. When I go in there now I can feel you. Feel the sunshine you must feel when you're out there in your garden. Sometimes when I can't sleep, I go down there and just sit. It makes me feel better. Like you're there with me. That's something else I wanted to tell you. I like the kitchen."

"Thanks." Helen let her hand brush against Richard's. She could feel the warmth radiating from his skin. It felt good.

"You left because I got angry you painted the kitchen, didn't you?"

"It was just paint," she said, pushing her little finger out just enough to touch the inside of Richard's palm.

"I was thinking about stripping off the old wallpaper and painting the living room so it would look as good as the kitchen."

"Yellow, like new sweet corn," Helen said.

"That's just what I was thinking," he said, smiling.

"Nice," Helen said. And with that, she took her index finger and traced the outline of his hand on the table.

Chapter 24

Helen stayed in the visitors' room for a long time after Richard left. She watched through the window as the doctor and Richard walked down the hallway together. She watched, and she waited. She was certain the doctor would come back. She knew he would want to talk to her. She was not surprised when the nurse came in to get her to take her to his office.

"Sit down," he said, motioning for her to take a seat in the smooth wooden chair across from his desk.

"I had forgotten how kind his voice could be," she said, fiddling with the big safety pin holding dress closed, hoping to make it appear less obvious the dress was neither hers nor one that fit her. She wished she had worn a pretty dress when Richard had come to see her, or at least one with all of its buttons.

"He had something he wanted to tell you?"

"Joe Nathan is gone."

"Gone?"

"He's leaving town."

"How does that make you feel?"

Helen considered the question. She didn't think the doctor would understand it made her feel like there was a God, not a perfect God, but a God in heaven.

"Richard told me he wanted to paint the living room yellow."

"What do you think about that?"

"Have you ever picked corn?"

"In a garden?"

"I always take the first ear I pick from each plant and peel back the husk to see if it's ripe before I pick the rest on the stalk. It's one of my favorite things to do in the garden. I grow a pale sugary-tasting corn called Silver Queen. It's a lovely corn with a small ear filled with pale sweet kernels. I love how, with new corn, the husks are still fresh and pliable and make this green squeaking sound as you pull them away to expose the plump ripened kernel beneath. It's the softest yellow you've ever seen."

"Yellow is a nice color."

"I told Richard I wanted to paint the living room yellow, like new sweet corn."

When Richard left the house to go to the hospital to see Helen, he had not told Linda where he was going. He did, however, say he had something to do in town and would be back in time for dinner. Linda seemed reluctant for him to go and asked if there was something special he wanted for dinner. He was surprised by her question. He couldn't ever remember Helen or anyone ever asking him if there was something special he wanted for dinner. He thought about it a minute, then said he wanted roast chicken and mashed potatoes.

He figured, if Linda made a roast chicken and mashed potatoes for dinner, there would be more than enough for all of them if Helen came home.

Linda peeled the potatoes slowly, letting her knife slide right under the skin in a clean circle around the potato. One by one the peels fell in long ribbons into the sink. She was making mashed potatoes and roast chicken for dinner with a cucumber salad and some green beans from the garden.

She thought about using her grandmother's china from the hutch in the dining room but decided it didn't feel right. Fancy wasn't what she wanted. She wanted to tell her father she was fine, in fact, happy with a family with just the two of them.

Although she decided not to use the good china, she got out her mother's pale pink Fostoria water glasses. She loved the delicate twining flower pattern etched into the glass and how light and wonderful the thin rim of the glasses felt against her mouth when she drank from them. They were the glasses she and her mother used for iced tea when they sat outside at their stand reading in the afternoons, waiting for customers to come. They were her mother's favorites. She had found them at the Goodwill. One of them had a tiny chip in the rim.

Linda hadn't used them since her mother had left. Something about them made her feel both sad and angry and she didn't understand why, when her mother left, she had left everything behind.

Linda was glad her father had asked for roast chicken and mashed potatoes. More than anything right now she wanted a normal dinner. A normal life. A normal family. She wanted to put an end to the troubles they'd had and the loss they'd felt. A good roast chicken could help do that. Chicken and creamy smooth mashed potatoes topped with melted butter and lots and lots of salt and pepper. She wanted to make food that would make them feel like they were full: warm and full of life.

She opened the freezer in hopes of finding something for dessert. There were no more cakes left from Tommy's funeral.

"Good," she said out loud. "We'll go out for ice cream."

That's what they'd do. They'd have dinner together and after they cleaned up the kitchen and put the leftovers away, they would get in the car and drive into town and have an ice cream, just like a real family.

School was going to start in a couple of weeks: her senior year. Linda missed her mother. Her mother would know what to say to her about going to college. She'd know what to do. But, her mother was gone.

Linda had decided she'd ask her father where he thought she should go to college. It was time to make him be part of her life.

She didn't want to be alone anymore.

Richard left the hospital and walked out to the back of the parking lot where he always parked his car. He unlocked his door, slid into the driver's seat and put his hands on the steering wheel. He knew he should have told Tommy and Linda where their mother had gone when she left, but he couldn't. He just couldn't bring himself to tell them she'd gone crazy and he'd had her locked up. At the time, he didn't understand why Helen acted so crazy and painted the kitchen or why she cried all the time. In truth, there was something shameful in all of it for him.

Maybe he was the one who was crazy. Sometimes he felt like he had spent his lifetime in a foxhole, crouching with his face pressed against the damp mushroom-smelling earth, just waiting. Waiting for some mortar shell to explode so it would light up the sky and he could see where the others were hiding. He felt like he'd spent his lifetime waiting for a night when he could sleep without seeing dead bodies floating in the water. He was tired of the shadows playing against the walls of his mind: scared soldiers running from the cross fire. He grew weary waiting for Tommy to grow up and quit being so wild. His heart was heavy with the many hours he had stood by the window waiting for Helen to come home. He was tired of wrestling with his dreams and just plain tired of waiting, hoping God would whisper in his ear and tell him what to do next.

Ironically, as much as he hated fighting, the fight with Joe Nathan had given him the best night of sleep he could ever remember. When he woke up he felt rested: different, like he was somehow a new person.

When he came down to go to work the next morning and walked into the kitchen he felt like the walls were alive. The room was pulsing with life. The sun was streaming through the big picture window, and the African violets Linda had collected from around the house were in bloom. They were so beautiful. He couldn't figure for the life of him why he used to be annoyed by them.

Suddenly, the air felt fresh with morning and he wished the house were filled with African violets. He felt full of hope, as if he'd at last found salvation for all he'd done in the war.

That's when he decided he was going to go the hospital to talk to Helen. He wanted to tell her about Joe Nathan leaving. Richard wanted to see if she might be willing to come home.

The Devil was gone. For too long, the war had been trapped inside of Richard, eating at him, tempting him to hide, to be afraid, to run. Right after Warren had been killed, Richard had hit the beach with the other men on his boat and he ran as hard as he could run and when he couldn't run anymore, he stopped and began shooting. He shot and shot until the repeat of the rifle in his ear made him deaf and he couldn't hear anymore. He killed as many Germans as he could, foolishly believing killing the enemy would bring Warren back to life.

When the sun finally set, and Richard could at last sit down to rest, there was blood and bodies everywhere and the air was foul with death. The killing had not changed anything. Warren was still dead. So many people were dead. Richard didn't know how many he had killed. He knew, however, he would never again be able to sleep without wondering whose son or good friend he had killed in the name of war. The killing was awful. It haunted him.

Sleep became a dangerous thing. If you slept you might get killed. Someone could sneak up on you and slit your throat or put a gun to your head. He'd found a German soldier once, sleeping in his foxhole, his coat pulled up around his shoulders. Richard had aimed his gun and was ready to shoot the sleeping man, but something about the way the man was sleeping made him hesitate. He watched in wonder as this man, this German enemy whom he should kill, had pushed his back against the wall of the foxhole, pulled the collar of his coat up around his head and was sleeping the near dead exhausted sleep they all felt, day in and day out in the blood-soaked mud of the war around them.

Then, before he could pull the trigger, another soldier shot. One shot. That's all it took. One ear-splitting shot that felt like it cut him in half. But he wasn't the one who was dead. The sergeant screamed at Richard to get the dead man's gun and get moving. Get moving. They were always moving. There was never any time to sleep.

Richard had tried a thousand times to tell Helen he couldn't sleep because he was afraid to sleep. He also wanted to tell her he worked every overtime shift he could because the noise in the factory drowned out the sounds in his head. Being in the factory was like sleeping. He couldn't hear anything. He couldn't feel anything. His heart beat slower. His hands moved automatically from one task to the next. He felt safe there.

It was crazy. He knew it was crazy. He didn't talk to anyone about how the relentless flowing river of the line in the factory brought him comfort and made him forget. Even Greyjack didn't understand. Greyjack couldn't go into the factory. He'd told Richard the smell of metal and the heat from the machinery in the factory made him sick. Greyjack had been a gunner.

Maybe if Richard had been able to sleep at night, holding Helen in his arms, letting the warmth of her body heal the wounds he felt, she would have understood he was scared, not angry. Maybe she would have known how much he needed her, how much he loved the way she didn't care about what other people thought. He also loved how, every year, she would spend hours and hours studying her notebooks and planning her garden as if nothing in the world mattered more than what kind of green beans and tomatoes to plant in spring.

He wanted Helen to come home so he could hold her. He wished with all his heart he had been a better husband, a better father, but it was too late for wishing. Tommy and Mindy were dead and there was nothing he could do about it. That's what he had wanted to tell Helen: there was nothing they could do about it anymore and they needed to find a way to love again and get on with their lives.

Wishing wouldn't bring Warren back to life anymore than it could bring Tommy or Mindy or their baby back to life. Richard wanted to tell Helen he had done the one thing he could do, the thing Linda had asked him to do: he made sure Mrs. Nathan would be safe and would never get hit by her husband again.

Richard's heart had raced when Helen let her fingers brush against his hand. It gave him hope.

The doctor had warned him to go slowly.

He didn't need a warning. He knew all too well what had already been lost: his marriage, Tommy, Mindy and her baby.

He checked his watch. It was 4:45 p.m. There was still time to go by the hardware store to pick up some yellow paint before he went home to have dinner with Linda.

Linda was standing by the sink, looking out the kitchen window when her father drove up. She wanted to run out to the driveway to greet him, but she had held back.

"Hey, hello," he called out as he came in the front door carrying two gallons of yellow paint.

"Looks like you've got a plan," Linda said, watching as her father put the paint down in the middle of the living room.

Her father came over and put his arms around her and hugged her. Linda took a deep breath and let her arms slide across his back. When he kissed her on the top of her head the way Tommy had kissed her, she let go.

"Thought we'd paint the living room tonight."

"What color?"

"Yellow."

"Yellow?"

"Like fresh sweet corn."

"What about the wallpaper?"

"I should have taken it down years ago."

Her father wanted to get started right away with removing the wallpaper, but Linda insisted they sit down and eat dinner before they did anything else.

Richard really didn't feel hungry, but when he started to say something about getting started he saw Linda looking at the table she'd already set and remembered he'd asked her to make chicken and mashed potatoes.

"I thought, maybe after dinner," Linda said, pushing a big soft glob of butter into the middle of the mashed potatoes, "we could go out for ice cream."

"Sounds good," he said, but even after he said it, he went out to the back porch to get some newspapers and old sheets to cover the floor and furniture.

"Dinner now, please," Linda urged.

When her father at last sat down, Linda picked up her water glass to propose a toast.

"To my favorite parent. To the one who stayed," she said, raising her glass.

Richard sat, still as stone. He wasn't ready, not yet, but he had to tell her before it was too late.

"I..." he stammered.

"Pick up your glass," she said, her voice on edge.

When he raised his glass, she pushed her hand forward, across the table. The fragile pink glass in her hand smashed against his. Water and glass shards rained down on the table and onto the floor.

"It's okay," Richard shouted, but it was too late.

Linda was sobbing. She threw back her head to draw in a breath. Tommy's funeral, Mindy's phone call, the damned Easter basket with her mother's note and the empty house raged through her like a storm.

"I'm sorry," she started, but then she couldn't say anything, anything at all because she was on the floor on her hands and knees trying to clean up the mess with her napkin and crying.

"No," Richard said, getting up from his chair so he could wrap his arms around her, "please, please don't cry. There's something I have to tell you."

Chapter 25

Helen was standing by the window at the end of the hall looking out into the parking lot, hoping to see Richard's car.

"Your dinner is in your room, getting cold," the nurse said, pushing the meds cart down the hallway. "I wondered where you were. The aide told me you haven't touched your dinner. You okay?"

"Do you think she hates me?"

"The aide?"

"My daughter."

"Why would she hate you?"

"Because I left, and she doesn't know where I am. Maybe Tommy would be alive if he had known. Maybe he wouldn't have gone into the Army. Maybe he and I could have talked, could have worked things out."

The nurse reached into her pocket, took out her patient list, and sorted through the pills on the cart.

"Where you are or what you did has got nothing to do with what happened to Tommy. Sometimes I think what happens is what was planned in heaven to happen. But it doesn't matter, because it did happen, and nothing you can do can change that now.

"Look, I can't tell you what you should or shouldn't have done, but a lot of people keep it a secret when they come here. You've got nothing to be ashamed of. If she were my daughter I'd go on and tell her what happened and where I've been. If she loves you she'll understand. If she doesn't love you, it won't matter one way or the other."

"I hated my mother when she left."

"She run away with another man?"

"No."

"What happened then?"

"She died and left me."

Richard held Linda until the potatoes and the chicken got cold and the fresh-cooked green beans shriveled and turned a bit grey. Linda had some crying to do and he had been wondering when it would come.

"I miss Tommy so much," she cried.

"I miss him too," Richard said as he rocked her back and forth in his arms the way he used to hold her and rock her when she was a little girl who got scared in the middle of the night and couldn't sleep.

He let Linda cry as long and as hard as she needed to. He had already cried all he could for Tommy.

"Mindy killed herself, she killed herself." A flood of warm raw tears came streaming down her face.

"Yes," Richard said, stroking her hair.

"She was right. It was a boy, a baby boy."

Richard closed his eyes and tried to image what it would have been like to have a grandson to hold.

His heart felt like it would burst with pain, but he couldn't let it. He held on tight to Linda until the sun went down and the room grew cold and dark.

When Linda had exhausted herself with crying and had closed her eyes, he rested his cheek against the top of her head and waited. When she began to stir, he kissed her forehead and spoke to her.

"There's something I want to show you," he said. "Something you need to know. Will you take a ride with me?"

When they got into the car Linda realized they hadn't eaten any of her special dinner.

"I ruined our dinner, didn't I?"

"You hungry?" her father asked.

"Not really."

"Want an ice cream?"

"There's chicken. I hadn't put it on the table yet. I'd turned off the oven, but left it in to keep it warm. There was a cucumber salad too, in the refrigerator. We could eat that."

"We could eat ice cream and save the chicken for breakfast."

"Tommy ate chicken for breakfast once," Linda said, remembering the last time she'd seen Tommy and how he kissed her head and held her.

"Forget about the chicken. Let's have ice cream," Richard said.

They each got a double scoop in a dish. Richard ordered one scoop of chocolate and another of strawberry, and Linda got orange pineapple and vanilla.

"Let's take our ice cream with us," Richard said after he paid, "I told you there's something I wanted to show you."

Linda held onto her father's dish while he drove through town.

"Where are we going?" she asked.

"Not far," he said, driving through the main entrance of the hospital.

"This is the state mental hospital," Linda said, wondering why they'd come there.

"I know," Richard said quietly as he carefully maneuvered the car to the very back of the parking lot and stopped.

"This is where your mother has been."

Chapter 26

"In a couple of weeks Linda will be starting her senior year."

"What do you think about that?" the doctor asked.

"She has the money. In the bank. From the garden stand. The two of us, we raised all the money with the garden. She began helping me when she was just this big."

Helen leaned forward in her chair and showed the doctor how little Linda had been when she started helping her in the garden.

"Was the garden Linda's idea?"

"Lillian had a garden, and when I married Richard, I started working in her garden."

"So, is it your garden or Lillian's garden?"

"It used to be Lillian's, but it's mine now. Mine and Linda's. But the money from the stand is hers. To go to college."

"You want Linda to go to college?"

"Of course."

"What do you want? What kind of dreams do you want to plant in your garden?"

"My dreams?"

"It's okay for you to have dreams."

"I want to paint the living room. I want to buy books. I want a whole garden that's just mine, bursting with roses and dahlias and snapdragons. I want to travel."

"Have you ever asked Richard about his dreams?"

"I didn't before, but I want to now."

"And what about Linda? Does she want to go to college?"

"Who wouldn't want to go to college?"

"Did you or Richard go to college?"

"No, there was the war."

"So you want Linda to go because you couldn't go?"

Helen braced her hands on the seat of the chair and took in a long slow breath. She hated all the questions but knew her leaving depending on being able to answer all of them.

"Yes, I want Linda to go because I didn't go and because she's smart. She's really smart."

"What about Tommy? Was he smart?"

"Tommy didn't want to go to school. School was too much sitting still for Tommy. It wasn't good for him. He was wild."

"Why was he wild?"

Helen let her head fall back against the back of her chair and shifted her weight. She began to laugh. It was a soft private laugh at first, but it grew until it filled the room.

"I think," she said, a smile spreading across her face, her hands relaxing at her sides, "I was hoping you could tell me."

"Some people are just wild," the doctor said, studying the smile on Helen's face. "Do you think Tommy was angry?"

"Angry?"

"Jealous of Linda and your garden?"

"Good heavens, no."

Helen was surprised at how good and sweet the words tasted in her mouth. They were sweet because they were the truth. Tommy, for all his wildness, had not been angry. He had also not been jealous. He had been righteously wild and impetuous. She couldn't protect him, and she also couldn't stop him.

"Why did he drink?"

"Why does anyone drink?" Helen shot back.

"Why do you want to go home?" The conversation had just become a tennis match, and the doctor felt like he had scored. Helen had become strong enough to question him. She was strong enough to go home.

Helen sat up straight, her hands pushed, once again, against the seat of the chair. Her heart was racing.

"I want to go home," she said, calmly and slowly, "because I want to help Richard paint the living room. I want to ask him about his dreams. I want to learn to dream my dreams as well as dream with him."

"Anything else?"

"Yes, I want to see my daughter. I want to help Linda with the garden. I want to drink coffee in the morning sitting at my kitchen table and reading the morning paper. I want to cut my hair short, short and curly so I can feel pretty again. I want to cook dinner and dream about what I'm going to plant in my garden next year."

"Dreaming is good."

"Yes," said Helen, her hands relaxing at her sides once again, "dreaming is good. Richard told me after he had the fight with Joe Nathan he was able to sleep."

"Yes, he told me also."

"If you can sleep, you can dream. That's what I told Richard. I told him if he could sleep he could dream. I think it would be wonderful if Richard and I could dream together."

"What would you like to dream about?"

"Tomorrow," she said, her hands resting in her lap. "I want to dream about tomorrow."

The day after her father had taken her to the mental hospital and told her about her mother, Linda woke up at the crack of dawn as usual but didn't go into the garden. Instead, she made herself a cup of tea and a slice of toast and started peeling wallpaper off the living room walls.

She peeled and scraped until her fingers ached. As she worked, she imagined how her mother must have felt all alone that day and on into the night when she painted the kitchen by herself.

"Want some help?" Her father had come down the stairs wearing an old t-shirt and a pair of grease-stained pants he used to wear to work.

"Want some breakfast?" Linda responded coolly.

"I can get it."

"Why didn't you go visit her?" she demanded.

"I told you. I went to the hospital everyday, but I didn't go in. I sat in the parking lot, watching and waiting, trying to figure out what I should do. I once saw her standing by the fence."

"Why didn't you tell us?"

"I didn't know how."

"So she's been there all this time alone?"

"The doctor said she needed time."

"How much time?"

"I don't know."

Richard picked up a scraper and began peeling paper off the wall. Linda had already sprayed the section of wall he was working on with water. The old paper came off in long soggy clumps and strips. Richard scraped for a while, then, like Linda, picked up the fallen pieces and put them into the trash. It was a slow process.

"How do I do this?" Helen asked.

"Do what?"

"Go home."

It was the doctor's turn to laugh.

"You've already done the hard work," he said, "the really hard work. You're more than halfway there. You're better, you know that, don't you?"

"Yes, I feel good. Much better, thank you."

"That doesn't mean you won't ever feel sad again. That's not what coming here is about…never feeling sad again. Feeling sad is as much about being well as learning how to feel happy."

By lunchtime, the living room walls were stripped bare. The whole house smelled faintly like wet mulch.

"You hungry?" Richard asked Linda.

"There's cold baked chicken."

"Anything else?"

"I threw the potatoes and the green beans away. There's a cucumber salad."

"I'm sorry."

"I was so angry when she left. I hated you both. Hated everyone in the world. Everyone but Tommy. When he died…"

"I know."

"How would you like to do this?" the doctor asked.

"How would *I* like to do this?"

"Yes, you. It's your life. How do you want to go home?"

"When?"

"You can go whenever you want."

"I can go now?"

"Yes."

"Can I have my earrings back? And my clothes, the ones I had on when I came here. I want to wear my clothes when I go home, not one of these ugly dresses."

"Of course."

"Just like that?"

"Just like that."

"Should I call Richard?"

"It's up to you."

"Can I call Greyjack?"

"If you want."

"He brought me here, didn't he?"

"Yes."

"Then I think he should take me back home."

Richard and Linda had just sat down at the kitchen table to eat their lunch of cold chicken and cucumber salad when the phone rang. Linda got up to answer it.

"It's Greyjack," she said, handing the phone out for her father to take, stretching the long tangled cord so he didn't have to get up from the table in order to talk.

"Greyjack," Richard said. A smile spread across his face. "We'll be here. Thank you."

Linda stood, waiting to take the phone back and hang it up for him, but he didn't hand it to her. Instead, he got out of the chair, hung up the phone, put his arms around her and kissed her head.

"Your mother's coming home."

Helen stood quietly by the nurses' station when Greyjack came. She had her discharge papers in her hand. She fiddled with her garnet earrings, pushing her hair behind her ears so Richard would see she still had them. She had on her own clothes. The clothes were too big and smelled of the strong disinfectant soap they used in the hospital laundry, but they were hers and she felt like herself again.

"You ready?" Greyjack asked.

"Thank you."

"For what?"

"For being a good friend. For bringing me here."

"I didn't know what else to do."

"I didn't either."

Linda cleared the table, stacking their dishes in the sink and washing them as quickly as she possibly could. Richard grabbed a fresh towel and started drying the dishes and putting them in the cupboard.

"She's on her way?" Linda asked.

"Greyjack is bringing her."

"But the house, the room, we're not finished."

Richard looked around at the mess of sodden wallpaper stuffed into the waste can and the damp plaster walls.

"It'll be fine," he said.

He went into the living room to where he had put the paint cans. He grabbed a screwdriver and carefully pried the lid from the can. He found a paint stick and began stirring.

"Yellow, like fresh sweet corn," he said, holding up the stick so Linda could see.

"I think it's going to be perfect," she said.

Richard had never done anything crazy in his life before. He had never ran away, never knocked a mailbox off a post with a baseball bat, never jumped off a barn, never got drunk or howled at the moon like he knew Tommy had done.

"Tommy was a wild one," he said to himself, picking up a paintbrush and testing the bristles against the palm of his hand.

"They're coming," Linda said, running to the window.

"Give me a minute," he said, "go out to meet her. Don't let her in the house, at least not yet. Tell her I'm coming."

Linda wiped her hands on the dishtowel her father had been using. She no longer cared what other people said or what they thought about her mother. Linda just wanted her mother to come back into her life. She ran out to the driveway to greet Greyjack's car.

Richard dipped the fresh paintbrush deep into the bucket of paint, and painted a message across the now bare living room walls: WELCOME HOME.

Roundfire Books put simply, publish great stories. Whether it's literary or popular, a gentle tale or a pulsating thriller, the connecting theme in all Roundfire fiction titles is that once you pick them up you won't want to put them down.